CROSSING THE BLUE RIDGE

A Tale of King's Mountain

A Novel by

L. E. DENTON

To My Brother
Robert Bennington Conklin
(Benny)

Contents

Chapter One

The Susquehanna River runs peacefully enough down its course, relieving lush farmlands and wooded forests of their excess. Broad and deep, its tranquil shores offer a broad vista that brings calm and amicability to all those who view it. But sometimes deep gray storm clouds appear on the horizon, leaden and heavy with their burden. The thunder crashes and unleashes a torrent of rain, pounding down, thrashing and hammering all it touches.

Rivulets form, and turn into creeks, streams and floods, and the Susquehanna turns into a roaring monster, leaving its bank and sweeping away all in its path. It rushes towards the sea, scouring the landscape and all before it, both natural and man-made.

At times, in the course of human events, the same sort of phenomenon occurs. Thunderous dark clouds of dissent and dispute come across the horizon, darkening all below. A deluge of riotous, tumultuous events come about, and sweep before them everything in their path, changing the direction of history, much like a raging river fed by a flood will change its path.

My name is Caleb Anders. I am the fourth child and only son of Jeremiah and Celia Anders, and was born on March 7, 1757. I was raised in what is now Harford County, Maryland, not far from the Susquehanna River. My older sisters – Jane, Susanna and Martha – were my seniors by many years. By the time I was ten, all were married and had left home. Jane and Susanna married men from Baltimore and moved there to start their lives anew. Martha, closest to me in age, being but seven years my senior, married a local farmer, Jacob Finley. They farmed acreage left to Jacob by his grandfather, and lived an hour west from us by horseback.

My mother, Celia Smith Anders, was the kindest woman I have ever known. She was tall and angular, with pleasant features and bright blue eyes, which I inherited. She was keen on seeing to it that my sisters and I could read and do our numbers. Her well-worn copy of the "New England Primer" from her own youth was the foundation of our education. With it she instilled in me a love of learning, though I think a part of it was due to my love and affection for her. She was a godly woman, who saw to it that we attended church whenever we were able. At a young age, on Sunday mornings, I was able to hitch the horse to the buggy with the help of my older sisters, and without my father we would make our way to church.

My father, by contrast, was short and stout, and as gloomy and unhappy a man as you would ever want to meet. Where this glumness came from I have no idea. He farmed the 120 acres left to him by his father, acquired after he left the old world for the new. Thus, from his youth his path was set. How he managed to marry such a thoughtful, industrious and intelligent woman as my mother is unknown to me.

He was a brutal and uncaring man. He treated my mother with contempt. Any shortcomings she had were dealt with harshly. He grumbled and fumed at the hours she spent teaching her children, and if his supper was late because of it she would see the back of his hand across her face. He never noticed, but my sisters and I saw the bewildered looks and silent tears that came from his cruel treatment of her.

His treatment of us was no less harsh, which I believe led my sisters to marry and leave home at a young age. We rarely heard from Jane and Susanna, safely ensconced in Baltimore City. They were busy raising children of their own, and the less they had to do with our father, the better. This added to the weight my mother carried in her heart. She sorely missed her eldest daughters, but I believe she understood the reason why they so rarely wrote or visited.

Starting at the age of about eight, I had regular chores on the farm, and these grew in size as I did. My father was a harsh taskmaster, and expected more than I was ever able to give. I suffered terribly at his hands, which he freely used to beat me with anything handy – the staff of a pitchfork, the reins of the draft animals, or the fallen limbs of a tree. His ill treatment of hired workers was so well known that by the time I was ten he was never able to hire anyone else to help. Even slave owners refused to lease out their slaves to him because of the harsh abuse he would heap on them. As a result, the burden laid on my shoulders during planting and harvesting season was sometimes almost impossible to bear.

The only respite I would have was during the height of summer, when the crops needed little tending, and during the hard, cold winter months. During these times, Martha's husband Jacob would ride east and cajole my father into letting me stay with them, claiming he needed my help with maintenance on his own farm, which was twice the size of ours. He would bring a half dozen chickens or a few smoked hams to recompense my father for my absence. Grumbling mightily, my father would usually agree, while warning Jacob of my laziness or incompetence.

"Make him work! I can't seem to get much out of him," he would state with disdain, as I climbed into Jacob's buggy. "And don't let him eat you out of house and home!"

And so I would be off, often feeling guilty for leaving my mother with such a man.

Jacob and Martha were the only light I had, other than my mother, in those dark days. The time I spent with them were the best of my young life. I helped Jacob repair fences and barns, and Martha with her chickens and kitchen garden. In the evenings we would often play cards by the firelight, or read from the Good Book Jacob had inherited from his grandfather.

But it was my time with Jacob out in the woods that proved most useful in my later life. He had a great fondness for hunting, and it was he who taught me the proper way to load and fire a flintlock rifle. He had two – one that had been passed down to him from his grandfather and one he had purchased on his own. He taught me how to track game in the woods and how to read the prints they left. He taught me how to throw a hatchet, and how to set up a camp. How to read the signs of the trail, to see who else had used it. How to build a roaring fire, or a small, smokeless one if need be. He taught me which plants were edible and which ones were poisonous. He showed me how to trap small game using snares like the Indians, and the proper use of metal ones.

"How did you learn all this?" I once asked.

"My parents died when I was young, from a fever. I was raised by my grandfather, who came over from the old country when this was just a trackless forest. He learned his skills from experience and some friendly Indians in these parts." he replied.

"Why are you teaching these things to me?"

"Caleb, we have no way of telling what will befall us in the future. We must be prepared for whatever circumstances might arise."

At times, while we watched and waited for game, Jacob would wile away the hours by sharing with me what he knew of the politics of the day. He explained the Stamp Act, those despised taxes imposed on us colonists by the British, and the Townsend Duties, which were more taxes thrust upon us.

"The main problem as I see it," he would exclaim, "is that we have no say in it whatsoever! We have no one to plead for mercy from those grasping rascals in Parliament!"

He went into great detail about the incident we knew as the Boston Massacre. How the British had killed those who were protesting the heavy hand of the British Army on our necks. "It's getting worse, not better for us, son. Those fellows up in Boston are aching for a fight. I fear the worst is yet to come."

Being young and foolish, I paid little mind to these speeches. I had no notion these events would have any impact on my life, or what they would lead to. I was just content to be surrounded by the lush woodlands and meadows, a rifle in my hand and in company with as fine a fellow as Jacob.

And so we spent many happy hours in the woods. I discovered I was a good marksman, even better than Jacob. The rifle felt comfortable in my hands, as if it was meant to be there. I yearned to possess one of my own someday and told Jacob.

"Perhaps you will one day. But until then, you are welcome to use one of mine." he smiled in reply. Many times we would not make it back to the farmhouse until darkness had fallen. Martha would smilingly fuss at us.

"I tried to keep your supper warm. Why the late hour? Did you get lost?"

"No, Martha," Jacob would reply. "This boy is difficult to drag home. He would live in the woods if we would let him!"

We used everything we hunted. Jacob knew the proper way to preserve our game, and taught me how to skin them for their hides. His smokehouse was often full with our harvest from the forest – venison, bear meat, fat turkeys and ducks, geese, squirrels and rabbits.

"If you would like, Caleb, I know a man who would buy these hides from us. I could easily sell them. And some of the meat as well. Martha and I cannot eat all we have brought in."

I paused and thought a moment. "Can you hold the coins for me?"

"Certainly." He looked knowingly at me.

"It's just that my father would gladly relieve me of anything I earn."

"I am aware of that," he replied. "I will hold your portion of the earnings until you have need of it."

When it was time to travel back to the small but sturdy farmhouse of my father, I would grow quieter the closer we would get. As we drew near, I could see the cornfields that made up the bulk of our farm, either the growing stalks, laden with their bounty, or the stubble left after the harvest, in stark contrast against a blanket of white snow. The red brick house would appear first, with the outbuildings and barn peeking from behind it, like an overprotective mother shielding her young. I worried as to what condition I would find my mother upon my return. Most often, I would get a happy smile from her weary face, and a strong berating from my father.

"It's about time you made it back!" he would declare sullenly.

Jacob would often intercede for me. "Caleb was a big help and very useful to me, Jeremiah. I would have been hard pressed without him these last few weeks."

"It may be so. But he will have to work extra to make up for lost time."

The days of my youth passed, and I anxiously awaited for the time I could strike out on my own. In those days, the only thing that kept me at my father's house was my mother, who continued my education as best she could, despite the querulous nature of my father. She was quiet and strong, cooking and tending house and gardens for a man who held her in low regard. I admired her strength, and determined to stay as long as she had need of me.

And yet, I always anxiously awaited Jacob's return each summer and winter, and used my time with him and Martha to learn and grow in the ways of the woods. Jacob continued to sell our stockpile of furs and hides and meat, and showed me the coins that were my portion of the earnings.

"I bartered my measure of our little enterprise, Caleb, and managed to get these coins for you. I thought they would be more useful to you."

"Thank you kindly. There must be five pounds here!"

"Yes. Enough to give you a fresh start. A beginning, when you start your own journey in life."

I bowed my head, grateful he understood my situation. I dared not voice my objections to my father's mistreatment, but I could easily see my brother-in-law understood it.

"It's fine, Caleb. Your sister Martha has voiced her concerns over what goes on at your father's house."

He stopped, ruminating. "I'm grateful to have found your sister. Even though I am a good ten years older than she, our marriage has been a happy one. We hope to have children of our own one day." He sighed. "The Lord moves in mysterious ways. Although he has not blessed us yet, I am grateful to have such an astute student as you. I hope you don't mind if I treat you as the son I hope to have one day."

I looked at him quizzically. "Not at all," I gulped, trying hard to duck my head and hide the feelings I was sure showed plainly on my face.

"Then, let us get back to the woods you love so much, and work on your education!"

Laughing, we headed off.

While I learned much from Jacob during those years, many of the lessons he taught me had little to do with the woods. He taught me how to be a husband and father. How to be positive about the future – and even to look forward to it. During my years on this earth, I have found that some of those around us teach us how not to be. My father was a perfect example of that. He gave me little in the way of guidance when it came to life. But Jacob – he stood out in stark contrast. I'm grateful I had his example in those early days, or I fear my life would not have prospered as it has.

As I entered my sixteenth year I had grown to be a full head taller than my father. The years of hard work on the farm had given me a muscular frame, which came in good stead, as it turned out. As I grew, my father's punishments became less severe. He would hesitate to strike, as he could no longer look down on me, but must turn his face upward. At times, I could see a flicker of fear come across his face as he gazed into my defiant eyes. I had even begun to step in front of my mother when he berated her.

"So that is how it is to be," he would sputter angrily.

"Yes," I would obstinately reply.

As the year 1774 dawned, bitterly cold with snow heaped all around, I began to contemplate my future. I knew there would be a time when I could no longer stay under my father's roof. What would happen then to my mother? What course would my life take? I did not know the answers to these questions yet, but a tragedy would catapult me forward, into a life I could not have imagined.

CHAPTER TWO

As I sit here now, quill in hand, before a roaring fire to ward off the chill, with my wife sleeping comfortably in our bed, I recall vividly those terrible days in the spring of the year 1774. I had just turned 17 years old when my beloved mother became ill.

It began with a racking cough and a high fever. After a few weeks, as she weakened and was unable to keep up with the chores my father expected of her, he became irate and berated her mercilessly.

"Woman, I expect a warm supper when I get home from the fields! Are you not capable of completing the simplest of chores?" He would shout at her.

"Father, she's ill. You cannot expect any more of her!"

"I'll ask your opinion if I am interested in hearing it," he would growl.

"I think we should ask old Doc Howard to come check on her."

"No."

"But father, she's not getting better."

"I don't care. She should be able to keep up with her duties, even if she is sick."

"Fine. Then let me take the saddle mare and ride over to Martha and Jacob's. Perhaps she could come and tend to her."

He grudgingly gave his consent. I immediately went to the barn and saddled Sadie, our mare, and took off at a fast clip for my sister's home.

As I rode, I meditated on the obstinate folly of my father. His lack of concern for my mother's health was typical. My indignation grew as I rode, and by the time I reached Martha's home I was in a rage.

I rode Sadie straight into their front yard. As I passed the full, tidy fields of their farm, the tops of crops just breaking the surface of the rich loam, the cows feeding hungrily in the meadow, the pigs safely penned beside the well-kept barn, my anger soothed. I knew I had reached a calm in the storm.

I rushed up the steps of their farmhouse, red brick like ours, but with a full second story. I could see that Martha had been busy with her spring cleaning. The steps and stoop were swept clean of winter's debris. Tidy and orderly, Martha knew how to keep their home in good order.

I hurriedly knocked on the front door, calling out for Martha. She soon bustled to and opened the door, a look of surprise on her face. "Caleb! What's the matter? Why have you come?" she asked in surprise.

"It's mother. She's taken ill. Father won't get Doc Howard, so I've come to see if you could be of any help."

She opened the door wide to let me in. "What ails her? How long has she been ill?"

"About 4 weeks. She is feverish and coughing up blood now." My voice quivered as I explained.

"Go to the north field and get Jacob. I'll gather my things together," she replied, bustling off.

I headed for the fields and found Jacob working on a fence. I explained to him the dreadful circumstances as he eased himself into his coat and hat.

"Let's head back to the house. I'll help in any way I can."

By the time we returned to the farmhouse, Martha had filled her portmanteau with necessities. She had donned her hat and coat, and immediately said, "Hitch the buggy, Jacob. We must be off."

Jacob helped me carry the heavy portmanteau to the barn, and I helped him hitch up his horse to the buggy.

"Has Doc Howard been called?"

"Father refuses to call him," I answered, gulping.

"Fine. I'll take my saddle horse and find him and bring him to your place. Tie your horse to the back of the buggy, Caleb, and take good care of my wife."

"Yes, sir," I answered, thankful to have someone to share my burden with.

When we arrived home, Martha went straight in to the bed where my mother lay. "Caleb, see if you can get my trunk in here by yourself. Mother, I've brought some medicines that might help."

Mother lay limply in the bed, her face bright red from the fever that had overtaken her body. She looked so wan and thin, lying there. Yet she smiled quickly when she saw I had brought Martha.

"Thank you, my dear, for coming. I'll be better soon."

"Until then, you must rest."

My mother nodded. A look of relief came over her face. Her daughter's presence seemed to bring her some small comfort. As Martha busied herself with her trunk, I went and found Father.

"Martha has come. Jacob has gone off to find Doc Howard," I told him.

"All this fuss. Your mother will be fine," he replied, annoyed.

"Perhaps we should let the doctor decide." I spoke rather sharply, looking down on him as leaned against his shovel. He was in the barn, busy cleaning out the stalls. The rank odor of manure tinted the air, and I must say I took some small satisfaction seeing him perform a chore that normally fell to me.

I went and fetched Sadie and Jacob's buggy horse and returned. I put the horses in the stalls and made sure they had fresh water and were fed properly. My father continued with his task. No more words were spoken between us.

Martha was diligently tending to mother when I returned to the house. She had laid out an array of bottles and potions, and was solicitously tending to her needs. My mother looked content as her youngest daughter bustled about.

Within hours, Jacob rode up, Doc Howard following in his buggy. I was relieved to see them, and hoped the doctor could be of some assistance.

He hurried into the house and shooed us away. "Stay outside. I will come out and inform you of everything I find."

Jacob, Martha and I sat on the stoop. Father never joined us, although I knew he was aware of the proceedings.

It seemed like an eternity before the doctor came out of the house. He had a long-suffering expression on his tired face, lined as it was with the heavy burden of his occupation.

"Jacob, Martha, Caleb, I'm sorry I don't have better

news." My heart sank at the words. "I believe your mother is suffering from consumption."

We balefully looked at each other. We all knew about the ravages of consumption, and that there was no cure. I gulped repeatedly, trying to control the tears I could feel gathering in my eyes.

"The best advice I can give you is to keep her comfortable. Try and get her to eat when you can. She will have good days and bad. Don't let her become overtaxed. Now I must hurry away. Other patients, other patients. . ." he mumbled tiredly.

Jacob escorted him to his buggy, while Martha and I sat on the stoop, stunned at the news.

I choked up. "What are we to do now, Martha?" I pleaded with her.

She leaned over and put her arm around my shoulder. "We will do as the doctor has ordered. We will make her as comfortable as we can."

I nodded in reply.

After Jacob saw the doctor off, planted snugly in his buggy, he returned to us on the stoop.

"I will gladly break this sad news to your father," he stated.

"Thank you, kind husband. I don't believe I would like to converse with him at this time," Martha replied, somewhat vexedly.

Jacob returned shortly. He shrugged his tall, thin shoulders, and even his whiskers couldn't hide the look of bewilderment on his face. "It seems we will not get much help from that quarter."

I could feel my face grow hot, anger welling deep within me. I had always known my father was a coward, and his lack of reaction to the news of his wife's illness only added further proof.

"What are we to do, then?"

Martha grabbed my hand. "I will stay for the week. I will help you as best I can." She rose and hastened into the house to see to our mother.

Jacob and I spent a few moments together on the stoop. He assured me of his concern, and that all would be well. I knew deep in my heart that would not be true. I knew my mother didn't have long for this world, and that fact would hurl me into the unknown without the anchor I had always depended on.

Weeks passed and the season turned. My mother was able to be up and about for short periods of time. I tried to help as best I could. She taught me to cook simple foods, directing me from a chair I had moved into the kitchen for her. I remember those times with fondness. Despite her constant cough – so deep they would double her over – I learned how to pot meat, and even pickle and brine vegetables from the garden and prepare meats from our own pasture. Helping her, as well as maintaining the chores my father insisted I continue to carry out, left me exhausted by the end of the summer.

My father's reaction to his wife's condition was puzzling. At times, he seemed to bend just a little. He would hesitate before he spoke to her, a sure sign he understood what the future held. At other times, he would rant and whine, a sure indication that he could not truly change.

Martha would ride her saddle horse over regularly, staying a week at a time, which helped to relieve me of some of the responsibilities I was carrying on my young shoulders. While she was there I could go about my work, satisfied in the knowledge that my mother was being cared for.

Inevitably, consumption took over. My mother, always on the thin side, began to look all skin and bones. Her complexion was sallow, her hair turned completely gray. Seeing her, shriveled and shrunken under the blankets wrenched my young heart, as nothing else at that point in my existence had.

She passed one evening, while my father and I slept. He had taken to sleeping on a mat in the kitchen near the hearth, while I slept in the loft, as usual. I awakened early that morning, and while I stretched and yawned, it came to me that I could not hear my mother coughing. I rushed down the ladder and into the room we used to nurse her in, only to find her stiff and silent, her bright blues eyes opened and staring at nothing, her mouth rigidly formed into a half smile. I gasped and sobbed, and called out to my father.

"So she's gone," he said, hunching his shoulders as he stood in the doorway.

"Yes," I sobbed, as I reached over and clutched her cold hand. "I will be off this morning to get Martha."

"We will need help digging her grave. We will put her out by my parents in the family plot."

I nodded, rose, and headed for the barn, where I quickly saddled Sadie and was off.

We buried my mother the third week of September, 1774. The preacher, Tom Hankins, was there, as was Martha and Jacob and a few of my mothers' friends from the church. It was a bright morning, the sun gleaming off the shovels laid beside the grave. The smells of early September were heavy in the air. The leaves had begun to fall, and their rich aroma rose up to mix with the loamy smell of the dirt piled alongside the grave. The preacher spoke a few words of comfort, and the friends gathered with us in the front room of our house after her grave had been filled. Martha and Jacob stayed but a short while, as it was getting close to harvest time and there was much to do at their place.

My father's reaction to my mother's death was what would be expected of him. He showed very little sorrow, and carried on his duties after her death as if it didn't much matter. He never spoke of any regrets, but did manage to sniffle a few times during her burial for the benefit of the neighbors.

I had made my plans during the final weeks of my mother's illness. I had slowly gathered some supplies I knew I would need and hid them out behind the house, in the roots of a tree near the barn.

I had found a bit of oilcloth, which I used to wrap around my meager supplies – a sharp knife, a small hatchet, some needles and thread, a small cooking pot, and various and sundry other articles I knew would come in handy.

On the evening of the funeral I lay stiff as a board on the straw tick mattress that was mine in the loft. I waited anxiously, fully clothed, as I heard my father perform his evening rituals before going to bed. After a few hours, I eased down the ladder and listened anxiously. His snoring assured me he was asleep, peacefully, despite lying in the same bed my mother had died in but a few short days ago. I eased back up the ladder and gathered my belongings – an extra pair of breeches, two shirts, two pair of stockings, a bit of soap and a razor. I wrapped them carefully into two blankets, rolling them tightly into a bundle.

I calmly made my way back down and then went to the front room. There, hidden behind some other objects on a shelf, was my mother's copy of the "New England Primer." I removed it, added it to my bundle, and then slipped silently out of the house.

I made my way first to the mound of dirt in the family graveyard, newly dug, but enclosing the body of the woman who had done so much to make my life meaningful. I saw in my mind's eye the dress with the little blue flowers – her favorite – that she lay buried in. I tried not to think of how it last appeared on her – loose and shapeless on her dead body – but how lovely she looked in it on those Sundays when we made our way to church. She would sit, back straight, her hands folded in her lap, while she listened with rapt attention to the sermon of the day. She appeared almost beautiful on those occasions, the light shining in those bright blue eyes that matched that dress so perfectly.

I whispered some soft words to her, the tears trembling on my eyelids. I determined then and there I would do all I could to make her proud, as if she still walked the earth like the rest of us.

After I said my goodbyes to her, I swiftly found my stash of supplies in the tree roots where I had secured them, and then directed myself to the barn. I quickly saddled Sadie and secured my bundles behind the saddle. I spoke gently and kindly to the animal, hoping my exit from my father's domain would be swift and silent.

We left the barn and headed west, along the route I was most familiar with. I took one last look over my shoulder at my father's house, and silently cursed the man who had made my life and the lives of those I loved so miserable.

Chapter Three

The impetuousness of youth often leads us down paths we have no way of foretelling. As I gaze back over the decades, I know full well I had no true purpose in mind when I fled my father's house. All I remember is a yearning to be free, to make my own path, and to leave a cruel and heartless situation that had caused me much turmoil and pain.

I arrived at my sister's house in the wee hours of the morning, after galloping madly along once I was a short distance from home. I'm sure I looked a fright when I knocked loudly on her door, which was answered by Jacob, disheveled in his nightshirt and holding a lantern. Once he saw who had knocked so forcefully, he quickly swung the door wide and ushered me in.

"Why are you about at this late hour, Caleb? What brings you here?"

I answered breathlessly, "I cannot stay at home. I've decided to strike out on my own. My father's house has become intolerable."

"Martha, it's just Caleb."

She peered down the stairway, her hair disheveled and her eyes sleepy and half-closed. "Caleb?" She said, drowsily. "What brings you here?" She asked as she descended the stairs.

"I have to leave, Martha. I can no longer be part of my father's house."

"Let's go to the kitchen," Jacob suggested.

We made our way into the still-warm room, the embers of the evening fire still glowing in the fireplace. Jacob stirred them vigorously and added wood from the neat stack alongside.

"I'm sorry for disturbing you this late in the evening. I've come to gather my things here to be prepared for my journey," I stated, quickly.

Jacob looked at me thoughtfully. "What are your plans?"

"I've been reasoning it out for some time now. I cannot tolerate living as I've lived. I must strike out on my own and make my own path. I've heard about the great wilderness west of here, and I've decided to go and see what there is to see, and be my own man," I uttered forcefully.

Jacob nodded his head. "I understand that times have been hard, but are you sure this is the best choice for you?"

"Yes." I answered. "I'm unsure how I can handle my father any longer." I clenched my fists. "I've struggled with it long enough. I believe I can make it on my own, and that is what I plan to do."

Martha leaned over and grasped my hand. "I understand full well. But we dread your leaving. We're both so fond of you, little brother."

"And I you. I will never forget the kindnesses you have both shown me. The knowledge you've shared. And the affection you've shown me." I gulped. "But I must be off, and I will be off this very night."

Martha rose and bustled about. "I'll gather some food for you. Some meal and other necessaries. I have some fresh bread, and some smoked pork. I'll pack you a bundle."

Jacob rose from his chair. "I have your currency. And don't forget, you have a hunting shirt and leggings here that Martha fashioned for you. Come, let's gather it all together."

We went to the front room, and Jacob loosened a stone in the hearth of the fireplace and pulled out a small leather pouch. "You have close to seven pounds here, Caleb. I suggest you separate it and place it in various parts on your person and in your belongings. That way if you happen to fall into bad company, you won't lose it all at once."

I nodded.

He reached over the fireplace with his long arms and

pulled down the flintlock rifle he had purchased from the hooks that secured them there. "Here, I want you to have this." He reached into a box near the hearth. "I also have some extra powder and balls."

I stuttered, "But Jacob, I cannot take your good rifle!"

"Nonsense. I want you to have it. You cannot go unarmed, Caleb. There may be all sorts of people you'll meet on the road before you find a place to settle. You must have something to protect yourself. Besides, I still have my grandfather's. That's all I need," he insisted.

I reluctantly grabbed hold of the gun. "How can I ever repay you?" I asked humbly.

"Don't worry about that, Caleb. You have been a light in our lives. Your love for hunting and learning about the ways of the woods has brought me great pleasure. I only hope one day I will have a son that brings me as much joy as you have."

Impulsively, I grabbed hold of the man who had been more of a father to me than my own and hugged him. "Thank you so much, Jacob. I will always remember you."

Martha hurried in with food neatly tied into a burlap bundle. "This should last you a few days." She looked up at me fondly.

I quickly put my leather hunting shirt and leggings on over my clothes. I grabbed the rifle, the extra ammunition and the bundle of food and headed for the door.

"Don't travel on the main roads, Caleb. There are dangerous folks about, and you are traveling alone,"

Jacob warned me. "Have your firearm loaded and ready at all times. Avoid any Indians you come across until you can be sure they are friendly. Light small fires, as I showed you. Martha has provisioned you, so I'm hoping you won't have a need to light a cooking fire for a few days."

"Before you leave, what shall I tell father?" asked Martha. "You know he will be here first thing to search for you."

"He will be after me, all right. Only because I have taken Sadie and a saddle and bridle. And, of course, because he will no longer have free labor," I responded angrily.

"I cannot lie to him. You know that. What would you have me tell him?"

"Tell him I was here, but you don't know for sure where I was heading. That will be the truth, as I'm not sure of that myself," I replied ruefully. "Who knows? Maybe I'll head south and visit Jane and Susanna in Baltimore City."

"He will be very angry."

"I know. And I'm sorry you will have to bear the brunt of it."

"There will be no display of anger from your father while I'm here, Caleb," Jacob interjected.

Martha and Jacob joined me outside and watched me

arrange my packages on Sadie's back. "I'm frightened for you, brother. Will we ever see you again?" Martha asked wistfully.

"Write us when you get settled somewhere, if you are able. We will be here, waiting to hear from you," added Jacob.

"I promise to write as soon as I can. Don't worry about me. I'll make a go of it, you have my word."

With that, I mounted Sadie and headed off. I looked back at the two of them – Jacob, tall and lanky, still in his nightshirt, with his arm around the shoulders of Martha. She had the size and shape of our father, being on the short side, with a pleasing plumpness to her. But, like I, she had the blazing blue eyes of our mother, and a sweet softness around her face that reminded me so much of her. I blinked back tears as Sadie and I left their farmyard. I had no notion if I'd ever set eyes on them again, but I was determined to make it on my own. What lay before me I had no idea, but I was sure the path I had chosen was the right one. There was a place for me, somewhere out there in the wilderness. I was determined to find it, whatever the cost may be.

CHAPTER FOUR

Before the sun rose I had made good progress along a path heading west. Sadie was in fine spirits, as if she could sense the tension and excitement that rumbled through me. She had a spring in her step, and tossed her head merrily as we made our way. I took Jacob's advice and stayed off the main thoroughfare. Even at seventeen, I knew good advice when it was given. I could sense a vulnerability that I had yet to this point in my life experienced. It wasn't precisely fear – at that young age, I could not gauge what true fear was – but it was a feeling that I must be vigilant and careful, mindful of my surroundings. This sense of watchfulness would stand me in good stead in the course of time.

As the sun peeked over the eastern horizon, its rays striking the early autumn colors of the hardwood forest, I determined to find a place for Sadie and I to rest. I found a spot near the edge of a meadow, the green of summer competing with the yellows and browns of the fall season skittering across its surface. I picked a tall stand of pine, well off the path I had been following. I divested Sadie of her saddle, bridle and the various packages I had tied to her back and rubbed her down.

"Good girl, Sadie." I whispered to her, as I tied her to a tree. "For now, it's you and I." I gave her a handful of oats and a long lead, so she could forage for herself. I unpacked the bundle Martha had given me and enjoyed a quick repast, then wrapped myself up in my blanket and found a spot soft with fallen pine needles heaped about in great quantity, and took some rest.

I awoke in mid-afternoon, the sun brightly streaming through the branches and boughs of the pines. Sadie grazed nearby as I stretched myself awake. I had dreamed of my mother, sitting next to me, her face lit with a smile, reassuring me with her soft voice. What she said I could not recall, but a sense of calm was upon me. I knew in my heart she understood my need to flee, and I felt better for it.

I gathered my belongings and loaded patient Sadie again. I continued on the side path I had been using since I left Martha and Jacob. I could see the main thoroughfare through the forest, occasionally peopled by wagons and buggies, stirring up the dust in clouds, as folks passed to and fro, some with frowns, others gaily laughing and talking in groups. I was satisfied I had made the right choice in staying on my own. I was too close to home to make myself known to others. I knew my father was probably already at Martha's, questioning her as to my whereabouts. I did not want word to get back to him as to my location.

And so, we made our way west. The landscape changed as we moved along. Farms and fields grew further apart. There were large stretches of broad forests, foreboding in their stillness and quiet. An occasional bird call sounded but could do little to disturb the tranquility. I had an urge to explore those vast stands of trees, shrubs and vines, but knew I was still too close to home to wander. I forced myself forward.

I stayed true to the path well into the evening before I found a suitable place to make camp. The moon had appeared brightly in the cloudless sky, winking and nodding at me through the trees while I found a satisfactory place to rest and refresh. There was a small stream from which Sadie drank thirstily. I filled my canteen and splashed water on my face. I washed myself as best as I could and then built a small fire, which I used to warm the victuals Martha had sent with me. The air had turned cool and crisp, typical for that time of year. I rolled myself up in my blanket and slept.

When I awoke, refreshed, I unwound myself from my blanket, checked to see that Sadie was safely where I had left her, and poked and prodded the embers of my evening fire, adding kindling to it as I did so. As I sat warming a piece of ham, skewered on a stick over the fire, I began to understand the enormity of the task before me. I had no real plans as to my final destination.

I suppose the cool crispness of the morning, the sun just beginning to peak over the eastern horizon, partially shielded by the foliage of the forest, cleared my head somewhat. I needed to think.

"I'm away from my father's house, which went as well as anyone could expect. I imagine he's already been to Martha's, searching for me and Sadie. I'm tracking west, and have put a good 25 or 30 miles between us," I thought to myself. "It's perhaps another fifty miles to Frederickstown, if I continue as I have come. Perhaps I could inquire once there as to what lies further west. Surely someone there will have knowledge of what lies in that direction."

My decision made, I gathered my belongings and saw to the needs of my horse. She had fed herself quite nicely from the undergrowth around her tether. I fortified her further with a handful of grain and brushed her properly before bridling and saddling her.

"We're off again, Sadie!" She nodded her head briskly, as if in reply.

I started the day out on the main thoroughfare until traffic became more congested. I still had a fear of my father's wrath, and so by mid-morning I found myself once again on a faint trail, to the north of the main road. Few houses and farms could be found in the area in which

I traveled, so I knew I was still some distance from any form of civilization.

I decided in late afternoon to pull off and make camp. We had made good time that day, and I decided we would rest early and try to rise well before sunrise to continue our journey. The more traveling we could accomplish without the impediment of heavy traffic, the better. Before long, I knew, we would encounter the scattered farms and fields outside of Frederickstown, and I wanted to avoid any chance of coming upon someone who might recognize me.

We rested once again in a stand of pines, not far from a clear running creek. The weather turned cooler as the sun set, but thankfully the skies remained clear and bright. The winking stars in the vast blackness of the sky made me wonder at the vastness of the universe as I lay tightly wound in my blanket, the cool autumn air biting at my cheeks. As I drifted off to sleep, I convinced myself that my choice to leave had been a good one, and that I would one day find my place in the world.

The following morning I arose to a cloudy sky, and the north wind had taken over, with an icy sting in the air. I once again took stock of my situation. I was aware that I was drawing close to the town of Frederick, and that the possibility of being recognized, or that my father had made it this far west, were growing slim. I determined my best course of action was to make my way to the main highway. I could travel faster if I wasn't impeded by the shortcomings of the trail I had been traversing. After taking care of the needs of Sadie, I loaded her once again with my belongings and made my way to the road.

Congestion on the thoroughfare had increased. There were farmers, with their creaky carts loaded with all sorts of goods, heading west. Some were loaded with cages of squawking chickens, others with grain or corn. Some folks were shepherding small herds of cattle or pigs, bellowing their displeasure at such treatment. Occasionally, there were empty carts, heading east and back to their homes. Every now and then, I spotted a family with all they owned in the world tied down in the back of their cart, the husbands walking patiently beside the draft animals to lighten their load. Small children frolicked along the roadside, until their mothers screeched at them to keep up.

Within a few hours it was plain to see that no one along the road was interested in a lone rider. I rode along quietly, past fallow fields and small, well-kept farmhouses, the front yards neatly swept, the barns beside or behind them orderly and in fine condition. Some of the houses were clapboard and others were made of logs. Yet they all exuded a sense of prosperity and good fortune.

"I see now I have nothing further to worry about. My father would not have continued this far to look for me. Perhaps he headed to Baltimore City to make inquiries there."

Still, I kept my rifle across my saddle, keeping in mind Jacob's warning about the dangers of traveling alone. All by myself, I knew I could be in danger of being set upon by someone with bad intentions. I had no stomach for such an incident, and hoped my rifle would dissuade anyone with such a notion.

By noon, an icy cold drizzle had begun to fall from the leaden skies overhead. Before long it turned into a steady rain. The ruts of the road turned into a muddy mess, and many who traversed along with me pulled aside, to cover themselves and their belongings with tarpaulins, or shaded themselves under overhanging branches of tall birch and oaks along the route, though most of the leaves from those grand trees had already fallen. I determined to keep moving forward, and pulled my cap closer around my ears. All that was left moving along the roadway were those farmers herding their stock to market. As I passed them by, I could hear many of them cursing the weather, and asking among themselves why the weather had turned cold so early in the season.

I myself didn't know the answer to that question, but quietly cursed to myself with the same vehemence as those unlucky herders. By late afternoon I was drenched and hungry. Sadie's brisk walk had slowed, and I understood her circumstances all too well. The fields and farms had grown closer together, but I was able to find a grove of mixed woods, not far from the highway, to spend the night. As I bedded down that evening, under an oil cloth I had slung along the low branches of an old maple tree, I counted my blessings to have had some days of clear weather to make my escape, and talked calmly to God and asked that the following day would bring better weather. I piled up the fire, and created a large blaze to dry my things before it. I watched the embers of the fire from under my blanket and slowly drifted off to sleep. I had no way of knowing that the next day would bring me great good fortune, and a new direction for my life.

Chapter Five

When I awoke shortly before dawn, I checked Sadie and rekindled the fire, which still had some embers glowing beneath the charred wood. The rain had stopped, and as the sun rose I was thankful to see some clear skies. Most of the belongings I had placed before the fire were now tolerably dry, so after stick-frying a piece of bacon I repacked my meager possessions and headed out. A mist hung over the woods, giving the trees the look of ghostly apparitions, their limbs askew and awkward. I picked my way carefully along, heading toward the highway. Suddenly I came into a small clearing, not far from my campsite.

When I first entered, all I could see were the very broad shoulders of a man, buckskin clad, as he crouched over a small fire. As I entered he heard me and slowly rose, towering over his fire. His hat was jammed over a tumble of black curly hair that fell to his shoulders. His mouth was hidden by a tremendous black beard and mustache, the skin of his face as tanned as leather. I gripped my rifle a little tighter as he lifted a hand, as large as a good-sized ham, in recognition of my presence.

"Howdy, stranger! Were you the one with the roaring fire over yonder?"

I blinked rapidly as he spoke. I stood close to six feet tall, but this man was a good six inches taller than me. Yet his voice was high pitched, almost as high as a woman's. I did my best not to smile at the incongruousness between his stature and his voice.

"Yes, that would be me," I replied.

"Where are you heading?" he asked.

"I'm headed to Frederickstown."

"You got business there?"

Cautiously I replied, "I may have, or I may not."

I took a careful look around his campsite. He had a rather large black horse – he needed one to accommodate his bulk – and a fully loaded pack mule. They were tied to a tall pine, patiently waiting for their master.

"Well, I left Frederickstown yesterday. Didn't make it far before the rain. Not much happening there, if you ask me."

I slowly dismounted, still grasping my rifle in my hands.

"That's a fine looking rifle you have there, stranger. I only have a musket myself, but will be looking for something better once I get where I'm going."

"And where is that?"

"I'm looking to get into the fur trade. Came south from Pennsylvania. Have you ever heard of a fella named Evan Shelby?"

"No, can't say I have."

"Well, he used to live around these parts. An Indian fighter and fur trader, he is. Lost lots of money trying to trade with those red devils west and north of here. He packed up a year or so ago and headed south. I figured what was good enough for old Evan is good enough for me. I aim on heading south to see what I can find."

I walked back to Sadie and sheathed my rifle among my packs. "I was thinking of getting into the fur business myself. I was heading to Frederickstown and then west. I figured business would be good in that direction."

"Don't bet on that, stranger. The British have those Indians all riled up. They've been raiding and killing all along the frontier. Most folks are steering clear for now."

He poked the fire viciously. "No, it's south for me. I hear Shelby has built a fort down there, with plenty of opportunities for a man to make a living."

"I thought the British wouldn't allow us to settle south of here. West of the mountains."

"Most of us aren't too worried about what the British want. They can take their proclamations . . . well, you catch my meaning." he grinned slyly.

"But aren't there Indians down there too?"

"Plenty, I hear. But we got something they don't – Evan Shelby. He's an Indian fighter from way back. He's fought 'em out west, and if he's decided the ones south are easier to handle, that's all I need to hear. South is the way to go."

I impulsively stuck out my hand. "I'm Caleb Anders."

He grabbed it in his huge paw and replied, "Nate Daniel. From Westmoreland County. Where do you hail from, Caleb?"

"I'm from Baltimore County. North of the city, close to the Susquehanna."

"Nice to meet you. Perhaps it would be wise if we rode along together for awhile. Too many strangers hereabouts. Having company would prove a benefit to us both."

I thought briefly about Jacob's advice. About using caution and avoiding trouble. I had my currency hidden in various parts of my packs and person, to keep it secure. No doubt there was safety in numbers. Nate Daniel seemed to be a good traveling companion. His size alone would certainly dissuade anyone from molesting us, if they had a notion. I hadn't determined yet if I trusted him completely but thought I would give him the benefit of the doubt, for the moment. It certainly wouldn't hurt to travel a few miles down the road with him. His rationale for heading south seemed reasonable and well planned out.

"Yes, that sounds like a fine idea," I replied.

With that, Nate quickly extinguished his fire and mounted his horse, tethering his mule behind him. We headed for the road, and once upon it set out at a quick pace. We soon slowed, however, because of the mud that covered the deeply rutted highway. The rain from the day before had been a curse – not just to us, but to all the other travelers we encountered. Oaths flew out of the mouths of the cattle and pig drivers, their charges slipping and sliding through the muck. Those farmers with their carts heaped high were equally profane. The squawking and the racket set our teeth on edge.

"Look here, Caleb. There's a trail heading south just a little ways up yonder. Let's leave these fine folks to their business and be about our own."

With a sigh of relief, we left the churning mud of the road and struck off on a faint path leading south. The going was much easier, as there had been little traffic to pass that way. Being in unfamiliar territory, I nestled my rifle across my lap as we maneuvered our way through the tangles of underbrush.

"Isn't much of a trail, but at least it's heading in the right direction," I opined.

We remained mostly silent as made our way through deep forests and across streams and meadows. Occasionally, we came across a crude cabin, usually nestled under a grove of pine or cedar. They seemed empty and forlorn as we passed them by. We saw not a single other human being the rest of that day.

As we picked our way along the faint trail, concealed as it was with dead and dying leaves laying thick all around, we could hear the skittering and crashing of wildlife in the underbrush. The hardwoods were ablaze with color – bright oranges, reds, yellows and browns. Immense oaks and beech, elm and maple trees were everywhere. Fine country, I thought to myself. Yet, it was not far enough away from my troubles to want me to remain there. I clutched my rifle tightly, just in case we stumbled upon something that was less afraid of us than we were of it.

We decided to make camp as soon as the sun began to set. We busied ourselves taking care of our animals, seeing to their food and water before we started a fire and pulled out our blankets. We shared our rations that evening, both of us ravenous from the travails of the day. I glanced at Nate's ruddy features as we ate. I noted that he was a huge specimen of a man, but there didn't seem to be an ounce of fat on him. Some sort of hard labor had made him strong as an ox. For that I was thankful. It was good to have a traveling companion, I decided. I fervently hoped I'd made a good choice of one.

We settled ourselves before the fire, each with our own thoughts.

"You seem to be on the young side, Caleb. What draws you away from home?" Nate asked curiously.

I leaned over and poked at the fire. "My father and I didn't see eye to eye," I replied. "I'm seventeen. Old enough to make my own way."

He cackled, with a high-pitched tone that reminded me of a gaggle of women gathered together at the back of the church after services. "That seems mighty young to me."

I grew defensive and fired back. "What about you? What brings you here?"

"I already told you. I aim on getting into the fur trade," he countered. "Besides, there wasn't much there for me at home. I'm the youngest of eight. My Pa and Ma already have plenty of help around the place. Being the youngest and strongest, I always got the most difficult tasks, like mucking out the stables, the plowing, any heavy lifting." He shrugged. "But still, I did learn some useful trades. I know how to shoe a horse, that's for sure. And I'm pretty handy with a knife. Any game we got – I did the skinning if it was needed. Yes, I'm pretty handy with a blade." He pulled out a knife from inside his buckskin shirt and flashed it until it twinkled in the firelight. He laughed at the look I threw him.

"Don't worry, son. I only use this knife on animals, not people," he chortled.

"Well, let's hope that's all you'll need it for where we're going," I replied.

"You just never know. There's bound to be Indian troubles where we're heading. Seems there's Indian troubles everywhere nowadays," he said. "You're tall but a might lanky. I sure hope you can hold up your end if we meet up with any trouble."

I laughed. "Compared to you, most everyone is lanky. Don't worry about me. I'm pretty handy with this rifle. I can hold my own."

"That's what I aim to get, one day soon, instead of this old musket." He slapped at it disdainfully. "Easier to load, but it ain't worth anything for distance."

"So you told me." I patiently replied.

That was a peculiarity I learned early on about Nate. Once he got his mind set on something, he would worry it to death, like a hound with an old bone. Sometimes he would bring up what was on his mind at odd intervals, in moments that seemed completely inappropriate. For instance, in the midst of a hunt he would start complaining about his hunger, knowing full well we could do nothing about it at that moment. He would carry on about it until we found something to fill his belly. Or perhaps the fireplace wasn't drawing to his satisfaction and we needed to get it fixed. He would fret about it endlessly, while in the midst of the woods, where nothing could be done about it. Not a thing would satisfy him until we could return and work on that fireplace. But I accepted his shortcomings over time, as he did mine. Friendship demanded it. All in all, as we settled in to sleep that first night, I determined I had made a good choice for a comrade. One day, he would save my life, and I his. Our lives would become intertwined, in ways I could not imagine back then. I was just happy at that moment that we had stumbled into each other.

Chapter Six

We awoke the next morning when it was still dark, the air crisp and cold. We stirred the embers of the fire from the previous evening and warmed ourselves for a bit. At the first rays of daylight we gathered our belongings and slung them on the backs of our horses.

Nate's big black mare, Bessie, was a beautiful animal. She stood a good 17 hands high, with rippling black muscles and a long, thick neck. Considering Nate's stature, she was a good fit for him. His mule Daisy proved to be good tempered for a mule, which would benefit us greatly in our travels. She was loaded with various bags and pouches, which included a kettle and other cooking implements and a few skins Nate had brought with him.

The trail we had been following became fainter as the morning progressed. I thought in my own mind we would have to find a better path before long. The tangled underbrush was becoming a nuisance and was slowing us down considerably.

About mid-morning I spotted a small flock of turkeys on the edge of a clearing. I gestured to Nate, who was riding behind me, to stay still. I dismounted slowly, raised my rifle, steadied it, and took a shot at the large, fat tom turkey I had spotted. My shot rang out, echoing through the dense foliage. The flock scattered in fright. Nate rushed over, grabbed our prize by its feet and raised it in triumph.

He shouted, "You shot his head clean off!"

"That's what I was aiming for."

He strode up to me, a huge smile showing through his monstrous beard. "I guess you do know how to shoot!"

"I had a good teacher."

"Well, let's tie this bird up on Daisy's back. We'll have fresh meat for supper!"

That evening, we ate well. We chopped up our turkey, and added parched corn and some chickweed we had found during the day. It was tasty and filling. We used part of the turkey to dry for another day. We cut it in thin strips and arranged it on a rock close to the fire.

After supper, as we stretched out before the fire, our bellies satisfyingly full, we discussed our situation.

"Look here, Nate, this trail we've been on . . . " I started.

"I know. It's becoming increasingly difficult to follow."

"I'm of a mind we should head off to the eastward tomorrow. Perhaps we can find a better path that leads us to where we are going."

He thought for a moment. "Why not west?"

"We haven't seen any Indians in these parts. That makes me uneasy. If there is something brewing, they most likely would head west, wouldn't they?"

"There was talk in Frederickstown of some trouble west of us. Those red devils were causing all sorts of difficulties in that direction. I heard tales of settlers getting burned out and plenty of scalps being taken. Also heard tell of a couple of companies of militia heading out that way. I think you may be right. We should head east. We may stumble upon trouble, so we should take precautions. No sense us losing our lives before we get to where we're going."

The following morning we headed south southeast. Before long, we came upon a rocky overhang and decided to climb it to see what was before us. We scrambled up, and then stood silently as we viewed our surroundings.

We had been traveling through a valley that snaked its way through a stretch of high hills, but they were nothing compared to what we spied from our vantage point. Off to the west, a good distance, we saw great mountains, sheathed in greens and the colors of autumn, standing majestically against the western sky. But it was to the east that we eyed a most remarkable sight. Through the veil of lowered clouds and morning mist, a blue tinge showed through – a magnificent mountain range the likes of which I had never seen before. Although a good distance off to the southeast, they were close enough to cause me to catch my breath. To this day, I will never forget my first sight of the Blue Ridge Mountains. Their mysteries and secrets seemed to call to me. They beckoned me to come closer, to explore them, to welcome them as a part of me.

I trust Nate had the same response to those monstrous, shimmering crags and valleys, those mist shrouded heights that lay before us. We both stared in silence for a few moments.

"Should be good hunting," he said matter-of-factly.

"Should be good hunting for a whole lot of us," I replied.

We slipped and slid down the overlook, mounted up once again, and moved off. A sense of anticipation overcame any fears or misgivings I had harbored in my heart. We most certainly were choosing the right course. We were following a path to home. I just knew it.

Before long, we spotted deep heavily laden storm clouds heading toward us from the southeast that didn't portend well. We discussed the possibility of seeking shelter for ourselves and our animals before the storm came upon us. We found a north-facing pile of rock near a stream and a thick grove of pine and cypress. We opined it would be a good place to make camp. We attached our tarpaulins to the rocks and tethered our animals in the grove. After we set up, we decided to explore for a bit and found a high-piled beaver dam just upstream from our newly minted camp.

"I brought along a few traps. While we're waiting on the storm, we should set them out. Beaver pelts are worth a pile of money!" Nate exclaimed.

"Might be worth a try," I responded.

We went through the ponderous packs Nate carried on Daisy's back, and found four traps he had brought along. We carried them to the dam and began reconnoitering. We began at the edges of the stream, where there were fresh marks on felled trees and downed branches. Scores of tree stubs, gnawed and worried by the industrious beavers stuck straight up into the sky.

"Looks like they've been busy along here recently."

"Yup. First trap goes here."

We waded into the stream, chillingly cold and clear. We found an entrance hole close to the waterline and placed another. We set the other two along the top of the dam, at a muddy crossroads used by the diligent beasts.

We no more than got through setting our traps when the storm burst over our heads. Torrential rains beat down upon us, soaking us to our skins. We slipped and slid through the underbrush to our shelter. By the time we reached it, thunder and lightning crashed and flashed overhead, and we could hear the restless neighing and shuffling of

Bessie, Daisy and Sadie. We did our best to reassure them, while making sure their tethers were secure.

We had stowed all our baggage inside our shelter, and Nate had the foresight to gather dry wood and kindling before we left for our trapping. While the wind howled around us, driving the wet under the flaps of our makeshift tent, we waited out the storm.

"We'll have to get more traps once we reach our destination."

"I'd say we could use about a dozen between us."

"My brother-in-law Jacob also taught me how to rig up traps in the style of the Indians. I can easily teach those to you also. They're simple but they are very effective."

The wind finally slackened. Nate busied himself getting a fire going at the entrance to our shelter. We huddled close to it, as the temperature had dropped. We made do with a simple meal of dried turkey and boiled greens.

And on that day, our partnership was formed.

Following a wet sleep we arose to a damp and blustery day. The wind drove the now-spent raindrops, clinging to every limb and leaf, through our clothing and down our necks as we made our way to check the traps we had set the day before. Two had been triggered, loaded with fat, healthy beavers. We removed them, and then reset the traps.

We returned to our camp, where Nate deftly relieved our catch of their pelts. He worked swiftly, his flashing knife speedily removing their skins with the ease of one who had an abundance of experience.

"Good eating tonight, Caleb! Nothing better than beaver meat."

"The Indians sure think so."

"I'll set this meat to cooking." He grabbed up the kettle, filling it and setting it in the fire. He added dried corn and some greens that grew outside our tent flap. A quart or so of water was added. A smidgen of salt from our supplies was thrown in on top.

We then took up our newly acquired prize of pelts and did our best to scrape them as clean as we were able. We had no way of drying them – that would have to wait for later.

"What say we stay here an extra day. Any hides we can get here will help us later. That beaver dam can yield us some good rewards."

"An extra day won't hurt." I replied.

Before we left our snug camp, we had gathered six beaver pelts. A very good start to our new enterprise.

Chapter Seven

The underbrush had gotten thick as our journey continued, with brambles and brush intertwined with fallen dead timber, limbs and branches. We were forced to dismount and lead our horses, cursing and swearing all the while.

It was hard going, not just for us but for our animals. We used our hatchets to clear a path where necessary. Time marched by, and it seemed we were doomed to wander forever through the wilderness we had encountered. We stopped for fresh water whenever we could and to rest our animals.

We came upon a clear, deep stream after three days of wandering and decided to set up camp. Nate reached into his packs and miraculously pulled out some hooks and fishing line. Our food supply had gotten low by that time, and yet we were hesitant about using our firearms to replenish it for fear we would draw the attention of any nearby Indians. After taking care of our animals, we set ourselves down on the bank to see what we could catch. With nothing else for bait but dried corn, we were not hopeful of our chances of catching our supper.

It had been a clear fall day. The sun shone brightly overhead as it made its way westward. We lazed in its warmth, thankful for it. Nate spoke. "Seems to me we should have come across a better path by now."

"We haven't made many miles, Nate. Not through this twisted mess we've encountered."

"Maybe tomorrow we ought to head more east than south. Surely we will come across a trail of some sort in that direction."

"You could be right. I'm willing to give it a try."

With our plans set, we concentrated on fishing, and soon enough caught two healthy-sized trout. We gutted them and started a small fire. We skewered them over the fire and finished setting up our camp. Both of us famished after the travails of the day, they disappeared as soon as they were cooked.

All along our route we had heard the howling and yelping of wolves after dark. That evening, they were uncomfortably close. I built up the fire to a roar as we turned in for the night. Both of us had our hands on our firearms as we fell asleep.

It was slow going again the next day. We confronted the same tangles and twists that had previously delayed our passage. We doggedly persisted, determined as we were to find a way to those shimmering blue mountains we had viewed from afar.

A nagging doubt had crept into my mind by that time. I was tired and hungry. Our progress had been much slower than I had anticipated. I dared not voice my concerns to Nate, for fear he would see my weakness. My youthfulness foolishly persuaded me to keep silent. Would we wind up spending our lives wandering through this trackless wilderness? I did not know.

About mid-morning the next day we heard from a distance the bellowing of oxen and the shouting and cursing of a man off to the east. We urged our horses toward the sound, through a thick tangle of roots and brambles. Within a few minutes, we burst through the brush and found ourselves on a deeply rutted road, heading south. We glanced to our right and saw a small covered wagon stuck in a boggy area, with mud halfway up its wheels.

There was a man, covered in muck and mud, urging two oxen harnessed to the rig. Hat jammed down on his head, he was bellowing at them, exhorting them onward. We could see they were hopelessly stuck. We dismounted to lend a hand.

Samuel Hayward wasn't a large fellow. Most of his face was clean-shaven, with a jutting jaw and jet black eyes. His wife, Chastity, was a diminutive woman. She stood on the roadside clutching a baby to her breast. I could see tendrils of auburn hair drooping from under her bonnet. Beside her were three small boys, all with blazing red hair. Timothy was the oldest, about ten, followed by Ezra, eight, and Elijah who was six. They stood quietly enough, their gazes all directed toward Samuel and the Herculean task that lay before him.

After introducing ourselves, we set to work to see what we could do to help.

"First off, we need to unload some of these goods off this wagon," Nate declared.

We set to work unloading barrels and bundles and some small household goods. It was amazing to me how Samuel and Chastity had managed to load so much into such a small space. There were numerous cooking utensils, boxes of hand tools, a small plow, jars of pickled produce, even a rocking chair!

Once we got about half of the wagon unloaded, Nate spoke. "Samuel, you direct the oxen while Caleb and I give a heave to at the back."

While Samuel coaxed the oxen, we put our shoulders to the wood. With a tremendous push, I saw Nate's end of the wagon clear the rut it was stuck in and sail forward. Not to be outdone, I pushed with all the strength I could muster and got my end out also. The oxen moved forward, and the wagon was clear.

Samuel was effusive in his thanks. "Don't know what we would have done if you boys hadn't shown up. We got stuck here late yesterday and have been trying ever since to get this darned wagon out."

"Thanks aren't necessary," I responded. "We've been trying to find a decent route south and are grateful we heard you. Where are you heading?"

"We haven't got our eyes set on any place in particular. Just heading south. We've been hearing tales of open land and figured we could make a place for ourselves there."

Nate and I both nodded.

"If you boys don't mind, we surely would be happy to have you ride along with us for awhile. Chastity here is afraid of Indians, although we haven't seen any yet. Both of us are pretty good shots, but the more of us there are, the safer we'll feel. That is, if we wouldn't hold you up too much."

"Sounds reasonable. We don't mind it. There is safety in numbers," I replied.

We reloaded the wagon and secured the bundles and boxes. Samuel and Chastity, still clutching her infant, along with their youngest boy Elijah mounted the wagon. The two older boys scampered alongside as we moved out.

Nate and I took the lead, with the wagon following

behind. We were in good spirits. The road was passable and the weather was good. I knew it would be slower going with the Hayward family now a part of our convoy, but believed the good of it outweighed the bad.

We made fine time that day, traversing a good ten miles, despite the drag the wagon made on our little company. Towards sundown we made camp alongside a bubbling creek that crossed the road. A fire was started, and Chastity laid her baby down on a blanket close to it, and then busied herself over a kettle that she hung from a spit. In it she placed dried pork, salt and some pickled carrots out of a crock, along with water her eldest son fetched for her from the creek. I searched through my pack and found some parched corn I had managed to save to add to the mixture.

As we waited for our supper to cook, we set up the rest of the camp. Samuel and Chastity and the baby, a little girl named Mary, slept under a tarpaulin, while the three boys made their beds in the wagon.

"We need to find some fresh meat," I told my partner. "These folks don't have provisions for all of us, and we need to do our part in providing. Let's take to the woods to see what we can find."

With that, Nate and I took our guns and moved into the forest. We found a few squirrels chattering in the trees, their tails swishing and flicking back and forth. We dispatched them easily and brought them back to camp.

"Ma'am, these here squirrels will help with our suppers tomorrow night." Nate addressed Chastity.

"Thank you kindly, boys. They're big and fat and will make a nice stew, that's for sure!" she responded happily.

After we ate, she got busy fussing with the boys and got them settled in the wagon. Samuel, Nate and I relaxed before the fire, our bellies full of the fine meal we had just consumed.

"So where do you hail from, Samuel?" I asked.

"Just north of Philadelphia, close to the Delaware. You?"

"Baltimore County. Nate here is from Pennsylvania also. North of Frederickstown."

"I had a pretty nice place. Not big, you understand. But we were pretty well fixed. Forty acres I had, well fenced. Grew some corn and hay and had some pigs and chickens. Chastity inherited the place from her grandfather. He had no sons, and she was the only grandchild he had when he passed."

We grew quiet as he talked.

"If it weren't for the dad-blamed politics, I'd have stayed." He grew heated. "I don't know why folks can't just mind their own business! Committees of Safety, they're called! Bunch of rabble rousers if you ask me! Tarring and feathering! Riding people on rails! Burning folks out! Happening all over! It's gotten so bad, a man can't feel safe in his own home!" Even in the firelight I could see his face turning red. He leaned over and punched at the fire with a stick. "I didn't want to raise my family in all that ruckus. I'm not a fan of those lousy British, mind you. They keep poking at us, with their silly rules and taxes that don't make any sense. They're even quartering their troops in people's homes up there in Boston. But I have a family to take care of, and I aim to do it where there's peace and quiet!"

"But you're heading into Indian country," I pointed out.

"Maybe so. But I figured they can't be any worse than those folks tearing up the countryside, destroying and raising hell. At least I can shoot Indians."

"So what did you do with your place?" Nate asked.

"Sold it. My sister and her husband bought it from us. Got a pretty good price, too. Packed what I could into this here wagon, and have some hard money to find us a place where we're heading."

Nate spoke up. "Well, we're heading south to find Evan Shelby. I heard he has a place down here, close to the Blue Ridge. He's an old fur trader and Indian fighter, and we figured it would be a good place for our fur business. As soon as I can, I'm going to replace this old musket with a rifle. Better for hunting."

"Sounds like a fine idea." Samuel replied. "Might work out for us as well. I've heard of Evan. I didn't know he had moved. I thought he was still in Maryland."

"Nope. He got swindled out of his property. At least,

in my opinion he did. He tried trading with the western Indians, but that old Pontiac put a stop to it. That war took everything he had, I heard. He headed south a few years ago – two or three, maybe. The lousy redcoats can't keep us penned in. We'll spread out as we see fit, whether King George likes it or not!"

With that, we turned in for the night. The wind had picked up, causing the flickering flames of our campfire to jump and dance. After a weary day I fell fast asleep, a deep dreamless one.

The covered wagon of Samuel and Chastity Hayward crossed the clear, cold stream with relative ease the following morning, and we continued on our journey. It was the first week of October, and the hardwood trees were in their full, fall glory. We traveled through the rolling hills and lush meadows with little difficulty. Off to the west, the mountain range we had spotted but a few days ago grew further away. The hulking mountains to the east, shrouded in mist and clouds as they often were, beckoned to us, as if challenging us to discover their secrets.

All in all, we were a happy group. The boys scampered about alongside the roadway, laughing and catcalling to each other, their red hair glinting in the sunlight. They weren't much of a nuisance, unless they decided to bedevil Daisy, Nate's patient mule. Chastity would sternly put a stop to their antics as soon as she became aware of them. Daisy, her ears laid back as if she took their mischievousness as a personal insult, maintained her steady pace in spite of them.

We made good time most of the day, but just before dusk a heavy rain overtook us. We pulled into a grove and decided to call it a day. We managed to form a covering in the trees and soon had a fire blazing. Nate and I skinned the squirrels we had killed the day before, and quickly gutted them and stuck them in the pot Chastity had boiling over the fire. We would be damp, but at least we would have a hot meal.

Nate and I talked after we bedded down for the night. It was wet and cold, but we were not discouraged. We happily anticipated what lay ahead of us. Before long, we would have the opportunity to forge our own paths and make a future for ourselves.

CHAPTER EIGHT

We slogged on through misty rain and mud for the next two days. The Hayward boys no longer scampered along the roadside but were confined to the wagon by command of Chastity. Although she was small, her young boys knew not to cross her. She was not one to tolerate any nonsense from her offspring. She could break off a twig and use it liberally on their backsides if she had a mind to, and they knew it.

Despite the dreary weather, which clouded my view of the distant mountains that had drawn me so powerfully, my outlook was cheery. I had no cause to complain about much of anything in those days. I had companions, a good horse, and enough food and water to get by. I was away from my father and the troubles he had caused. Life was good, and I had much to look forward to.

We were about three days out from our destination when we were joined by three men that evening after we made camp. They were a scruffy looking lot, bedraggled from the rain, their horses spattered with mud up to their withers. They hallooed when they spotted our campfire, and we cordially invited them to join us around it.

"Where are you fellows heading?" Samuel asked.

The tallest one spoke up. "Don't know for sure. Just heading south, looking for a little adventure, I guess. My name's John Williams. I hail from Baltimore City." He added, "I met these other fellows along the way and we decided to ride together, seeing as three guns are better than one if we run into any trouble."

The short one with the full beard and broad smile spoke. "Henry. Henry Fallwood. I hail from just west of Philadelphia. Looking to get into the fur trade if I can. I have a good rifle and a steady hand, so I'm looking for opportunities to use them."

The last one said, "George Simmons." He offered no other information.

We all introduced ourselves in return. Henry and John smiled and nodded as we did so, but George paid little attention. I must say I took a dislike to the man from the very start. He had shifty eyes. I kept an eye on him as the rest of us conversed, and I noticed he was carefully taking stock of the wagon and the items around our camp. He eyed Chastity in a way that I found particularly distasteful. There was just something about him that made me uncomfortable.

I expressed my concern to Nate after we had all bedded down for the night.

"I tell you, Nate. I don't like the looks of that George fellow. He's got a look about him I find troublesome."

"Me too. He took some time checking out our belongings. We should keep an eye on him."

"Agreed."

The next morning we got an early start. Nate and I offered to scout around to see if we could round up some game. Our little party had grown. With seven of us able to use firearms – Chastity informed us she could wield a musket about as well as a man and had her own – we felt safe enough to use our weapons with impunity.

On our hunt we found ourselves in rock strewn terrain, with stunted trees that strained to reach upward with very little success. We did stumble upon a small meadow and positioned ourselves close by. Dew was still dripping from the weeds and bushes in the meadow, as it was still early and perfect feeding time for any game in the area. Luck was with us, and we spotted a small herd of deer along the opposite edge of the clearing.

"Caleb, you take the shot. Your rifle is more accurate. I see a big buck there. You see it?" Nate whispered.

I nodded. I lined it up, took steady aim and fired. The buck dropped where it stood.

We rushed over. "Clean through the head. We'll be eating well for the next few days. And look – his hide is unmarked," Nate pronounced with a wide grin.

We bundled the buck on the back of Bessie, Nate's mare. I felt a little sorry for her. Not only did she have to haul Nate's big frame, but now had the added burden of a buck that weighed a good 150 pounds. We made our way back over the rocky slopes and caught up with our traveling companions within an hour.

There were catcalls and shouts of joy when we rode up with that big buck. Chastity clapped her hands and laughed. The boys climbed out of the wagon and scampered around us, whooping and hollering.

"Good going, boys! Perhaps we should make camp a little early this afternoon so we can dress him and get him ready for the pot!" Chastity said.

The rest of the day, we traveled in high spirits. Nate told the story of my shot with great detail. The men nodded and eyed me with a new respect. I noticed George taking stock of my rifle, a little too intently for my taste. I clutched it tighter as he did so.

We made camp late that afternoon. Nate and I tied the buck we had killed to a tree limb, its head pointed downwards. The two of us got right to work skinning the beast, carefully removing the hide with our skinning knives. We then removed its innards and brought the heart and liver to Chastity, who had her kettle placed over a fire, already boiling. She placed the parts in the kettle and added some parched corn. She smiled happily at us.

Samuel had another fire going and fashioned a makeshift spit. We butchered the rest of the buck and brought the chunks of meat to him, and he carefully speared them and hung them over the fire.

Our three new companions were busy fetching water and firewood and tending to our beasts of burden. They staked them out in a field, after watering them at a small creek that ran beside the road.

Henry cheerfully offered to refill the water barrel lashed to the side of the Haywoods' wagon, and Chastity happily nodded her approval.

After our meal, the boys scampered about around the fire. The baby Mary rested comfortably in Chastity's lap, smiling and gurgling at her mother. I noticed George sat a little distance away from the rest of us, his eyes moving furtively among us and then at the wagon and animals staked out beyond it.

I tried to ignore him as best I could.

"So what news do you have for us?" Samuel asked eagerly.

"Not much," Henry answered. "You heard about the Congress meeting in Philadelphia..."

"No," Nate replied. "We've been on the road for a few weeks. What Congress?"

A satisfied grin spread across Henry's bearded face. He patted his full paunch contentedly. "Well, it's all about those dang fools in Boston throwing good British tea overboard last year."

I spoke. "I don't recall hearing about that."

"Where you been, boy?" Henry asked, aghast at my ignorance.

"I don't pay much attention to politics," I responded.

"It's gotten way beyond politics now. Folks up around Boston had enough of Parliament assigning taxes on us without our say so. A bunch of them raided a ship in Boston harbor and threw all the tea – bales and bales of it – overboard." He chuckled. "Safe to say the lobsterbacks were none too happy with them. So, being the sole of wisdom…" he rolled his eyes upward "…Parliament decided they would get back at them with even more restrictions."

I thought a moment, and then remembered Jacob telling me about the Boston Tea Party while we were on one of our hunts. I had paid little attention to it at the time, being caught up in my own cares and concerns. I had little idea then that such an incident would spark a fire that could not be contained.

"More restrictions?"

"Yup. First off, they closed the port at Boston, and demanded those folks pay them back for the tea they dumped in the harbor. Most of them hadn't had anything to do with throwing that tea over the side, so they were none too happy. Then they took away the charter for the whole colony of Massachusetts and decided Parliament and the King could control it better than its own citizens."

A look of satisfaction spread across Henry's face. He appeared to be very happy to end my ignorance.

"That's not all." John spoke up. "Don't forget the part where any of them bigwig Britishers don't have to stand trial in Massachusetts. They get to have a free ride to England and stand trial there."

"So no witnesses then?" Nate inquired.

"Yup. Witnesses have to go to England to give a testimony. Now how many ordinary folks can afford to take off and sail away to England? Who's going to support their families while they're gone/"

"And the Quartering Act," Henry said. "Don't forget that. Lousy lobsterbacks get to live in any house they choose. If it puts you out, so be it. No one in the colonies has a say in that either."

"That's why they're having a Congress," John continued. "All the colonies have elected folks to get together in Philadelphia to try and resolve all this mess. Not that I think it will do any good. Too many people are fed up with all the new laws. They want to have a say in what goes on here."

Samuel stood. "That's why I left. I'm tired of talking about it. All I want is to live in peace, without all this squabbling and fussing about. Not anything we can to about it, so I say we just live our lives and take care of our families."

"Well, you did ask for news," I pointed out.

"Yes I did. And I'm sorry I asked," he replied huffily.

With that, he and his family retired for the night.

After we bedded down, Nate and I had a whispered conversation. "I sure hope all this hullabaloo over those lousy redcoats don't interfere with our plans," Nate complained.

"I don't see it. We'll be safely away in the mountains. Surely it won't travel down that far."

"You never can tell about it. People have a strange way of bringing their problems with them," Nate answered.

"We'll just have to deal with it the best we can if that happens. We won't have to get involved either way."

"Maybe. I just don't like it, that's all."

"Surely you heard about all this before you left home?" I asked.

"Yes, I did, but I didn't pay it much mind. Didn't figure I had to get tangled up in it. My big brother Josiah was all put out about it. Claimed he was part of one of those Committees of Safety. Don't know for sure if he was or not. He isn't one to tell the truth, you know. Anyway, he said he's ready to fight if it comes down to it. He got my Pa and Ma all riled up about it, too. Not that I like the King's government, mind you," he interjected. "But as I said, I've got other plans."

I spent some moments contemplating our situation before I fell asleep. A sense of unease descended upon me.

We were up before dawn and ate a cold breakfast before heading off. While hitching the oxen to Samuel's wagon and loading up our own horses and mule, two wagons passed us by. They were both loaded down and accompanied by six or seven riders. We conversed with them briefly. The party consisted of two families – brothers. The wives were driving the wagons while the men and older children were astride the horses. More children rode in the wagons, sitting across various and sundry household items. They seemed tired and agitated, as they told us they had heard gossip of battles and war taking place to the west.

"Militia is out, trying to teach them Indians a lesson. They've been bedeviling the settlements again. Lots of folks burned out, and scalps taken. We're trying to get south as quick as we can, in hopes things will be calmer down there," a tall, bedraggled man wearily informed us.

We watched them as they passed, the wheels of their wagons creaking in agony as the women who steered them flapped the reins to encourage their horses to go even faster. The children huddled in the back were quiet. At that moment I was thankful I had no one but myself to worry about.

During the day, we began to see a few cabins, smoke curling from their chimneys, scattered through the rugged country in which we passed. There were fenced pastures and garden plots, barren at this time of year except for the wilted tops of carrots and turnips and a scattering of pumpkins and cabbage.

Despite its ruggedness, it was a marvelous country we passed through. The Blue Ridge mountains leered at us from the east, always inviting and enticing us. There were broad valleys, lush with stands of tall hardwood and pine sporadically making their presence known. The Haywood boys, Timothy, Ezra and Elijah, scampered and skipped about, their mother admonishing them to mind the horses and not interfere with our progress.

Around noontime we came across a great Conestoga wagon, its wheels mired in mud, alongside the main road. Great cursing and lamentations could be heard as we came abreast of it. There was a horde of people milling about. The wagon, pulled by a team of four oxen, was escorted by a dozen or so horses. While the women stayed astride theirs, about six men had dismounted and were arguing about the best way to free their wagon. It must have been heavily laden to be so bogged down. I was a bit curious as to why the party chose such a heavy wagon, usually used to haul freight, for their journey but I asked no questions.

We paused and offered our help, but they injudiciously declined it. As we moved away, Nate made the comment, "Must be city folks. Anyone knows to lighten the load. Maybe they'll figure it out before next Sunday." I couldn't help but chuckle to myself.

Anticipation was high that evening as we gathered around the fire after hungrily consuming our supper. It had been a fine day for travel, with clear skies and a light wind. We had found an excellent spot to make camp, with water nearby. We had spotted no trouble along the road, and for that we were thankful.

As had been his custom, George Simmons had separated himself from the rest of us, choosing to size us up from about six feet away. Whenever I glanced at him I felt a cold, clammy feeling running down my backbone. I didn't like his standoffish attitude, nor the way he had continued to coolly appraise our gear and animals. I noticed Nate occasionally glancing his way as well. Our eyes met at one point, and we nodded together. I was not alone in the feeling of unease George stirred up.

John Williams was busy telling a tale of his childhood days in Baltimore City, while the others around the fire guffawed at his antics. Not to be outdone, Henry piped in with some stories of his own youth. While the men were thus entertained, Chastity roused herself from the fire and took the boys to the wagon to settle them down for the night.

We politely refrained from talking about the political

situation back north, to keep from upsetting Samuel. He was a good man, sturdy and devout in his duties as husband and father. By tacit agreement, we spoke of other subjects.

"It's a bit of a curiosity to me that we haven't seen any travelers heading north along this road," Nate mentioned, his face lit by the glow of the fire. "Does it seem odd to anyone else?"

"I find it a bit curious, too. I would expect a steady stream of traffic heading in both directions, considering it's harvest time and all," Henry said.

"Maybe the weather has held things up. The road, although well worn, would be an impediment to any heavy traffic," I shared.

"Perhaps so," said Nate. "But we need to be watchful tomorrow. Something tells me to be wary of what we may find."

Chapter Nine

There was an eerie stillness in the air as we made our way through the valley in which we found ourselves the next morning. The mountain range still loomed over us to the east, tufted clouds obscuring its crags and peaks. There was a bracing, cold wind from the west, but the clouds that clothed the mountains remained unperturbed, obstinately clinging to them, like a young child clings to the skirts of its mother.

We spoke little as we traveled, as the anticipation of reaching our destination occupied our thoughts. We were enveloped by a strange silence. We passed a few homesteads, their chimneys cold and smokeless, with no signs of human occupation. Even the birds up above were silent as they flitted across the sky, going about their business noiselessly and purposefully.

And then we spotted it. The first sign of trouble.

The charred remains of a cabin came into view, small curls of gray smoke still rising from the logs. Chastity herded the boys into the wagon, while the rest of us went to examine it.

Whoever had started the fire was determined to destroy it and all its contents. Little if anything remained except for a few blackened clay pots close to what remained of the fireplace. We stepped carefully among the ruins, searching to see if there were any clues as to whom this dwelling had belonged, but found nothing to give us any indication.

"Careful, boys. I hope to God we don't find any bodies among the ashes," Henry said quietly.

As near as we could tell, there wasn't any evidence that someone had been consumed by the fire, but it was difficult to be sure, as so little of what remained was recognizable. We carefully backed out of the burned heaps of ashes and blackened wood and gathered together, the grim faces of my companions showing the panic and fear I felt myself.

"What's to be done?" Henry looked at us, worriedly.

Samuel shook his head. "I don't know. We've come too far to turn back."

"I agree," Nate said. "But moving forward will be dangerous. We'll have to keep our guns loaded and ready. No hunting or firing off our weapons until we reach our destination. We don't want to draw any attention to ourselves."

"Samuel," he continued. "You'll need to get as much speed out of your oxen as possible. We can't be that far from Shelby's, by my reckoning."

Samuel nodded somberly. "I will."

"Let's move out, then. Two men to the front, two to the back. One alongside Samuel's rig."

We mounted up and our little party continued south. The ominous silence that had plagued us all morning continued. We could see nothing stirring except the leafless limbs of the hardwoods that lined the road, their bare branches creaking and groaning in the westerly breeze.

We saw two more burned cabins, tendrils of smoke rising from their ashes, but took no time to stop. We hurried forward, seeking shelter from whatever had caused the destruction we witnessed. Nate and I rode in the front of our little column, our eyes scanning the woods on either side and the road ahead of us.

"No question about it. Must be Indians."

Nate answered, "I can't figure it would be anything else."

Around noon, we spotted in the distance some brightly colored heaps in the road ahead. We pulled up and stopped. Nate went back to the wagon and spoke to Samuel.

"Trouble ahead, Samuel. Stay here and let us investigate."

The riders to the rear joined us, and we rode a short distance ahead. There we found the bodies of the party that had hastily passed us the day before. Most were clumped in the road, like they'd been huddled together. A few bloody forms were scattered in the field to the left. The sight of their mutilated corpses, bloated and covered in flies, caused me to lean over in the saddle and retch. The stench that arose from them was almost too much to bear. There were at least twelve bodies, best we could figure, although it was hard to tell. It was obvious they'd been scalped, and the horses that had accompanied them were gone. We soon spotted their two wagons, well off the side of the road, their hulks burned and lifeless.

"Now what?" Henry asked. "If we take the time to bury them, that will delay us from getting to shelter ourselves."

Nate thought a moment. "Nothing we can do to help these poor devils. I think it's best if we carry them over to what is left of their wagons. We have a woman and children among us, and we don't want to frighten them any more than necessary."

Henry rode back to inform Samuel of the situation while Nate, John and I performed the grisly task of moving the bodies. It was ghastly work, and the sight of the carnage inflicted upon these people, including the children, haunted my dreams for years to come.

Once the roadway was cleared we started south again.

Samuel urged his oxen on, a look of pure terror on his face, and on the grim visage of Chastity riding beside him in the wagon. I know their hearts trembled for the fate of their little boys, silent now, riding in the back.

By mid-afternoon we spotted the walls of a stockade in the distance, perched on top of a small hill. It was still some distance away, but I breathed a sigh of relief when I caught sight of it. Sunlight glanced off the barkless timbers, pointed skyward, that comprised the sides of the enclosure.

"Shelby's Fort ahead!" Nate bellowed to our companions who trailed us. He and I glanced at each other, and I saw a look of immense relief in his eyes. I myself was almost overcome, the terror of the day still rattling in my head as we surged forward.

The small hamlet of Sapling Grove was nestled inside the walls of the fort. Some of the buildings helped form the walls, with firing slits for windows. In one corner was a big, sturdy building, the original blockhouse from which the rest of the stockade had stemmed. When we first entered it was difficult to take any measure of the settlement, as all was in a tumult. A great crowd of wagons and tents was sprawled among the buildings and animal pens, with dozens of people rushing to and fro among them. There were children scampering about, with yapping dogs darting amongst them.

A couple of men rushed up to us as soon as we entered the gates, demanding to know if we had any news.

"We spotted your caravan aways off. Have you any news to bring us?" they asked desperately.

"See here," John spoke up. "We have no news, other than spotting some burned out cabins and the bodies of the dead left behind by some crazed animals. What has befallen you here?"

As we dismounted, a horrific tale unfolded.

"Captain Shelby and most of the fighting men left these parts some weeks ago, headed to the Ohio country to defend the frontier from the red savages that have been plaguing the settlers," a short man with a wrinkled hunting shirt and long stringy hair explained to us. "All the womenfolk and children have found shelter in these walls, on account of the raiding savages that have struck us whilst we are shorthanded."

"Which savages?" I asked.

"We aren't for certain. They could be Cherokee, but some are saying it's Chief Logan and his Mingoes that have wreaked this havoc among us."

Another man spoke up. "We are short of ball and powder. Our flour supplies are depleted, and we have very little else on hand. I sure hope you brought some supplies."

"Very little. We had hopes of resupplying ourselves

once we reached here. You say you cannot supply us?" John asked.

"Not likely. We are in dire straits here." The man shook his head.

"Well, let us get settled in, and then we will council with you," Nate spoke kindly.

We found a small opening close to the western wall of the fort and got to work setting up a camp. We got a fire going and stripped our animals of their saddles and bridles and unhooked Samuel's oxen. We asked a family situated next to us about water and feed and were directed to the small stream that ran beside the fort, known as Beaver Creek. There were very few provisions for our animals within the compound, we were told. We would have to depend on what we had brought with us, which was less than adequate.

After watering our beasts we returned to our spot. Chastity had already started a kettle to boil on the fire. She was sitting beside it, holding baby Mary, as the boys took stock of their surroundings.

"Will you be all right here? Me and the boys are going to find out some more information about our situation." Samuel said.

"I'll be fine. I will work out something for us to eat while you're gone," Chastity replied.

So Samuel, Nate, John, Henry, George and I made our way through the crowds of women and children that were encamped around the outskirts of Sapling Grove and headed toward the center of town. There we found a group of men gathered – in total, about eight individuals.

They were all dressed in buckskin, died in various shades of blues, browns and greens. Each had their rifles, and bags of ball and powder horns adorned their belts. They were a hard looking lot. They each carried a somber expression and were deep in discussion when we joined them.

The tallest of the group spoke up. "Glad to have you folks join us. We've been in dire need of more guns." He was a tall, red-headed Scotsman, his accent still strong and clear. His craggy features belied his age, which I later found out to be twenty-five.

He introduced himself as Ian McTavish. The rest of the men huddled with him also identified themselves. Three or four others also spoke with the strong accent of Scotland, and were equally as capable looking as McTavish.

John Williams took the lead to introduce us as well, and gave a brief description of our journey to the fort. He detailed the burned-out cabins we found and the dead bodies of the group we had discovered only that morning.

"Our circumstances here are dire. We have run short of supplies and are in hopes that you have brought enough ammunition to defend yourselves. Foodstuffs are difficult to find, considering this great crowd we have to supply." Ian waved his arm wide, indicating the women and children crowded within the confines of the stockade.

"I believe we have enough ball and shot to supply ourselves, as we used our guns sparingly on our journey, not wanting to draw attention," Nate declared.

"Good! We haven't seen or heard the savages rampaging for a few days, but we don't know for sure if they are still nearby. This past Thursday they grabbed hold of a Negro woman who works in the service of the Captain – Captain Shelby," he explained. "She was able to work herself free, but not before they questioned her for some time about our defenses here. She claimed one of her captors was well-versed in the English tongue. We believe it may have been Logan, a chief of the Mingoes. We have worked out an arrangement to take turns along the walls to scout out for any savages that may remain in these parts. I will assume you fellows are amenable to taking your turn as well." Ian looked them all in the eye.

"We're more than happy to do our fair share," John replied adamantly.

"My wife Chastity is a good shot. I believe she would be willing to also participate," Samuel said.

"Good! We have a few other women helping out as well. The others will tend any children while she is on duty. Most of our women and older children are very handy with a rifle and a knife. One must always be able to defend oneself out here on the frontier."

And so, the five of us were integrated into the defense of the fort. Chastity also took an occasional turn, with Mrs. Wilson, our neighbor along the wall, watching the children while she perched herself at the top of the western wall. We readily took our turn as lookouts for the next three days.

When not on duty, the men would gather and practice their hatchet throwing skills. They set up a target near the center of the stockade and took bets on who could throw their hatchets most accurately and at the greatest distance. Nate and I readily participated, although I had no great skill at the task. I was encouraged by the others, however, and became more proficient.

"Caleb might not be the best with the hatchet, but he is an excellent shot with the rifle. One of the best I've seen," Nate bragged.

McTavish wandered over and eyed my rifle. "That's a beautiful weapon. Where did you acquire it?"

"My brother-in-law gave it to me when I left home," I answered.

"Keep tight hold of it. The Indians would love to get their hands on such a fine piece. Not to mention a few of the unsavory characters that can be found in these parts."

I nodded in response and determined to take his advice.

On our fourth day at the fort, October 14, 1774, as we were gathered together for a council, McTavish proposed that we should risk a dash south to the Watauga settlements to see if we could get any relief. "We haven't had word from Watauga since the raids. I'm thinking they may have some supplies or even extra men to aid us."

"What do you propose?" John Williams asked.

"I'm thinking we should send a couple of men south, under the cover of darkness, to inquire. We will need someone who knows the way and another for extra firepower. It will be a hard journey. Watauga is twenty miles south, so we'll need horses in good condition to make the journey." Ian turned. "I am willing to volunteer myself as I've traveled the route several times. The newcomer's horses are still in good shape. Do any of you wish to go with me?"

Without much thought I spoke up, "I would be willing. I'm handy with the rifle, and Sadie is still in good shape. I believe she could make the journey without much difficulty."

Ian came over and slapped me on the shoulder. "Good. We leave after dark."

CHAPTER TEN

It was a cold, windless night with the quarter moon peeking out from behind the gathering clouds when McTavish and I set out. We rode silently, side by side, along the main road that veered west not far past Shelby's fort. We came upon a wagon path that led south from the main road not long after we headed out. Nate had let us take Daisy, just in case we were able to find much needed supplies for our companions at the fort. She dutifully kept up with us to the rear, with a good nature not often found in mules. By this time she was used to my presence and had no quarrel with me leading her instead of Nate.

The road was smooth enough, despite the deep wagon ruts that marked it. There was frequent travel, no doubt, between the Watauga settlements and Sapling Grove. Even with the clear road, we knew we had to make good time if we were to get to our destination before sunrise.

We didn't want to be caught out in the open while there was a chance to be spotted by an Indian raiding party.

We rode hard, stopping only to water our animals and clear a space for them to graze along the banks of a creek we found along the way. Sadie, despite short rations for a few days, was in good form and seemed none the worse for wear. McTavish's beast, a brown mare very similar to Sadie's size, was a trifle thinner, and we had to pull her away from the banks of the creek before we could continue our ride.

The watery rays of the sun, filtered through the low-slung clouds appeared while we were yet short of our journey's end. McTavish urged us forward. "We're almost there. Let's make a run for it!"

With that, we pressed our horses forward, and within thirty minutes we saw a group of buildings nestled together on the banks of what I was soon to know as the Sycamore Shoals of the Watauga River. As we drew close McTavish shouted, "Halloo! We hail from Shelby's Fort! Let us pass!"

"That you, McTavish?" a voice replied.

"Yes."

"Come on in!"

We entered the town, which consisted of scattered houses around a large central square. I noticed men posted here and there, but just like the situation at Shelby's Fort, there were few of them. The square itself was full to bursting with canvas tents, populated with numerous women and children. It was early morning so the women were busy around their campfires, preparing food for the dozens of children that scampered about.

A tall, rangy man greeted us, his rifle slung comfortably in the crook of his elbow.

"Good to see you, Ian!"

McTavish greeted him with a warm smile. "Arthur! Arthur Brown! I didn't think I would find you here!"

A grim smile crossed Arthur's face. "I wouldn't be if I hadn't injured my knee a few weeks back. I would have ridden off with Shelby and the rest of the militia." He sighed. "But I suppose someone had to stay behind to guard the womenfolk. How about you? Why are you here?"

McTavish placed a hand on my shoulder. "This here is Caleb Anders. He and a few others have recently joined us at the fort."

Arthur Brown nodded his head to me, after taking a second to size me up.

McTavish continued. "Captain Shelby asked me and a few others to stay at the fort. Seeing as I don't have a wife and children, he thought it best for me to remain for guard duty. He figured the others would be too busy taking care of their families in the fort and wouldn't be as alert as they should be. Good thing, too! We've had several Indian raids – a few cabins burned, scalps taken and children stolen.

They haven't approached the fort, though. Not enough of them to take it."

"Any idea who they were? Cherokee maybe?"

"We have no idea. Some think it was Logan, raiding from the Ohio country. But we can't be for sure. How have things been here?"

"We're in pretty bad shape. With most of the men gone, the Cherokee have taken the opportunity to plunder the countryside, coming up from their towns south of here. We've had little means to stop them."

"Bad news all around," McTavish said. "We've run short of supplies. Caleb and I have come in hopes you all might have some flour and other necessities to spare. We can't carry back much, constrained as we were in getting here for fear of stumbling upon a raiding party ourselves."

Arthur shook his head. "We don't have much ourselves, but can perhaps spare some flour and parched corn, if that would help."

McTavish nodded.

"But where are my manners? You must have ridden all night. Let's see if we can come up with some food for you and tend to your horses."

Arthur bundled us off to his house. His wife busied herself before the fire and soon had a dozen eggs and some small slices of venison prepared for us. While McTavish and Arthur continued to talk, I found myself dozing off while I ate, tired to the bone. McTavish took note of it.

"My young friend is in need of some sleep. Is there someplace where we lie down? We'll have to be heading back at nightfall. They need our guns back at the fort."

Arthur led us up to the loft above the sleeping quarters of his home. He handed us blankets, and I immediately fell into a deep slumber. I was awakened by McTavish shaking my shoulder.

"It's almost nightfall, Caleb. We will have to be back on the road soon."

I arose and followed him down the ladder. Mrs. Brown provided us with a bundle of provisions for our travels, and we went outside to our horses.

"Our friends have fed and watered our horses and mule for us. They've supplied us with what they could spare. It isn't much, but it's more than what we had."

Arthur joined us. "I wish you a safe trip back, friends. It looks as if the weather will favor you."

I looked skyward and was thankful to see no indication of rain.

"Thank you, sir, for your help in this matter," I said seriously.

"No thanks necessary. I know the favor would be returned if we were in your position," he added,

"Take heed of Ian McTavish. He's been in these parts for some time, and he knows the ways of the wilderness."

"I will, sir."

We led our horses past the square to the spot where we entered the town, and then mounted. Daisy had several bags and bundles strapped upon her back, but not enough to weigh her down.

"We need to ride hard, Caleb. Harder than when we rode coming down. We must get back before dawn. I don't like leaving the fort short of our company."

Again we rode in silence. We pushed our horses hard, and took no time to feed or water them.

We reached the fort shortly before rays of the sun appeared. I was exhausted, but happy to return to what I then viewed as home.

The supplies we brought back were few, but were welcomed nonetheless. Nate grinned and slapped me so hard on the back I nearly fell over. McTavish went about distributing food to those who were most in need, and all were happy to have them.

The next few weeks were busy ones. During daylight hours, a few of us were sent out to scout neighboring farms, to see if we could bring in vegetables and livestock that hadn't been destroyed by the Indians. What we found was then shared between us. Some of the men set up a smokehouse within the walls of the fort, a large one, and the women were busy smoking and curing meat from the pigs and cows that were rounded up. There was a communal spirit among us. All shared what they had without a whisper of discontent.

Shelby's store, situated in the middle of the town of Sapling Grove, was short on many essentials, but was still chock full of useful merchandise. There were farm implements, clothing of all sorts, fabric, crocks and casks, soap and candles, and an endless assortment of other necessaries. Bartering was the most common means of exchange, as hard money was difficult to come by in those days.

In my first visit to the store I discovered a stack of steel traps, buried unceremoniously beneath a pile of shovels and hoes in the far corner. I pulled out eight good ones and took them to the counter, minded by a wizened old man with spectacles, his bald head gleaming, a pipe clenched tightly between his jaws. This was Mr. Eakins, who tended the store for the Shelbys and was known to drive a hard bargain.

"Well, young man? How do you aim to pay for these here traps?" he asked me.

"I have hard money."

"You do?" He pulled the pipe from between his teeth and looked at me quizzically.

"Yes I do. How much for each of these traps?" I replied.

"Well, now, I would say a shilling apiece," he replied matter-of-factly.

I looked at him shrewdly. It was an outrageous sum, but

I couldn't fault him for it. I was young, after all, and he might have thought I was easy.

I calmly replied, "These traps have been sitting in the corner for some time. Maybe you even forgot you had them." I paused. "I'll give you four shillings for the lot, if you'll throw in a few sheets of paper, a quill and some ink with it."

A smile cracked across his wrinkled face as he returned the pipe to his mouth.

"Well, sonny, since you're new here, I'll do this for you. I'll let you have the lot for five shillings."

"And the paper, ink and quill," I responded firmly.

He nodded briskly. I carefully removed the bag of coins I had hanging around my neck and removed five shillings and put them on the counter. He scooped them up, took a hard look at them to make sure they were genuine, and then reached under the counter and pulled out four sheets of paper. He found a small pot of ink and a quill on the shelf and shoved them towards me.

"Here you go. We hope to have a post rider before much longer, if you have in mind to write your family."

"Thank you." With that, I walked out, traps and writing material in hand.

It was difficult to write inside the shelter Nate and I had built for ourselves, being small and very ill-lit, so when I returned to it I set up a sort of desk at the entrance and seated myself on a log before it and began to write Martha and Jacob. I told them all about my journey southward and my new partnership with Nate. I glossed over our situation at the fort, not wanting them to be alarmed by it.

I finished by letting them know they could reach me by letter at Shelby's Fort, Virginia. I quickly folded the note, and as I was addressing it, I noticed Mrs. Wilson, our neighbor, had wandered over and was standing before me, watching intently. She was a kindly woman and had helped Chastity by watching her children while she took her turn standing watch over the fort. She was rather large and stout, with graying hair she tied neatly at the nape of her neck. I looked askance at her as she stood over me, her work-worn hands fidgeting with the apron that hung over her dress. She hesitated a moment, and then spoke.

"Excuse me, Caleb, I don't mean to intrude, but are you writing a letter home?" There was a plaintive note to her question, and a nervous tone in her voice.

"Why yes, Mrs. Wilson. I was just writing to my sister, letting her know I had arrived at a safe destination."

"We left Pennsylvania a year ago. I haven't been able to get hold of my folks, seeing as Mr. Wilson and I don't know how to write. Neither do any of our young'uns." She and Mr. Wilson were the proud parents of five children, ranging from five or six all the way up to thirteen.

"Would you like me to write a letter to them for you, ma'am? I have extra writing sheets here that I was able to get from the store," I suggested.

"Oh, would you?" she answered excitedly. "I would gladly share some of this dried meat I just prepared, if you would be so kind."

"Happy to. What would you like me to write?" I replied, pulling out a single sheet of paper from my little stockpile.

She directed me to inform her parents of her safe arrival to Virginia, and explained her husband's service in the militia, and that her children were well and healthy, although Josiah her eldest, had recovered from a bad fever the month before. I wrote as she directed, and then folded her letter and addressed it for her. She thanked me profusely as she grabbed the note. She hurried back to her shelter and gathered up a huge chunk of smoked bacon and handed it to me.

"My folks can't read or write either, but they have neighbors that can. They will be happy to hear from me. Thank you for your kindness, Caleb. It won't be forgotten."

I blushed a little at her praise and assured her it was my pleasure to be of assistance. It was also a pleasure to eat that bacon, which I shared with Nate. Soon the news spread among the campers that I could write with a good clear hand, and for many months after I would often find someone at my door with a sheet of paper obtained at the store, and some sort of useful item in exchange for my writing. I didn't mind, really. Lord knows I would never have been able to survive in that wilderness without the help and guidance of those very brave people.

Chapter Eleven

Nate was well pleased with my purchase of the steel traps. "Do you think the winter will keep us here at the fort, or should we venture out to the mountains in spite of it?" I asked, as much to myself as to him.

"Something to think about, partner. But you know we can't leave just yet. Even though we haven't seen any Indians since we arrived, and no new reports of attacks, we should stay put. At least until the militia returns. No good to venture out, only to get a shot in the head for our efforts."

"True. I suppose that would defeat our purpose." I grinned at him.

Late that very afternoon, a shout rang out from the north wall of the fort.

"Troops coming!"

Nate and I and a crowd of others rushed to the entrance of the fort and saw a group of men, seventy or more, headed south towards us. Some were on horseback, some walking. A couple wagons and carts in the rear carried others. A small group broke off from the main body when they neared the fort and headed on south. We were soon to learn these were men from the Watauga settlement that McTavish and I had visited but a short time ago.

I wish I could say these men were in high spirits with the good news they brought, but they were not. I would be hard pressed to describe a sorrier spectacle than what met our eyes. Dirty and disheveled, their buckskins were in tatters. Their rifles were slung over their shoulders still, but the eyes of these men showed a weariness impossible to describe. Yet, as soon as they spied their welcome, they endeavored to straighten their shoulders a bit and form a more orderly line as they marched through the gate.

The women and children who had been confined within the walls of the fort for many weeks were jubilant. They looked for their soldier husbands or fathers. Each clapped their hands and ran forward when they were spotted. The whole of them were encircled with a happy crowd, even the wounded in the wagons. Yet before long it became obvious that not everyone in the fort would be welcoming someone home. There were tears streaking the faces of some when they realized their loved ones had fallen in battle.

Hungry and exhausted, these brave men tiredly explained that a great victory had been won on October

10, a battle that would go down in history as the Battle of Point Pleasant. The evening fires were stoked and food was prepared. Even those who had lost a loved one or had no man in the fight pitched in what they could to feed the heroes that had returned.

As darkness fell, there were roaring fires spread throughout the compound, their flames dancing mightily in the cold evening air. Gathered around each one were groups huddled together, enjoying the heat and listening to the tales of the fighting men who had returned. Nate and I stoked a large one in front of our abode, eager to hear the tales the conquering heroes had to tell.

We were soon joined by McTavish and three of his friends from the militia – Tom Fitzhugh, Elliot Myers and Hugh McDonald – each with a bottle in hand. Between stories they would pull mightily from their bottles and sigh heavily. Tom passed his bottle to me and I took a gulp. It was my first taste of strong liquor, and I came up from it coughing and gagging. The other men had a good laugh at my expense. I can thankfully say that from that moment on I never had the urge to partake of it again. Sadly, this wasn't the case with some of my friends and neighbors. There were many tragedies that befell those of my comrades in ensuing years because of the bottle.

Once we settled around the fire, Tom, Elliot and Hugh began their accounts. Each had a way with words, I must say. Tom started with an explanation of their journey to the Ohio country.

"We left here, as you know, midsummer. We had about 150 of us, as some of the menfolk from Watauga joined our company." He paused. "We had plenty of supplies in the beginning. We headed northwest, and passed a few settlements during those first weeks. We couldn't travel very quickly, as most of us were on foot. We were in good spirits, though, and received extra supplies from the settlers we passed along the way. They were overjoyed to see us, as they had been subject to many an Indian raid and were happy to see we were taking on those red devils.

We joined up with Colonel Andrew Lewis. About eleven hundred all told, from Virginia. The plan was to meet up with Lord Dunmore. He was to come down the Ohio from Fort Pitt and meet up with us."

He paused and took a long drink from his bottle. "We had it rough, boys. We had to march overland, through a tangle of woods I had never before seen the likes of. It was deep and dark, boys, with nary a path or road to follow."

"How long did it take?" I asked curiously.

He gave me a long look. The firelight flickered before him and gave his countenance a frightful aspect, as light and darkness danced upon it.

"We was in that wilderness for nineteen or twenty days. Our food ran low, but we dared not take the time to hunt for provisions. We was in a hurry to get to our meeting point, you see."

There was a deep silence that fell among us, as Tom

leaned back and sighed heavily. I took a long look at him – a young man, but with the eyes of someone much older in years.

"It was strange, really. During those nineteen days we didn't see a single Indian. The forest was just plain empty. Sometimes we could hear the crashing of some beast deep within the timbers, but that was all," Elliot stated.

"I guess they were saving themselves for something bigger," McTavish interjected, knowingly.

"That's right." Elliot replied. "They were gathering themselves together, preparing. Their scouts surely knew we were heading their way. We too had scouts thrown out ahead, but got no word from them of any Indians.

We made camp after 19 days at the mouth of the Kanawha, where it runs east from the Ohio River. We had plans to cross the Ohio, then head west to our meeting point with Dunmore, close to the Indian village of Chillicothe."

Nate and I nodded our heads along with the others, but truth be told, we were wholly ignorant of the western country. Most of the names and places mentioned were new to our ears. We would glance at each other while the story was being told, but said nothing to show our lack of knowledge.

Elliot continued. "We were there three days. On the morning of the 10th of October, two scouts went out, hunting to fill out our meager supplies, and happened upon a large force of Indians, north of us and about a mile away. It looked as if they were planning a surprise attack. They killed one of the scouts, but the other raced back to us, hooting and hollering the whole way." He stopped. "You finish telling 'em, Hugh. You can tell it better than I can." With that, he leaned back and took a huge pull on the bottle in his hand.

Hugh cleared his throat. "Those Indians were surprised, all right. We figured they had no choice but to go ahead and attack us. But we were ready for them, thanks to that scout." His deep voice, tinged with a heavy Scottish accent, took up the story with relish.

"We roused ourselves and got our weapons ready. General Lewis had us spread out from the banks of the Ohio to the Kanawha. The attack began almost as soon as we were in position." He paused, the firelight flickering across his face. We remained silent, in anxious anticipation.

"They attacked us first from the right, shooting at us from heavy cover. That was the men from Augusta. They killed plenty, that first round. Lost some good officers and men." He paused.

"We were stationed on the left, and we were attacked next. The screams and howls of those red devils sent shivers up and down our backs, I can tell you. We were forced to take cover with whatever we could find. Trees, stumps, fallen timbers. They had pushed us back a good hundred yards or more. It was about that time we received reinforcements, which was a great encouragement.

We steadied ourselves and gave back as good as we got.

It was rough going, boys, but we decided we wouldn't give them any more ground." He paused again.

"I don't reckon how long we were pinned down like that, but it wasn't too long, thanks to those reinforcements. We steadily pushed back and caused those hellions to retreat. Slowly, at first.

About noon, we had pushed them back almost a mile. They were forced to cross some wet bottomland. It was a muddy mess by the time we reached it, but we didn't let it bother us none. We forced our way across it, finding whatever cover we could. I saw Tom over here," he pointed at his companion and laughed. "His face covered in muck, his eyes as red as a beet. He looked like a crazy man. Then I reckoned I probably looked the same."

"Those Indians didn't give up easily, friends. They kept at us, trying to break our lines. We could see Cornstalk clearly – you know, the Shawnee war chief. He was pacing behind his line, barking at his men to keep up the fire. Probably all of us took shots at him, but he was a lucky devil that day." Hugh shook his head and took a drink.

"Late afternoon, there was a lull. The fire from the Indians slowed, and we saw them gathering up their dead. It was a sight we took delight in. Before long, they had all departed and the field was ours."

"You're leaving out something," Tom interjected quietly.

"Well, I don't want to confuse these boys," Hugh replied.

Elliot jumped in. "What he's not telling is the part where Isaac led his company around the right side of those hellions and we hit them in the rear. Scared them so bad they gathered up their dead and wounded and lit out of there in a hurry."

"Who's Isaac?" Nate asked.

"Isaac Shelby. Evan's son," Elliot explained.

"Where was Evan?" Nate interjected again.

"See, I told you it would be confusing to these fellows," Hugh said.

"I suppose so," Elliot conceded. "It happened like this. We were hit early and hard. In short order we lost three of our top commanders – all Colonels. Lewis, Field and Fleming. It was quickly decided that Evan take command, which left our company without a captain. So Evan appointed his son Isaac to take his place. Evan's the one who directed us and two other companies to go around the right flank of those skunks and hit them where it hurts. It worked, too." Elliot stopped, satisfied.

"Sounds like we lost a lot of officers," Nate opined.

"Yes, we did. Too many," Hugh nodded.

There was quiet around the fire for a short while after that. We each contemplated in our own way the story we had heard. Those who had endured the trial seemed to me the quietest. My young mind could but imagine the rigors these men had been through. Little did I know at the time that I would have to endure my own trials before long.

Elliot resumed the story. "Turns out General Lewis had sent off for reinforcements during the battle. Colonel Christian was several miles to our rear. He hurried to us but didn't arrive until almost midnight. We were a sight to him and his men, I'm sure. By then we had our hands full with the wounded." He sighed.

"The next day, we buried our dead. We saw the Indians trying to drag off theirs, but we still found plenty on the field, especially by the river. We left them to the wolves and buzzards," Hugh said glumly. "We then went to work and built a stockade for the wounded. We were supposed to meet with Lord Dunmore and the other arm of our forces at Pickaway Plains but we had to tend to our wounded. We got the stockade built and gathered our horses and supplies together. We weren't able to leave Point Pleasant until the 17th," Hugh continued. "On the way we received news from that dirty skunk Lord Dunmore that he had signed a treaty with those red savages. We had them on the run, by golly! We could have taken the whole lot of them!" Angered, he fell to cursing under his breath.

"Listen, fellas, it only stands to reason that we got double-crossed by that red-coated weasel," Elliot said.

"How do you mean?" I asked curiously.

"Where do you think those savage skunks got their guns and ammunition? From the redcoats. All their supplies?

From the redcoats. The Shawnee, Delawares, Mingoes, Ottawas – they're all in good standing with the British. They're allies. They have been since the French war," Elliot replied angrily.

"But what would cause the King's troops to turn them on us?" I queried.

"There weren't any redcoats at Point Pleasant, son. They left us high and dry and then made peace with the Indians behind our backs. Word is they aren't too happy with us colonists at the moment. What with the ruckus they're raising in Boston and the actions of the Virginia Committees of Correspondence, the King would be mighty happy if all the fighting men of Virginia were dead. Well, we got the better of them this time. We outfought their thieving, dirty savages. And we'll do it again, if need be." Elliot sat back, satisfied.

With the telling of the tale finished, and the bottles all empty, we broke apart and made our way to our beds. As Nate and I settled into our shelter, I voiced concern over what we had heard.

"Do you really think the British used those Indians against us?"

Nate adjusted his blanket over his enormous chest. "I wouldn't put it past them. I never much trusted those lobsterbacks. I don't think they trust us, neither."

"But aren't we supposed to be Britishers too?"

"Not in their eyes, Caleb. If that were true, they would

let us have a say in how this country is run. I don't see that happening anytime soon. I'm afraid we have some hard times ahead."

Chapter Twelve

A heavy frost had fallen during the night and the air was frigid the next morning when I arose. Despite that, there was a bustle of activity all around the grounds of the fort. Many of the families who had sought shelter within its walls were gathering their possessions. Those soldiers who were in good enough shape upon their return were making plans to leave the safety of its environs and make their way to their own cabins and homesteads.

About mid-morning there was a shout from the lookout. Wagons, along with armed riders, were approaching from the north. When they rolled into the fort there was great jubilation. New supplies had arrived, as well as a post rider eager to deliver messages and take letters north. The siege had ended. The new arrivals shared that they had not seen a single Indian or any sign of fresh trouble along the wagon road. Food staples were unloaded – flour, salt, coffee, corn, great hogsheads of potted meats and pickled vegetables. There was a fresh supply of balls and gunpowder, and various and sundry other items necessary for survival in the wilderness.

Those of us who were able were helpful in emptying the wagons and securing the goods into Shelby's store. There was a new spirit among us. Not only had our little militia helped secure a major victory over the Indians, but the world had not forgotten us. The much-needed supplies were a blessing to all.

After we unloaded, we then helped pile the wagons with pelts and furs that had been bartered in the store. There were mounds of beaver, fox, bear, panther, wolf, buffalo and other pelts, wrapped into bundles and quickly loaded. The drivers and riders would spend the night, and then head back out the next morning. The women in the fort got to work cooking for these men who had risked so much to help secure what we so desperately needed.

Nate and I were before our campfire that evening when Samuel Hayward stopped by. Chastity and the children were already bedded down.

"Good evening, gentlemen!" he began.

"How goes it, Samuel?" I replied.

"I've been meaning to talk with you fellows about our plans."

"What plans would that be?" Nate asked curiously.

"You know, Mr. Wilson has returned with the militia.

He and his missus have a place south and west of here. They are alone with their children. He's got 200 acres of good land, and he's offered to help us get settled with them if we'd be willing to help him work it. It's too much for just one man to handle. It still needs clearing to get crops in the ground."

"I see," Nate responded.

"So Chastity and I figured it would be a good start for us. There's plenty of timber on Mr. Wilson's acres, and he will help us put up a cabin. Our womenfolk get along, and they would be able to watch all the children and share the workload of gardening and cooking."

"Is it safe where you are heading?" I inquired.

"Mr. Wilson says it's as safe a place as any other in these parts." He paused. "We don't feel right just leaving you fellows. You have been a boon to us in our travels. We would be happy to have you join us if you would like."

"That's a very kind offer, Samuel. But Nate and I have other plans. We wish you the very best though. When do you plan on leaving?"

"We will get our campsite packed up tomorrow and leave the following day."

Nate stood and clapped him on the shoulder. "We wish you the very best, my friend. It's been a pleasure knowing you and Chastity."

The following morning Samuel and Chastity were busy gathering their camp together, packing their wagon carefully for the journey ahead of them. The boys, as usual, scampered about, getting underfoot as much as they were able. Mary was left all alone on a blanket, wailing and squalling in her baby voice, oblivious to all the goings on.

Nate and I had guard duty that afternoon. Despite the lessened threat of an Indian attack, our little community was still wary of the imminent danger that lurked all around us. When we returned to our campsite, Chastity was calmly cooking over her outdoor fire. The Haywards were all packed up for the journey, as were the Wilsons. She called to us. "Come on over, boys! I've made a beef stew!"

During our meal, we all shared stories of our journey together south to the fort. Samuel smiled and Chastity giggled, curls of red hair slipping out of her cap, over their first sight of us, and the great heave Nate gave to the back wheel of their wagon that cleared them from the ditch.

"It would have taken a team of six oxen to get us out," Samuel said. "Lucky for us you fellows came along when you did."

"Glad to help, friend!" Nate smiled in reply.

"Now, if you fellows ever find yourself south and west of here, be sure to look us up. Mr. Wilson says it's about twelve miles from here, but over some rough terrain. We would be happy to see you at any time."

"Thank you kindly, Samuel. Be assured we would be

happy to have your hospitality if we are ever in your neighborhood," I answered.

After we saw them off, we took Bessie, Sadie and Daisy to the creek to water them.

"What are our plans now, Nate?"

"I was figuring we should go ahead and make our way to the mountains. There should be fewer people up there this time of year. Any Indians thereabouts would have departed for their wintering grounds.

"Maybe. But the snows will be an obstacle, won't they?"

"A little snow shouldn't hold us back," he chuckled.

About that time, a stranger approached. He was a short man – he could easily stand beneath Nate's arm if Nate had the notion of stretching it out straight. But he had a stoutness about him. Not the soft sort of stoutness, but the type that spoke of strength and resiliency. He had a way of moving that reminded me of a big cat – flowing motions with a spring in his step. His head was topped with wispy white hair, and his face showed the lines of time and experience etched clearly upon it. He had a long, straight nose and deep-set eyes, his cheeks a ruddy pink. If ever a man had a body that did not match his face, this one did. He was clothed from head to toe in neat, brand new buckskins, stained a pleasing shade of brown.

He smiled slightly as he approached us. "Who do we have here?"

We looked askance at him, but he had an air about him that prompted us to speak up.

"I'm Nate Daniel. This is my partner, Caleb Anders."

With that, the stranger cracked a bigger smile. "Don't tell me, son, that your parents named you Nathaniel Daniel!"

Nate fumbled for a moment and shuffled his feet uncomfortably. "Why, yes they did!"

"You must have a pile of brothers, then. They run out of names?"

"To be sure, I do have a sizable number of older brothers. Don't know why they named me as they did. But I go by Nate," my partner declared firmly.

"Fair enough," the stranger shrugged, still smiling.

"Where do you boys hail from?" he continued.

"Pennsylvania and Maryland."

"Both good places to be from. I've lived in both those places myself. But I'm glad to be here now." He went on. "I'm Captain Evan Shelby." He stuck out his hand to shake ours. "It's a pleasure to meet you boys."

"Thank you kindly, sir," I answered, a bit nervously.

"What brings you boys to Shelby's Fort?"

Nate answered, "We're looking to get into the fur trade."

Evan nodded. "I've spent many years in that profession

myself. I've made a fortune. And lost it, too." He smiled. "Do you plan on settling down whilst you ply your trade?"

I spoke up. "We like it here at the fort. We haven't made any permanent plans as of yet though. We were figuring on going out towards the Blue Ridge soon, to see what we can see. We would like to get to the business of making a living."

He nodded. "Not a bad time of year, although the snows will cause you trouble. Plenty of wildcats and buffalo. Beaver pelts bring a high price as well. I do a brisk trade for furs at my store. When you return, Mr. Eakins would be happy to set up an account for you."

"Thank you. We'll do that."

He looked us up and down with a sharp eye. "I'd like to speak with you fellows when you return. Stop at my house and call for me when you arrive back. It's the big house in town. You can't miss it." With that, he turned on his heel and sauntered off.

That evening Ian McTavish stopped by our campfire. We shared our plans with him. He nodded along as we explained our desire to head to the Blue Ridge as soon as we could gather supplies and break camp.

"There's already deep snow in the higher elevations," he pointed out.

Nate spoke, "We have no need of going to the higher elevations. There should be plenty of trapping and hunting opportunities before we reach the peaks."

"Oh, there is, to be sure. Now that Hugh McDonald is home safe, we will resume our own travels and trapping ventures. We put all that aside once the threat of Indian uprisings got in our way."

"I didn't know you were a trapper, McTavish."

"No, I don't suppose I've enlightened you about my business. But yes, I've been one since I left home on the other side of the Blue Ridge a few years ago. My folks and other family members live close to Salisbury, in North Carolina."

He continued, as the firelight danced around his face. "My father was but a mere lad during the Uprising in '45 in Scotland. Now, he and his family were no Jacobites. We are all good and decent Protestants. But after the rising, times were made difficult for our people, even though they had no hand in going against the King. The English came down hard on all Scots, no matter what allegiance they had. They took lands, handed out harsh sentences, raised taxes, did away with the clans. Many were bitter over the high-handed way the British abused the Scottish people. My father had heard of the opportunities that were offered in the colonies. He sold what he had and took us across the seas. We left in 1755, when I was but five years old." He paused, as if remembering the days he spent upon the waters of the Atlantic. "We first landed at Philadelphia. My father was a blacksmith and found work, but was unsatisfied with city life. It was noisy and crowded, and unfamiliar. There was no benefit to being a Scot there." He sighed.

"What brought your folks to North Carolina?"

"There was talk among the Scots of a land to the south, where there were rugged mountains and deep, rich forests. A land that looked and felt like their homeland. It was wild and untamed, but it brought back memories. My father saved and scraped. Times were hard for us the first ten years we were here, to be certain. Then in '65 we packed up what we had and left the dusty bowels of Philadelphia and made our way south with a group of other like-minded Scots. We found ourselves in such a beautiful country, one that truly flowed with milk and honey. My father set up a small smithy and soon business was good, as he was the only one to be found in that region."

"I do a little blacksmithing myself," Nate stated. "It's a decent and honorable profession. Why didn't you take it up?"

McTavish smiled. "Why haven't you?"

Nate laughed. "Perhaps for the same reason you haven't. A wandering foot?"

"Precisely." McTavish leaned back. "My younger brother is now my father's apprentice. I, however, had the urge to see what was on the other side of the mountains that towered west of us. One day I spoke of this to my father. He looked at me and said I should follow my heart, just as he had when we left Scotland. And with that, I packed my belongings, bartered the furs I had trapped for a horse, and made my way across."

"How long did it take you?" I asked curiously.

"It was midsummer then. The traveling was not as difficult as one would expect. I stopped often to hunt and trap and collected what I could for trade. All told, about a month, I expect. I arrived at Shelby's Fort three years ago, when it was just Sapling Grove. Captain Shelby had just retained his grant and was busy planning what would become the fort."

"You must know Captain Shelby well then."

"As well as any. And I know his sons – James, Evan, Moses and Isaac as well."

"What do you think of him?" I asked.

McTavish leaned forward, his shoulders hunched, his voice raised sharply. "Evan Shelby can outfight, outshoot and outdrink any man half his age, and that's the God's honest truth. Don't let his age fool you, boys. He's as hard a man as you will ever find. His sons are near as tough as he is, too."

"He's asked us to stop by and speak with him upon our return," Nate said.

McTavish laughed. "I suggest you do just that then, boys."

"Since you have had some experience in the mountains, do you have any advice?"

"Certainly. Here, let me draw you a map." He crouched beside the fire with a stick in hand. In the dirt, he drew an

X. "This here's the fort." He then drew a route that took us north for a short way on the road we came on, and then meandered this way and that for a good distance. He spoke of pitfalls and roundabouts to get us to where we were going, using a short line that cut across the main route as he explained each of them to us. "Once you find a spot for a permanent camp, keep an eye on your horses. If there are any Indians about you probably won't see them, but they will steal your horseflesh first chance they get. At night, keep them close by, because the wolves will form packs and attack them, particularly at this time of year. Make a mark on your traps, so others who might stumble upon them will know they belong to someone. Most folks in our trade are honest and will leave them alone."

"Supplies?"

"Bring feed for your horses. When there's snow on the ground, foraging is very difficult. For yourselves, some flour – not for baking, but for thickening soups and such – salt, plenty of parched corn, dried meat and beans if you can find them. Extra powder and shot. Always carry extra while in the woods. Sometimes a late snow will delay your return, or heaven forbid, you run into trouble."

"Thank you for your advice, McTavish. We will take it," I replied.

He nodded. "Hugh and I will be along in a week or two, as soon as he has regained all his strength. We'll keep a watch out for you." He reached out his hand and shook both of ours.

Early the next morning we got to the business of getting our supplies gathered and packed our gear onto the back of Daisy the mule. Bessie and Sadie also carried their fair share, along with us and our saddles. By early afternoon, we had set out. I looked over my shoulder at the fort as we departed. It stood in stark contrast to the scuttling gray clouds that spoke of new snow, and the broad pastures with spikes of oak, pine, spruce and maple interspersed about. I hoped to see the place again in the near future, but at the moment realized I might not be fortunate enough to return. I was determined, however, to make my way in the world, and willingly faced the dangers that might lay ahead.

Chapter Thirteen

We did our best to follow the map McTavish had drawn for us in the dirt before our fire the previous night. Nate had a better memory than I for such details. We headed north, then east, winding our way along through deep forests and broad meadows. At times we were able to find a barely discernible trail, and at other times not. We crossed streams and creeks, the waters bitterly cold but clear. On occasion we spotted wisps of smoke curling up from a fire in the distance, but dared not approach, not knowing if they were friend or foe. The possibility of stumbling into a situation we could not easily get out of was real enough. Anyone who wasn't an Indian would be on high alert after the recent raids, and we reckoned we wanted to avoid trouble if we could.

It was magnificent country. Enormous oak, maple, elm and birch trees, their naked branches reaching skyward, rattling in the stiff breezes of early winter. Interspersed between them were vast fields, fallow now, with dried grasses and leaves matted and tangled upon the ground. Outcroppings of solid rock were scattered about, with no rhyme or reason to them. We traveled along through the swells of the foothills, the mountains ahead covered in the blinding white of snow and ice.

We traveled for four days, climbing higher and ever higher, seeking a spot to set up camp. Although there was no snow on the ground at present, we knew it would be forthcoming. Not only did we need a place that would provide shelter for us and our animals, we wished for a spot close to where we could set up our traps and snares.

As we searched we came upon a vast beaver dam. It spanned a wide stream, frothing its way through a small canyon, tumbling over huge boulders and slabs of rock before evening itself out in a flat clearing meadow. This is where the dam had been built.

"Hoo boy, those critters have picked a fine spot to build!" Nate declared.

"I do believe that's the largest beaver dam I have ever spotted! We're in luck!" I replied joyfully.

"Let's make our way around it and head downstream. We don't want to make those little fellows nervous about our presence."

I nodded in agreement, and we carefully made a wide berth around the structure. We headed south then, searching for a place to set up camp. We found it, about a mile or so below the dam. There was a large outcropping of rock, with a spot facing south that would shield us from the bitter north wind. A large crack, barely discernible between trees and shrubs, could provide us the shelter we sought. As night approached, we patched a sort of roof over the crevice and built a fire before it. We fashioned a pen of sorts among a stand of pine that helped to both conceal and confine our three animals. We were worn out but well satisfied when we retired for the night.

It was bitterly cold the next morning with a deep frost on the ground. I quickly got a fire going and we sat before it, discussing our next move.

"We can't just leave our animals penned in, Caleb. They would be too easy of a target for any wolves or other beasts that might stumble upon them," Nate opined.

I thought for a moment. "One of us could stay and stand guard."

Nate shook his head. "I don't see how that would help us much. Only one man setting and collecting from our traps would be of no advantage to us."

"We could split up. One man take a horse and tend to the beaver dam. The other could go further afield and search for other game with the other horse and Daisy."

"That might work. For today, let's both go to the dam and set about catching those critters."

We saddled our horses and set out. We found some

small poplars not far from our camp and used our hatchets to chop and clean branches from them to use as bait. We approached the dam downwind, to lesson the impact of our presence, and set all our traps, hoping the guileless creatures would be foolish enough to take our bait.

It was still early afternoon when we finished. Not to waste a day with no snow and good visibility, we wandered east until we came to a broad meadow. We allowed our animals to feed among the fallen and tangled grasses and weeds while we eyed the tree line, hoping for game. As the day waned, we spotted what we were looking for – a small herd of deer wandered hesitatingly from the edge of the forest. Nate tapped me on the shoulder and nodded. I raised my rifle and took careful aim. I dropped a doe where she stood. Nate laughed and raced across the field. By the time I caught up with him, he had gutted her. We hung her from a nearby tree and began skinning her.

Nate worked swiftly and expertly, relieving our catch of her skin while I butchered her meat. The sun had begun to set as we finished, and we quickly made our way back to camp.

We kept our fire burning all night. In the blackness, we heard the yowling and howling of wolves and panthers, stalking whatever poor creature they could find. We slept little that night, and were up before dawn. We quickly made our way over to the beaver dam to check our traps, leading our horses and Daisy. Not surprisingly, all of them had been sprung. In one, we found what remained of a single beaver, half-eaten and useless for our purposes.

Nate cursed under his breath and exclaimed. "This will never do!"

"Let's use what's left of this one to set some of our traps in the meadow," I enjoined. "Whatever has taken this might be fooled, and we can only gain from its misfortune."

We reloaded half our traps about the dam, and then moved some distance away and set the others with the spoiled remains of the ruined beaver. We returned to camp.

That evening I began work on my powder horn. I had admired the ornate carvings I spied on McTavish's horn and had seen the same technique on the horns of those lucky men who made it safely back from Point Pleasant. I determined I would do the same. I used my knife and began, in my own fashion, to carve a scene of the Blue Ridge on my own. It would take many hours to complete, I knew, but I resolved to give it a try. I would carve a few lines and then used the ash from the fire to blacken them so I could see my progress. Nate watched me carefully. He had been busy stretching the hide of the deer we had killed in a makeshift frame, meticulously scraping off all signs of meat and fat.

"That's some neat work, Caleb," he grinned. "When you get done with yours, you can start on mine."

I snorted as a reply. "You're better with a knife than I am."

"True. But I don't have the patience for such tedious

work." He continued on quietly, "I'm not much for writing, either. I can read well enough, but these big fat fingers of mine have a time of it when I try to use them with a quill."

"Who taught you to read?"

"My older sister Cynthia. She had the patience of Job, she did." He laughed.

"That's fine, Nate. I can do the writing for us both."

The next morning, Nate suggested he stay behind while I checked our traps. "We have this venison that needs drying, and I want to work on this doeskin. We're in need of new moccasins, and I could fashion some good ones out of this hide. And these beaver need skinning. I think it best if I stay here and get these chores done."

So our routine was established. At times we would both venture out, and after checking our traps we would explore east and north of the beaver dam. Sometimes, one of us would stay behind and tend to housekeeping chores that needed to be done.

The snows came soon enough, deep and feathery, clinging to the landscape in deep drifts. Nate had fashioned us moccasins that came to our knees, tied off with a bit of leather. He left the fur on the hide, which kept our feet warm and dry. Despite his protests over the size of his fingers, he could handle an awl and needle as well as any man I knew. We struggled through deep snowdrifts that dragged unmercifully at our legs and feet, as well as those of our animals. Foraging for feed was now almost impossible for Daisy, Bessie and Sadie, and we dipped into the supplies we had brought from the fort.

The new year of 1775 dawned bright and clear, with a fresh three inches of snow deposited upon our makeshift roof. "Look, Caleb, we've got quite a pile of furs and hides. Several dozen beaver, fox, wolf, deer, even buffalo. We need to start planning on returning to Sapling Grove."

I nodded agreement. "Yes, that's true. But perhaps it would be best if we waited for just a little bit and hope the snow melts. It will be hard going if we leave now."

Another week went by, but the deep snow still clung on. We used the remaining feed we had, and fervently hoped the weather would break. It was a difficult week, I recall quite clearly. We tried to keep busy with our traps and tending to our animals. Then we got a stiff, warm breeze out of the southeast the second week of January. With that, the snowbanks began to shrink, and with relief we began breaking down our camp.

"Looks like we'll be home before the next snow!" Nate said cheerfully.

We loaded up our animals. Daisy's back was piled high with the furs and hides we had accumulated. Our horses were loaded down with most of our tools and other camping supplies, tied down behind our saddles.

The snow was still deep, and we struggled getting through it, until we got well east and south. It was with a sigh of relief when we spotted Shelby's Fort during the last week of January 1775.

The recent melting of snow had turned the grounds of the fort into a foul jumble of mud and manure, churned up and ghastly to the eye. We found a small spot in the northeast corner that sufficed and set up our camp. After we got a fire going, we set out in search of feed for our animals. Once that was acquired, we immediately went to Shelby's store to set up an account.

Mr. Eakins, the shopkeeper, was well pleased with the pelts and hides we brought. He dutifully entered our names into his register, and cocked his eye as he surveyed our goods.

"These are fine pelts. The beaver, of course, are worth the most. You have forty here, all of good quality." He stopped. "I would be happy to give you 10 pence for each."

"We will take nothing less than a full shilling for each," I replied.

He cocked his head at me. "That's a mighty high price you're asking for, Caleb."

"We aren't asking for hard money, Mr. Eakins. We are asking for store credit. You and Captain Shelby will make up the profit in our exchange for the goods you have to offer."

A half smile broke over his wrinkled face. "Fine. You win this one, Caleb."

We continued to barter over the rest of our furs, and wound up with a grand total of eight pounds, a sum we were happy to receive.

"There are a couple of fine Pennsylvania long rifles in that store. I aim to get me one as soon as I'm able," Nate said after we returned to our campsite. "I'll trade in this old musket for it, too." He slapped contemptuously at his firearm.

"It won't be long now, Nate, if our future ventures into the mountains are as successful as this one."

At sunset, we made our way to Captain Shelby's house. It was a fine affair, considering the setting. Large and rambling, with neat outbuildings and a fine, wide stoop across the front, it was sheathed in whitewashed clapboard, with an imposing second story.

We knocked and were immediately ushered in by a black woman, neatly dressed and dutifully welcoming. We stated our purpose and she showed us into the study. Captain Shelby was there, seated at a desk, with papers and books strewn across the whole of it. He had a quill in hand, bent over a sheet of paper.

When we entered, he raised his head. "Ah, boys, I see you made it back safely. I hope your trip was successful."

"It was, sir. Very successful," Nate declared.

"Good to hear. Don't just stand there. Take a seat." He

waved us over to a bench along a wall of the study. It groaned as Nate lowered himself onto it.

"You asked us to stop by and see you upon our return, sir."

"Yes, I did." He rose from his desk and stood before us. "I'm curious as to what your plans are."

"Why do you ask?" I replied curiously.

He began pacing back and forth in front of us, hands clasped behind his back. Dressed in fawn-colored breeches with matching waistcoat, a grimace crossed his face.

"We are in a tough spot, boys. Extremely tough. In case you don't know, I am in correspondence with many people throughout the colonies, and the likelihood of war with the King's men grows stronger every day. Boston is in an uproar. The Continental Congress was like a match thrust into a powder keg." He stopped momentarily and looked hard at us. "I am convinced that Lord Dunmore, the Governor of our great state of Virginia, was behind the plot to do away with us at Point Pleasant. If not for the quick thinking of a handful of men at an opportune moment, the only fighting force to protect this frontier could have been wiped out in a moment. In short, he was in collusion with the Indian nations we faced that day."

I blinked rapidly. My heart raced in my chest. "Surely that can't be true!" I said.

"It is true, young man," he replied fiercely. "The Indians that surround us to the south are hand in glove with the

British. They've been supplied by royal agents. They mean to do away with us at the first opportunity."

He continued to pace furiously in front of us. "My father was nearing the age of fifty when he brought us here to America from Wales. He was the father of five sons. He had property, to be sure, but not enough to provide for his children once he passed on. There was nowhere to obtain new land, you see. It was all taken up, mostly by rich landlords and the nobility. He was desperate to provide for us – quite desperate. He sold what he had and loaded us on a ship, and we made our way across the ocean. Here, he was able to do what he couldn't in the old country – he could provide us with opportunity. We had the freedom to seek our own destinies, and that is what we've done."

He stopped and pounded his fist in the air. "I will not see the British nobility once again put a stop to progress. I will not, I tell you!" His face had grown red, his voice raised to a thunderous howl. He glared heatedly at us as he spoke those last words. Even Nate, that great bear-sized man, shrank a little before his fury.

"Gone are the days when we let a Parliament thousands of miles away dictate what we can and cannot do, or bow down to a king who cannot possibly know the dangers and the chances we have faced here in the New World. The blood of many a fine man has stained the ground here, defending those of us who have dared to forge ahead – dared to strike out on our own. I have spent more than thirty years defending our rights against the red savages and the French and the British who have fueled their hate. I will not stop now."

He calmed himself and stopped in front of us. "And now we come to you two." He managed a smile. "I need men. Our militia is the only thing that keeps us safe. There will be those who choose to head north to take up arms against the King, I am sure. But we cannot leave the frontier open. It is vital to our people that we have men here who are willing to combat the scourge of the Indians that have been and will be directed against us by the redcoats."

As he spoke, I could feel the power of his persuasive personality roll over me like waves upon a shore. Whoever this man was, he most certainly had the qualities of leadership few others had. As he looked at us I glanced at Nate, and he at I. In unison, we nodded our heads.

"Good!" he nodded, satisfied. "Now, let's find a place for you to be situated." He returned to his paper-strewn desk and sat down. "Are you familiar with Beaver Knob?"

"I can't say that we are," Nate said.

"It's a small mountain about five miles southwest of here. I know of an empty cabin that could be had for the taking if you're interested. It's not in good condition, mind you. But with a little work it would be an acceptable place, I do believe." He continued, "I can't offer you any pay at this time. Your service would be strictly voluntary. I know you will be gone for stretches of time in pursuit of your livelihoods, but I would request you stop by here periodically to let me know you are around. If there is a need of you, I will send someone out to your place. Are those terms acceptable?"

"Yes sir," I answered.

"Fine." He picked up his quill and fumbled through a pile on his desk and found a small scrap of paper. "Here is a small map to the cabin." He took a moment, head bent over, and then handed the scrap to Nate. We both looked, and it seemed clear enough.

"Now, I have correspondence to take care of. Be sure to let me know how you are getting on." And with that, he turned to his papers. I could hear some profanities whispered rather loudly as we exited the room.

Back on the front stoop, we both paused.

"We're in the thick of it now, Caleb!"

"I suppose we are!"

CHAPTER FOURTEEN

It was not an easy task to find the cabin Captain Shelby had directed us to. There was no real path to follow, and the underbrush tugged mightily at the feet and legs of our animals. We were steadily climbing higher and higher into the deep forest that shrouded Beaver Knob. There was plenty of wildlife about. We could hear their crashing through the undergrowth as we proceeded. We found a small creek, and following the map, made our way up it until we came to a thick grove of pine.

"The Captain marked this as the spot," Nate said, as he examined the small paper in his hand.

"It must be here, then. Let's take a look."

We dismounted and peered through the trees until we spotted it. It was most certainly a ramshackle affair. We forced our way through the door, noting that the roof had partially caved in around the fireplace. We frightened a family of raccoons when we entered, and they began snarling and hissing at us as they made their escape through the hole in the roof.

Nate looked around and proclaimed, "Well, it ain't much, that's for sure. But with a little effort, we can make it habitable."

The structure was more spacious than I had imagined it would be – about fourteen feet square, which was plenty of room for the two of us. There was no furniture left. It was just an empty shell.

We spent the first night outside in our tent but the next morning we arose and proceeded to do what we could to fix the roof. We used our ax and hatchets to fashion shingles and used two or three crossbeams across the gaping hole for support. We dabbed mud into the cracks between the shingles. That evening, we spent our first night under our own roof.

It was just in time, for the following day, the snow came. It drifted down in large flakes, wet and cold. Undeterred, we began work on a pen for our animals.

"We want it close to the cabin," Nate stated. "Less likely to lose them to thieving Indians and prowling beasts."

We attached the pen directly to the eastern side of the cabin. It was about fifteen feet wide and twenty feet long. In one corner we fashioned a roof, big enough so Bessie, Sadie and Daisy could shelter under it. We found a large log and hollowed it out to hold water for them. We left it out in the open so that any precipitation that fell would help keep it full. Inside the roofed area we constructed a sort of trough to house their food and fodder. We were happy with the result, even though it took us more than a week to complete. Each day thereafter we would take them to the creek, to water and to forage for themselves.

Once that was done, we decided to make our way back to the fort for more supplies. We purchased nails, hammers, a saw and various other needed implements. There was produce to be had, so we bought a bushel of carrots and potatoes, parsnips and dried corn and beans, plus small kegs and crocks to preserve them in.

"Mr. Anders, before you leave I have a letter for you," Mr. Eakins said. He reached under the counter and pulled out a crumpled, sweat-stained letter and handed it to me. I recognized my sister Martha's neat handwriting – "Caleb Anders, Shelby's Fort, Virginia."

I eagerly broke the seal and read the following:

Dear Caleb,

I am thankful you have arrived at a safe and welcoming place after your journey. Father came by the day after you left, demanding to know where you had gone. We were truthful and told him we did not know. He did not ask us if we had seen you, so we could not be accused of lying. I got a note from our sister Jane. Father also went to Baltimore City to look for you. It is my opinion he was more concerned over the loss of Sadie than your disappearance. Jacob and I are faring well. We had a fruitful harvest this past fall, and are well stocked for the winter. We have had more than the usual amount of snow, which is quite vexing for Jacob. He says it will benefit us in the spring, but keeping our herds fed is a taxing chore for him. He is quite happy to know that we will be having a child come early summer. He sends his regards and says to tell you he misses you whenever he goes to the woods.

Your loving sister,

Martha

I blinked several times after reading Martha's note, happy at the good news of a baby, yet missing the times we had spent together. I was not surprised at my father's reaction to my departure. I would have expected nothing more from him.

When Nate and I returned to the cabin, I removed Mother's copy of the New England primer I had brought with me from its wrappings of oilcloth and placed it in the small metal box I had purchased, along with the letter I received from Martha. I then placed the box in my saddlebag until I could decide on a better place for its safekeeping.

We busied ourselves at constructing some furniture for our new home. We built two low shelves for our sleeping quarters, each with a lip around the edge to hold our bedding. We placed more shelves on one side of the fireplace to store our foodstuffs.

"Have you ever built any furniture before?" I asked Nate.

"Can't say I have. But I've seen it done, so I reckon that counts."

We spent a couple of days busily working on the construction of a table – simple enough with the plane we had purchased. We used pegs and nails to secure the legs. It wasn't impressive by any means, but it suited our purpose. Next we built a tall cupboard with doors. We used strips of hide for the hinges. It was crudely done, but we had high hopes the doors would keep the vermin out. Simple stumps of wood, the bark removed, served us for seating.

"Look, Caleb, there is plenty of trapping and hunting to be done right here on Beaver Knob. We can delay another trip to the mountains, at least until the weather clears a bit."

We spent the following weeks exploring our surroundings and hunted and trapped close to home. We spent our evenings before the fire, happy to have a roof over our heads. Sometimes we played cards, or I worked on the carving of my powder horn. Nate would share tales of his youth as I did also. We were quite content.

It was towards the end of February, I think, when we

got a visit from McTavish and Hugh McDonald. They hailed us a good distance from the cabin to forewarn us of their presence. We were working on the building of a smokehouse. We had found plenty of game on the Knob and were eager to preserve the meat we had acquired, rather than leave it for scavengers.

As they approached, Nate shouted out, "How goes it, fellows?"

They dismounted from their horses as they drew near. "All is well! How goes it with you?"

"Just fine and dandy. What brings you out to Beaver Knob?"

"The Captain told us you had taken up residence here so we thought we would pay a visit," McTavish replied. He glanced around at the small clearing. "I see you've been busy."

"Yes we have. Any news, McTavish?" I asked.

"Not much."

"Did you make it to the mountains?" I glanced at Hugh, who seemed well and healthy. He was certainly in better condition than when I last saw him after the Battle of Point Pleasant.

"Yes we did. A successful outing. How about you two?"

"Successful as well. How about we go inside? I have a stew cooking," Nate said.

We went inside and gathered around our makeshift table

and enjoyed a meal together. When we were finished, I offered for them to stay a few days with us. They agreed. We went outside and put their horses up in our pen, alongside our own animals. They stripped their saddles and bridles and brought them inside and stowed them next to ours in a corner.

As darkness descended, we moved the table close to the fire to catch the benefits of its heat, as it was a cold evening. Nate enthusiastically shared a tale of the beaver dam we had discovered.

"Biggest dam I ever saw! And some of the largest beaver I ever did see!" he gushed.

We chatted a little longer, and then McTavish spoke his mind.

"The Captain says you have joined the militia."

"Yes, we did," Nate responded.

"We could be in for some hot times, boys. The Cherokee have been busy south of here, looting and scalping. Sycamore Shoals has been hit several times. It's gotten bad enough they have begun building a stockade around the town."

"We haven't caught sight of any Indians around here thus far."

"The Captain wants you to keep an eye out for them." He stopped for a moment. "This cabin is well situated for such a purpose. The Stanton family built it a few years ago, then abandoned it to head further west. There's a reason it's so well hidden, boys. It's a good lookout point, perched as it is on the eastern side of the mountain. If you spot any savages, the Captain says you must head to the fort as fast as you are able. Don't attempt to engage them on your own. He will gather those he can reach and confront them with a larger force."

"I suppose he could have informed us of that before we left," I said quietly.

McTavish laughed. "Perhaps he didn't want to scare you off!"

"There isn't much to scare off Caleb and me!" Nate exclaimed.

"Even so, follow the Captain's advice. He knows the Indians better than any other man in these parts."

"That's fine. We'll take his advice."

Two days later, as McTavish and Hugh were getting ready to depart, McTavish asked us if we knew a man named George Simmons. Nate and I looked at each other and nodded yes.

"We had an encounter with him up in the mountains," Hugh said.

"We traveled with him for a short while on the way south to the fort. What's he done?" Nate asked sternly.

"We caught him stealing from our traps up in the mountains," Hugh answered.

"I'm not surprised. He's a sneaky one, he is. Didn't like the looks of him."

Hugh laughed. "McTavish and I gave him a good thrashing. I don't think he'll be stealing from anyone else soon. I doubt he'll make his way back to the fort either. He's a marked man now. No one here holds with stealing. Lord knows we get enough of that from the savages."

They mounted their horses.

"Keep your eyes out, boys. Ride to the fort if you see anything," McTavish reminded us as they departed.

It was the end of February when Nate and I decided to take the furs and hides we had accumulated to the fort. We had spent many an hour on lookout for any signs of Indians but had not spotted any.

We rode into Shelby's Fort in blustery weather, cold and cloudy, with sleet and ice slamming us from the north. The hooves of our animals broke through the ice encrusted puddles on the path we followed into town. The fort drearily beckoned to us as we approached. Despite the weather, there was a flurry of activity around it. Wagons, some empty and forlorn, others brimming full of bags, barrels and furs, were gathered around the store, like moths around a flame. Men and horses rushed to and fro inside the stockade walls. We steered our animals to the interior northern wall, where they could get some relief from the vicious winds that carried the freezing rain that stung our faces.

I dropped the letter I had composed for Martha and Jacob on the counter of the store, and requested that Mr. Eakins send it along with the next post rider. We then looked around to see if there was anyone we knew in the milling crowd outside.

"Ho, there's McTavish!" Nate exclaimed.

He spied us at the same time and hurriedly approached.

"Good to see you boys! Glad you came when you did!"

He quickly explained. Captain Shelby was organizing a foray south as a show of force to the Indians. They were to leave in the morning, at dawn.

"How many riders does he need?" I asked.

"He's looking for thirty or forty, if he can find them. He won't be leading us himself but wants us to head south to Sycamore Shoals and meet up with his son John. He has sent word to him, and there will be more men willing to ride with us there."

"We haven't brought our gear, but we can head back home and pick up what we need," Nate replied. We headed home as fast as we could, and gathered what we would need for the expedition. We loaded our tarps, cooking utensils, hatchets and axes, extra powder and shot, and the dried and smoked meat we had on hand, onto Daisy's back.

"Daisy, old girl, I wish we could leave you here, but that's just not possible," Nate spoke lovingly to her, patting and stroking her neck. "I promise to make it up to you upon our return."

We made our way back to the fort and arrived shortly after sunset. There were campfires burning all around the grounds, with groups of men gathered around, trying their best to stay warm in the freezing air. At least, the rain and sleet had stopped, but the ground was soggy and frigid as we tried to get some sleep that evening. I had a restless night, tossing and turning and doing my best to ignore the images of bloodthirsty savages with raised hatchets that danced in my head. I was almost eighteen, I told myself. It was time to assume the responsibilities of manhood.

Chapter Fifteen

The younger generation cannot fully appreciate the hardships and deprivations we suffered to make the life they now so easily enjoy. My oldest now attends Blount College in Knoxville, blithefully ignorant of the hazards we endured to make the life he now knows. I suppose it is the same with all generations. Retelling what occurred rather than suffering through it cannot produce the same results. At times I shudder to think what the future will hold for our fledgling country. Hard times are quickly forgotten, I fear. Will those who look back at the beginning of this great nation truly understand the sacrifices that were made? I most fervently hope they will, but I doubt that will be the case.

We set out on a frigid morning when the sun began its slow ascent from the east. There were thirty of us, hunched over our horses' backs, shivering and clutching our outer garments to our bodies. McTavish was there, and Hugh. There was the Fulton brothers, John and Jake, and Mr. Eakin's son Solomon. Most of the men neither Nate nor I knew but would become familiar with them on that particular undertaking.

We rode to Sycamore Shoals with determination. Once we arrived, we were greeted by the sight of the beginnings of the stockade being built around the small settlement. John Shelby was there, a sturdily built man who looked more like his mother than his father. He had black hair and dark brown eyes, steady and calm. There was none of the bluster that defined his father, but he exuded a quiet confidence that calmed my jangled nerves. He had gathered together another twelve men, so when we left the half-built stockade we were a force of forty-two.

We headed directly west, along a slight path barely discernible among the heavy forest and foliage. We were thankful for the cover of the woods, as it blunted the bitter wind that buffeted us from the north.

"It's the first day of March," Nate complained bitterly. "The good Lord should be sending us the warmth of spring, not this endless winter!" His great hairy fingers clutched the edges of his buckskin coat closer. "A man can only handle so much cold, Caleb. I've grown weary of it!"

"Your tune will change come July and August," I laughed.

"Perhaps so," he grumbled.

We camped, miserable and cold, at dusk that first evening. We huddled around the campfires we were able to build, after foraging for dry wood and kindling, our fingers numb and aching, in the deepest part of the forest around us. After we fed ourselves, John Shelby called us all together.

"Men, I know you've made a sacrifice to be on this expedition. I would be remiss if I didn't commend you for your courage and willingness to serve. I will do my best to lead us in a worthwhile venture. There have been scattered attacks by the Cherokee from their towns and villages south of here, all along our frontier. Livestock has been stolen or slaughtered, scalps have been taken, and they have captured some of our people for their own brutish uses. It is important for these savages to know their behavior will not be met by meek acceptance, but by force." He paused.

"My father, Captain Evan Shelby, has entrusted me to lead this group. If anyone here objects, please speak now." There was no reply.

"Very well. Here is our plan, then. If we happen upon any Cherokee in these parts, we take no prisoners. They will be shown no mercy. Is that understood?" There was a murmur of assent.

"Mr. Richard Henderson is now at Sycamore Shoals attempting to negotiate with the Cherokees, in hopes of attaining new lands for settlement to the west and north of us. This has no impact on the situation we now face.

There are at this time small bands of marauding Indians attacking our folks and destroying all they've worked for. We must put a stop to it." He eyed his audience with a fierce expression.

"We will make our presence known, boys. We will hunt and provide for ourselves. We want the Cherokee to know we are about, so that they understand their thievery and murder is well known to us. Are there any questions?" He paused. "If not, it's time to get our rest. We rise at the first rays of the sun."

The frigid weather continued the next day, and the next. The sun shown weakly but gave little warmth. We continued in a westerly direction, but because of our number and the lack of a path or road, it was slow going. We were grateful when on the third day we came upon the homestead of a grizzled farmer and his family, originally hailing from New Jersey. We were thankful John agreed for us to stay for a few days, to rest and warm ourselves.

The farmer, named Jenkins, was grateful for our appearance, and his wife and older children did all they could to make us welcome. They helped tend to our animals, and Mrs. Jenkins got to work making bread for us all, something that had not entered my mouth in many a day.

We spent the next few days doing what all men on such a journey enjoy doing. We played cards and had contests in hatchet throwing and shooting. Bets were made among us as to who was the best shot, and I'm happy to report that I won that contest easily. Nate was happy about it too, as he had placed five shillings on me and won that back and then five more.

"I told you fellows he was a fine shot!" he remarked with satisfaction.

The crowd that gathered around nodded in agreement, and I was now looked upon as a man of worth, even though I was nigh eighteen. I took pride in that, happy in the recognition of my abilities. Those abilities would prove to be very useful in the following years.

Farmer Jenkins told us that though his homestead had not been hit, there were others in the area that had suffered mightily. His wife and all his children were handy with the four rifles he kept, ready and primed, inside the front door of his cabin.

"I think those red skunks do a heap of spying before they swoop in. Our place here is well armed and fortified, and they prefer easier targets," he stated.

We left on a sunny morning, the temperature pleasing and warm for that time of year. We headed southwest, diligently looking for any sign of Indians. John threw out scouts in front and behind us, men who had vast experience with such things. We traveled this way for some days, but with no success in finding our prey.

We did come upon several small groups of homesteads, where three or more families had placed their abodes in close proximity to one another. All of them claimed to have sighted Indians and lost livestock to them, but they had not been molested other than that.

Two weeks out, we found a burned out cabin, its black timbers strewn about haphazardly in the middle of a small meadow, with green shoots struggling through the matted tangle of the dregs of winter, a sure sign of the changing seasons. We approached, each of us with the dread of finding bodies, but none were to be found. We sifted through what remained of the interior, looking for a sign of what might have become of the inhabitants, but found nothing to indicate their final disposition.

McTavish surmised the settlers had either been enslaved or had cleared out before their cabin had been burned.

"I see nothing to suggest this cabin was in recent use," he stated. "There are no cooking utensils or other household items that tell me otherwise."

"Let's hope so," I replied fervently. "There is no barn or other outbuildings. Perhaps this was a place used by hunters and trappers."

Later on that day, one of the scouts galloped in from the front of our company, shouting for us to come quickly. We urged our steeds forward and burst through the cover of the woods to find a cabin fully engulfed in flames licking furiously at the sturdy timbers that comprised it. The barn, which stood a good fifty yards behind it, was similarly ablaze. As we closed in, we found the unfortunate remains of three people, their heads a bloody mess where their scalps had been taken. The bodies were of two men and a woman, and it was a sad sight to see, their bodies at odd angles, mangled and blood soaked.

John spoke. "There is nothing we can do for these poor unfortunates. We must hurry forward to see if we can catch the scoundrels that perpetrated this monstrous act." He leaned forward. "I need a detail of five to remain and bury these folks. The rest of us will ride forward. Do I have any volunteers?"

Five men raised their hands.

"Good. Do it quickly. Catch up with us when you can." With that, we spurred our horses forward, galloping back into the deep woods. We gave chase as best we could, although we were hampered by the lack of any clear trail.

To say I was not frightened and uncertain at this point of our journey would be a lie. I had never shot at another human being, and being young and inexperienced, I dreaded the thought of doing so. Yet I knew our cause was righteous. Such atrocities could not go unpunished.

I was riding near the middle of our column when word reached me that John wanted me to come forward. I goaded Sadie until I was riding abreast of him at the head of our column. We galloped alongside each other for a short distance, and then he shouted at me.

"Caleb, we are not far behind them. I need you to take a shot at them if we come upon them unexpectedly."

"Yes, sir!" I replied.

We burst through the heavy woods into a large clearing.

Disappearing on the far side were at least a dozen horsemen, their hair flying in long strands behind them. I could see they were riding bareback, and about 150 yards ahead of us. I quickly yanked the reins and forced Sadie to the right of the column. I steadied her, and without dismounting, brought my rifle to my shoulder, took aim and squeezed the trigger. I saw the man I had targeted slump and tumble off his horse.

To the left, a couple of my comrades also took aim at the fleeing Indians and fired, but with no success. As if by magic, the rest of their party disappeared into the cover of the forest. We gave pursuit, passing by the one I had shot, but it soon became apparent we could not catch them. They had the advantage of knowing the woods thereabouts better than we did. After thirty minutes, John called a halt to the chase.

We returned to the body of the Indian. I had given him a clean shot to the back. I dismounted and examined him with dread in my heart. I had killed a man. It didn't much matter that he was an Indian – he was a man.

I felt no sense of pride in doing it. In fact, I was most unhappy. From his appearance, he was young, most likely my age or slightly older. Most of his head was shaved, save for a topknot of black hair, interlaced with feathers. His face was tattooed and painted with a red streak across his eyes. He wore a sort of tunic that fell to his knees, met by his long-legged moccasins of soft doeskin. He lay just as he fell, at odd angles. It appeared that one leg had broken when he fell off his horse.

Other men gathered around and congratulated me on my fine shot. Several suggested that I scalp him and take his topknot as a prize. Horrified at the thought, I angrily turned to them and replied, "No, I will do no such thing!" I remounted Sadie.

The others grudgingly followed my lead and remounted and we were returned the way we had come. We wound up back at the homestead where we had discovered the three bodies, with the five men we had left behind busily burying them. It was a good size clearing, and John decided we would camp there for the night.

That evening, I sat glumly by the campfire Nate and I had made. Nate was silent, unwilling to disturb my troubled thoughts. McTavish dropped by to share a word with me.

"That was a fine shot, Caleb. Not many here could have made it."

I nodded in assent but had nothing further to say.

"The first time a man kills another – it's a hard thing," he continued. "We have no easier way to deal with these troubling times."

I nodded at him again. There was silence for a moment, and then I spoke my mind.

"It's not just the killing, Ian. That was difficult enough. But I don't like the thought of scalping. Doesn't that make us no different than the enemy we are fighting? How can we condemn for such atrocities when we are committing the same one ourselves?"

"It's not for us that we take scalps, Caleb. It's for our enemies. They will come back at some point and take back the body of the man you killed. With his scalp still intact, it sends a message to his brethren. It tells them the victory over him was not won. Taking his scalp ensures they understand he was defeated."

I thought a moment.

"Have you taken scalps?"

He answered quietly, "Yes, I have. I took no pleasure in it, as some do. But the choice of it was mine to make. I wanted the Indian warriors who returned to the body to see I had vanquished them by doing so. Now, some of these men here are quite happy to do unto them what was done unto us. Again, that is a personal choice. No one will fault you if you choose not to follow the practice."

"That suits me fine," I replied angrily. "I will not debase myself in such a manner."

McTavish nodded, patted me on the shoulder and departed.

We continued on our scout for another two weeks. The weather had warmed, but the cold was replaced with lashing rains and high winds. Many nights we were unable to make a fire because of it.

It was with great relief that John told us we would return to our homes, as so many of our number were farmers and needed to get their crops in the ground. It was towards the end of April that we returned first to Sycamore Shoals, dropping off the men who had joined us there, and then turned our horses north, back to Shelby's Fort.

We arrived back, bedraggled and worn, our horses plodding slowly, after several weeks of being ridden hard through rough terrain and barely visible pathways. I still had thoughts in my head of the young Indian I had killed, and had slept fitfully since the incident.

We were surprised at the welcome we received. Families that had been left behind by our men had sheltered themselves within the walls of the stockade, and they gathered around us quickly, shouting the news.

"There's been a battle up north! Another Congress has been called for!"

Mr. Eakins strode on his short legs out of the store. A look of pleasure crossed his face when he spied his son Solomon, safely returned, but as exhausted and weary as the rest of us.

"Make camp. Captain Shelby has been informed of your return, and he'll want to speak with you directly," he told us.

Food was quickly prepared, and we gathered around the campfires that burned at intervals, women dutifully passing out helpings of what they had on hand. We were hungry and tired, and grateful for whatever provisions were supplied to us.

The womenfolk excitedly explained the details they'd heard of what would become known as the Battles of Lexington and Concord. How the King's regulars had marched out of Boston with the intent of stripping the colonists of weapons and powder, and how in defiance the militia had been called out. How they routed the redcoats and forced them to scatter back to the safety of Boston.

We listened but didn't understand the full impact of what we were told until Captain Shelby appeared before us, dapper in new breeches and waistcoat, and called us together. We grudgingly rose and obeyed.

"Thank you, men, for availing yourselves for the defense of your fellows. I know the trouble and travails that you have passed through. My son John sent me messages while you were gone, and I'm well aware of all that transpired. I commend you for your courage and willingness to serve." With downcast eyes, I nodded dully. Nate, standing next to me, shuffled his huge feet nervously, and I heard him cough uncomfortably.

"Now, to the business at hand." Captain Shelby's voice hardened. "I'm sure you've been informed by your families of what transpired outside of Boston a few days ago. A rider pelted through our gates with the news, and I believe you have a right to know the facts." He continued, "The royal Governor of Massachusetts decided it was within his right to strip from us the weapons upon which we depend for our safety and sustenance. He sent his troops on a fool's errand to Concord, intent on confiscating from us the tools we rely on for our very existence." His voice grew louder. "What did he expect? That we would cower before him and his blasted redcoats that have crossed the ocean to try to impose the will of the King of England? If so, he was sorely disappointed." He half laughed. "The militia was called out, my friends. Hundreds of them. They fought bravely and forced those lobsterbacks right back into Boston where they came from! It was a fine victory, men! A fine one!"

His voice quieted. "The leaders of the cause of freedom have been called together again and will soon start meeting in Philadelphia. Others have begun gathering troops to march against the British. It's war. It's not one we would have chosen, but it is here nonetheless. It will not be easy, friends. But it is a just cause, and one I proudly declare to you I am willing to fight for."

A half cheer rose among us. Nate and I looked at each other. Perhaps we did not know what lay ahead, but we were both in agreement. Captain Shelby would have our support.

Chapter Sixteen

After his short speech, Captain Shelby pulled me aside. We walked a short way, separating ourselves from the others. He reached up and grabbed my shoulder.

"My son John sent a message. It appears you have a talent with that rifle of yours."

"Yes, sir. It appears that I do." I looked down, not sure of what else I should say.

"I wanted to talk with you, Caleb. There will be a few men here that will turn their horses north and seek to join up with any military units they may find. I have it on good authority that Daniel Morgan is gathering men and arms up in the Shenandoah Valley right now. He should be ready to march within a week or two."

"Yes, sir," I replied.

"I'd hate to see you head that way, Caleb. We need men here, desperately. Now that the first shots have been fired, those lousy Brits will be stirring up the Indians even more than they already have. Our frontiers will be wide open to slaughter and mayhem."

I looked down at him, neatly attired as he was. I recalled him as I first saw him, dressed in buckskin from head to toe, walking with the purposeful steps of a man who knew his own mind and the cause he had determined was his.

"I have no intention of leaving here, Captain. I intend on making this my permanent home. I will admit I take no pleasure in killing. But if I intend on living here, I understand I must be willing to do what it takes to defend it with all I've got."

A rare smile broke across his face. "Welcome news. Welcome, indeed!"

Nate ambled up, his huge frame's shadow looming over us. The Captain looked up and spoke to him. "I expect you to stay as well, young man. No need of you to head north. Stay. We will keep you busy enough."

Nate covered his mouth with his huge paw, almost like a girl, to hide the smile that creased his face. "I'm staying with Caleb. If he remains here, so will I."

"Good!" Shelby exclaimed.

"I was wondering though, Captain," Nate continued. "Would it be acceptable to you if the two of us head east to the mountains and do a little trapping? I'm trying to make enough money to exchange my musket for one of those fine rifles you have in the store."

"You men have to make a living. I understand that. The two of you are free to go. Be back in six weeks if you are able. But if you see any sign of Indians while you're gone, you must make your way back here to inform me immediately." As we nodded in agreement, he said, "Now I must head back home. My wife will not be happy if I miss supper again. She likes me home whenever I am able. The good Lord knows she deserves that, as much time as I've been forced to spend away from her."

Nate and I left the fort and made our way back up the hills to our cabin. A bright moon served us well, a guiding light leading us home. We were thankful to find it just as we left it, and could find no sign of any intruders while we had been absent.

We rested our animals for a few days before we headed further east, to those magnificent cloud-shrouded mountains that seemed to draw me to them. The weather had warmed, and the fields and forests sung of spring, with green grasses and wildflowers strewn about, the new growth of the trees of the forest promising us a bountiful harvest if we had a mind to work for it. The streams babbled over rock-strewn beds, a sound I always found peaceful and inviting. The icy cold waters of those streams were teeming with fish, and we dropped our lines in whenever we rested beside them. We enjoyed our catches, speared on sticks and roasted over the fire. Fine, big trout and bass, crappies and bluegills, all provided welcome feasts to Nate and I. We smoked them over a low fire while we slept at night and packed them along with the rest of our provisions whenever we were blessed with an abundance.

We ate well, that first spring in the mountains. Not only was the trapping better than we expected, and thus we were supplied with plenty of meat, we also had the bountiful harvest of the green growing things all around us. We had plenty of chickweed for our stews, as well as sassafras leaves, wild leeks and onions, wood sorrel and edible mushrooms.

We hunted splendid, big buffalo and deer, doing our best to skin them carefully so as to bring us a higher price at Shelby's store. Panthers and wolves and wild boar also fell prey to us, and there was an abundance of them that spring. Big, black bears were our favorite targets, when we could find them.

One sunny cool morning, I left Nate beside a stream we had camped beside to gather some greens for our breakfast. I had wandered quite a distance away, and then realized I had spent far too long meandering around, taking in the sights and smells of a delightful meadow.

I hurried back. We had plans to hunt on the higher peaks above us that morning, and I was concerned my wandering would spoil our plans. I got back to our campsite and saw Nate was not there.

"Now where could he have gotten off to?' I complained silently.

I glanced along the creek and saw him downstream about fifty or so yards south. He had squatted down by the stream and was busy pulling in his catch. At that moment, just as I was ready to hail him, I spied a large bear coming towards him from behind, its teeth bared. He heard its approach, and just as he stood and turned, I lifted my rifle to my shoulder and squeezed the trigger. I hit the bear squarely between the eyes, and it fell lifeless at his feet.

I splashed through the cold, clear water of the stream. "Are you all right?" I called to him.

"Just fine, partner!" he replied.

It was a big female bear. We heard a rustling from behind us, and glimpsed a small bear cub, squealing in distress. There was nothing we could do for it. We didn't kill it, but simply shooed it away, in hopes it would somehow find a way to survive.

"That was a close call. I do believe you saved my life!" Nate exclaimed.

I shook my head. "You're bigger than this old bear. You would have bested it if given the chance."

We grabbed hold of the bear's feet and bundled it across the stream to our campsite.

"I'm going to save this hide for myself." Nate declared, with a self-satisfied look on his face. "It's not often a man can be kept warm at night by a critter that tried to kill him!"

We returned to Shelby's Fort and Sapling Grove in mid-June. It was slower going than usual, as Daisy was loaded down with the great amount of furs we had collected. On the way, Nate talked half my ear off how he would get his hands on a rifle when we got back.

Our first stop was the store. While I bartered with Mr. Eakins on the worth of our pelts and skins, Nate took his time examining the five rifles on display. They were all beauties, I must say. He finally set his sights on a wonderful piece, made of curly maple with a brass patch box, ornately embellished. He hefted it with both hands and looked down the barrel. He brought it to his shoulder several times and whistled.

"This is a fine piece, Mr. Eakins. How much you want for it?" he inquired.

"Well, now, that's one of the best rifles we've ever had in stock. I couldn't let you have it for any less than six pounds."

"Six pounds?" I interjected. "Why, it can't be worth any more than five."

Mr. Eakins shook his head. "Now you know I can't let you have it for five."

"What if I trade in my musket for it?" Nate asked.

"Muskets don't fetch much these days. Everyone here

wants a rifle." He paused. "If you trade it in for the rifle, I can let you have it for four pounds, ten shillings."

"Deal," Nate said before I could object.

Nate finally had his rifle. To be honest, I was happy. Not so much that he had his rifle, but that I would no longer have to hear him go on so about getting one.

We had no sooner gotten back to our cabin before Nate began pestering me to help him practice with his new firearm.

"Let's get the animals settled first, Nate. Go fetch some water and I'll see to their feed."

Afterwards, I helped him with the steps needed to fire his new weapon. Set the butt of the rifle flat on the ground. Take the powder horn and measure out the powder in the cap of the horn. Pour it down the barrel. Take a buckskin patch and put over the hole. Seat the ball in the patch. Use the short ramrod to secure it into the barrel. Then use the long ramrod to force the ball and patch all the way down the barrel. Open the frizzen and pour a few grains into it. Close it, and then pull the cock all the way back. Fire!

"I always cut my patches ahead of time. That way, I can reload quicker," I explained to him. "It takes longer to load, but it is far more accurate and can shoot a greater distance than your old musket."

He grinned. "Don't I know it!" He looked around, squinting. "We still have an hour of light. Let's make the most of it!" He busied himself reloading.

That evening we discussed the news of the lands purchased by Richard Henderson from the Cherokee at Sycamore Shoals while we had been out hunting their brothers, who had been wreaking havoc on our friends and neighbors.

"Captain Shelby said it is some mighty pretty country. He has seen it many times and told me his son Isaac will be helping survey it," Nate said. "An immense piece of land, he said."

"Did he say he trusted the Indians to keep their part of the bargain?"

"He expects most of them will. Henderson didn't cheat them. He gave them a fair price for it. But Chief Dragging Canoe was not pleased. He left in a huff. The Captain is afraid there will be trouble ahead."

Summer flew by. We spent the days setting traps and hunting. We made trips back and forth from the fort, and I got busy pickling the vegetables we purchased at the store. We kept them in large crocks, lining them up along the shelving we had made inside our cabin. We kept the small smokehouse we had built behind our cabin very busy. Sometimes we had such an abundance we took our excess to the store and used it to grow our account.

We purchased new clothing – brand new buckskins and moccasins. We bought all the powder and shot we could get our hands on, figuring to be prepared for whatever lay ahead.

We met new folks all the time. Often while at the fort I was asked to write letters home by those who had heard I had a fine hand. I did so willingly, without hesitation. Often when writing I silently thanked my godly mother, who had taken time to teach me properly.

I rarely thought of my childhood days. Those times were past, and I was more eager to think of the future and what it would hold for me. The only exception was when I received a letter from Jacob with the fine news that Martha had given birth to a son. They named him Jonathan. I was pleased, and remembered with fondness the kindness he and Martha had shown me during those difficult years of my childhood.

Nate applied himself to becoming more proficient with his rifle. We had competitions, the two of us, to see who could load and fire faster. By the end of the summer, he could load and fire three times a minute, which was an admirable feat. I myself, on a good day, could manage four a minute, but not always.

Whenever we went to the fort we were sure to find groups of men gathered together, talking of the latest news on the war – a war that seemed far, far away. We heard of the new commander-in-chief, General George Washington, and that Captain Shelby knew him from his time fighting in the French War. We heard about Bunker Hill, where our troops stood up to the British Army, the finest in the world. There was talk of the Continental Congress, and Thomas Jefferson, a Virginian just like us, who helped fund the war effort. A few of our comrades put their rifles on their shoulders and headed north. Men like Josiah Wilson, Thomas Smith and John Peterson. We wished them good fortune, but most of us stayed home. True, the Indians had been somewhat quieted after the treaty between Henderson and the Cherokees, but those who had spent time along the Holston River assured us this peace might not last.

"One thing about the Cherokee – a person can never be sure when they will get restless and decide to pick up their weapons again," McTavish told us. "Shelby is right to encourage us to stay put. Lord only knows what would happen if we left our homes defenseless."

That fall, Nate and I headed back to the mountains. We stayed about six weeks, gathering furs and hides, subsisting on what we hunted and what we could forage in the woods. It was another bountiful harvest for us.

One day we stumbled upon a makeshift hut, windowless, sheltered among rocky outcroppings about halfway up the side of a silent, boulder strewn mountain. A stream close by rushed over a bed of pebbles and stones. We hallooed as we approached but received no answer.

As we drew closer, Nate said, "Looks to be abandoned. I see nothing here to indicate otherwise."

We dismounted from our horses and approached, knocking loudly on the door. There was no response. However, the door gave way slightly to the ham-sized fist Nate had applied to it. Curious, he pushed and it slowly swung open.

There was no fireplace and no furniture in the room. The only light was what streamed in through the doorway. We saw a peculiar bundle in one corner of the room, a bright blanket of red covering it.

We slowly advanced towards it and I prodded it with my foot. We both drew back in horror when a moccasined foot escaped from the blanket and splayed out. We could see the only thing attached to it was a leg bone, stark and white against the blanket.

Nate reached down and drew the blanket aside. We found a perfectly preserved skeleton, enclosed by buckskin that had holes and tears and fell apart at our touch. The skull leered at us, frozen in a perpetual grin. We looked at it silently for a moment.

"This poor soul has been dead for awhile," Nate said. "Looks like the rats have gotten to him. See how his garments have been torn."

I shuddered. "Poor fellow."

"Let's gather what's left of him and give him a proper burial."

"What caused his death?" I wondered.

Nate replied somberly, "No way of telling. I don't expect he was done in by someone else. Maybe he just took sick. If he had a horse, it's long gone."

We took our shovels and dug his grave next to the bubbling stream. We carefully placed his remains at the bottom, covered in the blanket in which we found him, and then got to work refilling it.

Afterwards, Nate fashioned a sort of cross from a couple of sticks and some rawhide. As he placed it at the head of the grave, he spoke. "Lord, we don't know this fellow's name or where he came from. But we know he has a family somewhere, left wondering what happened to him. We ask that you welcome him home. Bring peace to his family. Amen."

"Amen," I added.

We never did find out who that gentleman was. When we returned to the fort at the first sign of snow, we asked around, but no one had any idea who he might have been.

CHAPTER SEVENTEEN

I first met Isaac Shelby, son of Evan Shelby, sometime in December of 1775. He had stopped by only briefly, as he was busy doing survey work for Richard Henderson and the Transylvania Company. Millions of acres had been purchased by the company, in hopes of starting a new colony.

He was a commanding figure, much like his father. He had the same ease and confidence about him that naturally drew men to him. He had auburn hair, broad shoulders, and the same long, straight nose and deep-set eyes of his father, but was several inches taller.

He was in the center of a group of men in the store, who were eagerly listening to him describe the rich lands and bountiful opportunities that lay just west and north of us. He described rich forests and meadows, rivers and streams teeming with fish, and the vastness of it all.

"There are already settlers arriving, men. Most of you know Daniel Boone from down at Sycamore Shoals. He's started a settlement along the Kentucky River. Named it Boonesborough. There's been a road established, leading out of Sycamore Shoals through the mountains. You've heard of it, yes?" he queried.

We all nodded.

"It's tough going along that road but wagons can get through, and it will lead you right to Boonesborough."

Nate replied. "We've seen a few families making their way there. What about the Indians?"

Isaac quickly replied, "There are Indians there as well as here. No getting around it."

I was much impressed with him, but not dissuaded from my plans to remain where I was. I had all I needed. For others, they were drawn west. I could understand it, but I could not get around the pull the Blue Ridge had on me. I had no interest in Transylvania, no matter the beauty and bounty it held.

A few days later, Isaac was gone. We heard a few folks had taken heed of his reports and packed up their belongings and moved west. Nate and I, however, were content with our situation on Beaver Knob.

Captain Evan Shelby was a prolific correspondent, and continually got updates on the progress of the war. We heard about the defeats of our struggling Colonial army, and the dogged tenacity of those who fought the British for our freedom. The expedition to Quebec had evidently failed, but what was even worse was the British leaving Boston and moving their forces to Canada. As the Captain explained, once they crushed our forces there, they could use the province as a stage to move south against us.

"What those lobsterbacks don't know about the countryside could fill a book!" he declared as we gathered around the crackling fire Nate had managed to start despite the dampness and chill of an April morning in the stockade enclosure. There were about six or seven of us gathered around it, warming our hands over the flames.

"I ain't worried about it," declared Henry Sampson, a weather-beaten old trapper who had joined our circle, as he leaned over and spat a stream of tobacco juice. Remarkably, none of it landed on his thin, straggly white beard, a feat few of those I knew who chewed tobacco were able to attain.

The Captain raised his head sharply, cocking it to the side. "Well, you should be. The stronger the British get, the harder it will be for the rest of us."

"I don't get your meanin'," Henry replied.

"Don't be a fool, Henry. You know full well the British are behind the attacks on our settlements hereabouts. They are the ones encouraging the savages to attack us. They've filled their heads with evil rumors about us. They call us 'Virginians,' and those red devils use it as a curse word.

Perhaps to you this war is far away, but it isn't. It's right here and right now."

Henry leaned over and spat again, with remarkable accuracy. "I dunno, Captain. I ain't seen hide nor hair of an Injun for a good while now."

The Captain's voice rose. His cheeks flushed as he retorted, "It's just that kind of thinking that will get folks killed. I'll not have anyone here believe such nonsense. We must stay vigilant, men. Vigilant. The Cherokee are not done with us yet." With that, he turned on his heel and left us.

I looked uneasily around the circle of men, and it was plain to see that the Captain's words had an impact.

Ever mindful of Captain Shelby's prophetic words, Nate and I stayed alert during the spring of 1776. We made a short trapping expedition to the mountains in April and May of that year, but spent most of our time at our little cabin at Beaver Knob. The hunting and trapping was still good there. We earned plenty for our upkeep, and then some. We had a satisfyingly healthy balance at the store, so we did not want for anything.

The warmth of summer burst upon us, with soft breezes that smelled sweetly of lush grasses and wild flowers. We traveled often to Shelby's Fort, to get the news and to gather with our friends there.

We made new friends, too. The road we had traveled south on brought a collection of newcomers. Some headed further south to the Watauga settlements near Sycamore Shoals, while others had it in mind to travel further north and west along the road blazed by Daniel Boone. Still others decided to head toward the Blue Ridge, eager to uncover hidden treasures on their own. Many of them traveled with families – wives, harried and worn from the journey, with children hopping about and causing a ruckus. Some came with full wagons of household goods. Others had little to their names but were intent on making a home for themselves and their families.

With the arrival of each, there were new stories to share and reports of the conditions of the places from whence they had traveled. Nate made friends with several who had ventured from his part of Pennsylvania. Maybe these encounters brought a yearning for home. At last, he shamefacedly asked me to write a letter for him.

"Caleb, these fat fingers of mine were not made to curl around a quill pen. Would you write a letter for me?" he looked pensively at me.

"I thought you would never ask. I would be happy to, partner," I replied.

I carefully composed his thoughts on paper for him. He told of his safe arrival and his plans to stay where he was, and of our partnership. He gave them news of the struggles we had with the Indians, and that he was happy.

He painstakingly signed his name to the bottom of the missive.

"There!" he exclaimed. "My Ma will be happy now."

By the middle of July the news of the Declaration of Independence had reached us. A group of us were settled outside the store when Evan Shelby came flying out if his house, a scrap of paper clutched tightly in his hand.

"We've done it, boys!" he yelled. "Fat, old King George will not like this one bit!"

He read the paper he held in his hands, his voice quivering with excitement. We listened, the words flowing over us like a quiet wind.

"What exactly does it mean?" I asked somberly.

"It means we no longer answer to the lobsterbacks," he sharply replied. "It means we have our own country now. That the King no longer has any authority over us. That we have chosen the future, and it doesn't include Parliament. Now, I must get back. I have letters to write." And with that, he abruptly turned and headed back towards his house.

"Well, we've certainly done it now," Nate said. "Those lousy British are not going to take this news lightly."

Ian McTavish spoke up. "Neither are the Cherokee."

About two weeks later we were awakened at daybreak by a furious knocking on the door of the cabin. "Are you boys in there?" a familiar voice called.

I opened the door to Hugh McDonald, disheveled and breathing heavily.

"What's happened?"

"The Captain says come quick. Waste no time. Sycamore Shoals has been attacked."

We wiped the sleep out of our eyes and gathered our belongings as quickly as we could. By the time we made it out of the cabin, Hugh was gone. We saddled Bessie and Sadie and tethered Daisy and made haste to the fort.

By the time we arrived, there were at least thirty horsemen gathered inside the enclosure. Captain Shelby was pacing back and forth, and nodded firmly to us as we entered.

"Good! We're still waiting for more of you."

By the end of the day, our number had grown considerably. The news spread among us quickly. A force of Cherokee had attacked the stockade at Sycamore Shoals and penned a large number of settlers and militia inside its walls. No one knew for sure the exact number of settlers, or how many Cherokee there were, but Shelby had determined to go to their aid.

We left before daybreak the next morning. We were one hundred strong, each fully armed and determined to render assistance to our neighbors. Each brought their own provisions. With grim faces and steely resolve, we made our way south. On the way, the news was passed that Evan Shelby had been appointed a Major in the militia.

"Now, what do we call him?" Nate joked.

"I guess just Major."

"How about Major to his face but plain old Evan otherwise?" he suggested.

"Seems disrespectful to me," I replied.

"It's hard going keeping all these Shelbys apart. We've got to do something!" he retorted.

"All right. I see your point. Major to his face. Evan otherwise."

The closer we drew near to Sycamore Shoals and its fort, the faster Evan urged us on. We entered the clearing surrounding the fortified stockade at a full gallop, expecting to find it under attack. Instead, we found the gates open and silent. We rode quickly into the enclosure and found it full of milling people, children and dogs. Men were posted on the fort's lookouts, muskets at the ready.

Evan bellowed out, "Where are Robertson and Sevier?"

The two men he called for approached us, guns cradled in their arms. They looked weary, their clothing rumpled and stained. The taller of the two, John Sevier, spoke out.

"Shelby! So glad you could join our little party!" He was a handsome man, with deep-set eyes, high forehead and a shock of brown hair. He smiled easily at Evan and stuck out his hand as he dismounted.

As they shook hands, he explained, "We believe it was Old Abram's war party that attacked us. We've managed to repel them, with all of us here in good health."

"Good to hear, John," Evan replied.

James Robertson spoke up. "But we got word the scoundrels have killed several of our folks out there." He waved southward. "We heard some dreadful screaming about two days ago, and we fear some of our people have been captured."

"We'll need to send out scouts," Evan replied. "McTavish, organize it. We need twenty good men to ride out and reconnoiter the countryside," he continued. "Is my son John here?"

"No, sir. He never came in. He's most probably safe inside his own stockade. As far as we can tell, the main thrust of the attack was right here."

As McTavish led his scouts out, the rest of us dismounted and scoured the woods past the fields that shielded the fort. We found signs of the savages, but none were still about. They had fled, most likely when they realized they could not breach the fortifications.

As evening fell, the scouting party returned. They brought grim news. They had found the earthly remains of four settlers, tortured and bloodied, with their scalps missing. But there was no sign that the marauders were still about.

Our contingent took over guard duty that evening, posted along the rim of the fort, while the brave men who had held their own against the red wave that had besieged them got an evening's rest. Nate and I took our turns together, within a few yards of each other. It had been a difficult day. Through an eerie silence, the moon shrouded by clouds and the scent of the sweet grasses that surrounded us, my eyes fluttered, and the need for sleep nearly overcame me. I struggled to keep from giving in to it until we were relieved a few hours before dawn. Exhausted, Nate and I curled up in our blankets close to a smoldering fire in the inner circle of the fort and I fell into a deep sleep.

We stayed a few days with those hearty settlers, as John Sevier, James Robertson and Major Shelby continued sending out scouting parties until they were sure the menace was over. As we all mounted and headed back north, some of the families that had been sheltered within the fort began to move out, back to the homes they had carved out of the wilderness.

CHAPTER EIGHTEEN

We arrived back at the fort late that evening, our horses spent and hungry, as were we. When we entered the gates I was surprised to see our old friend Samuel Hayward, who had traveled south with us with his wife Chastity and their children. His face was haggard and drawn. He rushed forward when he spied Evan Shelby and grabbed the bridle of his horse.

"I have to see you, sir. It's urgent." His voice was desperate and shrill.

"Can it not wait? I've just now returned."

"No, it cannot," Samuel replied.

"Very well. Meet me at my home in thirty minutes."

With that, Samuel released Evan's horse and stood aside. Nate and I dismounted and went to him. "What's happened, Samuel?" Nate asked in a concerned voice. It wasn't like Samuel to be impulsive.

"Them savages took my boy Ezra," Samuel gulped. Sweat glistened on his forehead.

"What do you mean they took Ezra?" Nate said sharply.

"While you all were down south, a band of Cherokee appeared at the edge of our clearing. We was all busy with chores, but Mr. Wilson spied them. We got our rifles and shot at them. They turned and headed back into the woods." His voice rose again. "Ezra must have been down by the creek. He had a habit of not minding us and taking off down there when we wasn't looking. After we scared off the Indians we went looking for him. He was gone." Samuel bowed his head to hide the tears that flowed down his cheeks.

"Do you know for sure they took him? Perhaps he just wandered off," I offered, as gently as I could.

Samuel raised his head and spoke sharply. "We looked high and low for the boy. We searched up and down that creek and in all the bushes beside it. We found one of his moccasins, but that's all. He was taken, I tell you."

Nate reached down and gently put his hand on Samuel's shoulder. "That's fine. We'll go with you to talk to the Major."

At the appointed hour, we followed him to Evan's house, and were greeted at the door by his wife. She silently waved us inside. We found him in his study, seated amongst the papers and books scattered about. For the first time I noticed how weary and worn he looked, but his voice was as vigorous as ever.

"So, young man, tell me your troubles."

"My boy has been taken by the Indians. While you all were gone south, a pack of them swooped down on our farm and stole him." Samuel's voice quivered.

"Where abouts are you settled at?" Evan queried.

"We're settled in with the Wilson's. We are southwest of here, about twelve miles out."

The Captain nodded. "I know the place. Wilson is a good man. He was with us at Point Pleasant."

"I need your help getting my boy back, Captain," Samuel pleaded.

"Where is the rest of your family?"

"We're all here, sir. After those savages took Ezra, my wife and I loaded up our wagon and came here, looking for help to get him back."

Evan nodded in reply. He then spoke as gently as he could. "I don't know that I can."

"But you must! He's a good boy," Samuel pleaded.

"We don't know for sure who took him. We don't know which band of Cherokee were out and about near your place. If we don't know that, we can't know where to look."

Samuel bowed his head, and his shoulders shook as he sobbed loudly.

"I understand your plight," Shelby continued. "Your family isn't the first that has had children captured. I've seen it happen many times." His voice was firm but kind. "Give me some time. Let me see what I can find out for you. We can then go from there."

"Thank you, sir."

We left and found Chastity and the children, their wagon moored under the eave of the west-facing wall of the stockade. She was thin and wan, a pensive look on her face as we approached. Samuel told her the news, and her lips trembled as she nodded her head. The two other boys, Timothy and Elijah, sat quietly before the fire, their hands idle as they heard the news. Little Mary lay asleep before it.

Nate and I set up camp next to them, just as we had when we first came to the fort. As we lay under the stars that night, we discussed the predicament the Haywards now found themselves in.

"I don't know what the Captain will be able to do," I said.

"Me neither," said Nate. "I only hope there isn't a small red scalp placed on a pole before a Cherokee lodge."

With no pressing matters for us to take care of, Nate and I stayed with the Haywards for the next few days, hoping with them that Evan would have some news for them. Their grief was difficult to watch. Their other two boys, Timothy and Elijah, were listless and glum, and never strayed from the side of their mother. Young Mary whimpered continually, as if she sensed something was wrong but knew not what.

After a week or so, Evan had news. A post rider had come in and personally delivered the mail to his front door. After a number of minutes, we saw him suddenly appear at our campsite. Samuel leaped up and asked him if he had any news. Evan nodded his head.

"It's not good, I'm afraid."

Chastity sobbed loudly.

"Now, now," he admonished. "It's not all bad. No one has found the boy, but I now have an idea of his whereabouts."

"Where is he? Who has him?" Samuel demanded.

"While we were facing Old Abram and his Cherokee followers at the fort by Sycamore Shoals, it seems Dragging Canoe and his band of savages were wreaking havoc west of here. Since you found no sign of your son and have reason to believe he was captured, it is most likely Dragging Canoe is responsible."

"When can we go to try to fetch him back?"

"It's not that simple of a matter, Samuel. Dragging

Canoe is hiding amongst the fortified towns well south of here. To go in search of a single boy is not possible. The number of men needed for such a thing . . .”

“But we have to do something! I demand it!” Samuel’s voice rose, and his hands clenched into fists.

Evan did his best to soothe him. “We cannot at this time. We must wait. We must pray that the boy is safe and in one piece. I’m sorry. But keep in mind you are not alone. There are others hereabouts who have lost loved ones, taken off by the Cherokee. I assure you, sir, when the time is right we will take action. But that time is not upon us at present.”

“When you do decide to take action, Mr. Shelby, I want to go with you. I want to find my boy,” Samuel replied quietly.

“No need to worry about that. I will send word when the time is right.”

The following day, the Haywards packed up their wagon and left the safety of the fort, headed back to their homestead with the Wilsons. A sadder sight was never seen. Samuel and Chastity’s faces mirrored the pain in their hearts. Their remaining children rode silently in the back.

The waning days of summer were spent making provisions for our fall trip to the mountains. Nate and I stayed busy repairing equipment and chinking any gaps we found in the walls of our cabin. We repaired the roof as best we could, using moss to fill in between the new shingles we added. By doing so, we hoped this would prevent any wandering rats or raccoons from taking up residence while we were gone.

We had another good harvest that fall and were in high spirits. Daisy's back was loaded down with our furs and hides when we returned to the fort the first week of November. We had purposefully cut our journey short, as we didn't want to be away from home too long with the threat of continued Indian attacks hanging like a cloud over the fort.

It was one of those drab, sunless November days when we entered the gate of Shelby's Fort. The skies were gray and overcast, the icy winds from the north forced us to lower our hat brims and stand our coat collars up as high as they would go to protect our necks from the cold fingers of wind that tickled them. There seemed to be a sense of gloom about the place. There were few people out and about, and we hadn't seen any travelers on the road heading south.

Mr. Eakins was in an ill humor when we entered the store. Nate was having none of it.

"Why so glum, sir? Is there something we should know?" he inquired.

Eakins slammed down the account book he had brought out from under the front counter. "Oh, nothing much," he answered sarcastically. "Just that damn fool Washington has lost New York, that's all. Where have you fellows been?"

"We've been in the mountains."

"Just as well," he replied grumpily.

We could see we would not be getting much information from him, so we concluded our business and wandered out into the fort, hoping to find answers to the questions that dogged our minds. We couldn't find a single soul, and decided to take the risk and approach Evan Shelby's door. Nate's loud booming soon had someone open the door. It was Mrs. Shelby, dressed neatly in a green dress, a clean white apron pinned to it.

"We hate to bother you, ma'am, but is the Major at home?" I asked quietly.

"I believe he's locked in his study with his correspondence. Let me see if he is willing to talk to you," she replied.

A moment later we were ushered in. Evan sat in his usual place behind his desk, a scrap of paper before him, his hand furiously writing as we entered the room. He looked up to us and nodded.

"Be with you in a moment, boys."

Shortly thereafter he laid down his quill. "I suppose you heard the news," he said.

"Not really, sir. Mr. Eakins just said Washington has

lost New York. We were hoping you could give us more information," I responded.

Evan chuckled. "It's not quite as bad as all that. But he was maneuvered out of New York town and its harbor. Those blasted British and their navy . . ." His voice trailed off.

My heart sunk just a little bit at the news. At my tender age I didn't quite understand what that meant, but I did know any loss was a difficult one. The weather north of us at that time of year was fierce, that much I did grasp. I knew a few of the men who had left to join Washington in the fight, and wondered how they were faring.

"It's not a total loss," Evan continued briskly. "Washington is no fool. The British had him dead to rights. He withdrew to spare any more loss of life. He will save his troops for another day."

Relieved, I nodded.

"This is no easy task we've embarked on. Declaring our independence is one thing, but winning it is another. We must be willing to continue on for as long as it takes. Don't be discouraged, boys. All is not lost." A brief smile flitted across his face.

"Now, return to your home. If I have need of you I'll let you know. The Cherokee won't move against us while they're wintering. But be prepared for anything, I always say. Keep a lookout. If you see anything, anything at all, that might prove me wrong, make your way here as quick as you can."

We both responded with a "yes, sir" and he dropped his head, picked up his quill, and began busily scratching once again.

CHAPTER NINETEEN

We returned to the fort in the middle of December, on a warmish day for that time of year. We were happy to see McTavish and Hugh McDonald camped within its enclosure, just recently returned from their own trip to the mountains. McTavish somberly filled us in on details of the Continental Army's string of defeats, including the disastrous loss of Fort Washington, but claimed to be somewhat heartened by the fight the beleaguered army had made at White Plains.

"They made a stand. They were outnumbered, but they fought. It's a good sign in my view," he reported with a note of satisfaction in his voice.

"Where are they now? Does anyone know?"

"The Major says they're in New Jersey. Washington is keeping them together despite their losses. If he can combine with the army under Charles Lee I reckon they'll be able to hold Philadelphia."

We weren't much cheered by the news. I had received a letter from Martha, who said Jacob was excited to share that he had joined the local militia and was prepared to take the field if the redcoats showed up. I didn't like the sound of it. I expressed to Nate that perhaps it was my duty to go back home and join in the war.

"Well, now, I don't rightly see that," he calmly replied. "We have our own fight on our hands down here. What would happen if we let these red devils take control of the frontier? Do you think they would stop here? Not with the British urging them on, I can tell you. They'll head right up north. Then, the home folks will have the British in front of them and the redskins to the back of them. I don't see us going home, Caleb. Evan is right. We need to stay right here and do our part."

I saw sense in what he was saying but couldn't help the feeling of anxiety that overcame me in those days. I was torn about what sort of direction to go. Stay where I was and hope I could make a difference, or head home and take up arms against the British. It would be safe to say that many of my friends and acquaintances in those days felt the same way.

Our cabin appeared much as we left it. The repairs we made had held, and we were happy to have a warm place to lay our heads down when darkness arrived each evening. Each day, without fail, we would hike up to a clearing about three hundred yards north of our cabin, with a clear view southward. We would scan the horizon, looking for any signs of an Indian incursion. The sights we had seen of what such an incursion might mean for our fellow settlers weighed heavily on our minds.

The new year of 1777 arrived. In the middle of January we gathered up the skins and furs we had collected – not many, but enough for an excuse to make our way to Shelby's store for any news that might have arrived since our last visit. Mr. Eakins fairly beamed at us as we entered, shaking off the snowflakes that had clung to our buckskins on our ride into town. Despite the scudding clouds that churned out freezing ice pellets, thus ensuring a slow business day, he was as happy as I'd ever seen him.

"All smiles today, I see," Nate smirked at him. Although it was always hard to tell a grin with him, as a vast portion of his face was covered with a prodigious black beard and mustache.

"Yes indeed. Good news does have that effect on me," Mr. Eakins smiled in return.

"We could stand with some good news," Nate replied.

"Well, there are others that can tell it better than I, but let me just say that George Washington has done the impossible! He turned around and whipped the British twice up there in New Jersey! Good news, boys! Very good news!"

At that moment Isaac Shelby, Evan's son, entered the

store. He looked wan and thin, but seemed amiable enough despite his feeble appearance. We introduced ourselves again to him. He nodded. "I remember you boys."

"Anything wrong, sir?" I inquired.

"Nothing that a few good meals and my Ma's home remedies won't fix. I've been up doing survey work for Richard Henderson, you know. For the new lands he bought from the Cherokee. I got taken with a terrible fever. But I'm mending now. Getting stronger every day. What have you boys been up to?"

"We arrived back from the mountains a few weeks ago. We just came to town to see about the news. Mr. Eakins assures us that Washington has done the impossible," I replied.

Isaac laughed. "I suppose he did. He did something the British weren't prepared for. He went after them in winter." He rubbed his hands to warm them up. "The British get pretty nervous when their enemies do the unexpected. They think their own rules must apply to everyone else. Although to be fair, it was only Hessians that Washington defeated at Trenton. You know, the German mercenaries those lousy redcoats hired and sent across the ocean to attack their own people."

"Mr. Eakins said there were two battles," I interjected.

He cocked his head and shot a look at me that reminded me of his father. "There were. A few days later, the British believed they had us cornered in Trenton. We were a little outnumbered, for sure. But that great fool Cornwallis took for granted that Washington would play by his rules. The General slipped our forces out at night without the British knowing, and then attacked them at Princeton. It was neatly done. We won, fair and square."

He spoke with great conviction, although it was obvious to me he was still in a weakened state. His eyes were red and watery, and his hands quivered slightly as he talked. I suppose the look on my face gave my thoughts away. He reached over and clasped my shoulder.

"I'll be fit as a fiddle before you know it. Meanwhile, I must carry on my duties as best as I am able. I've been given a commission by Governor Henry to gather supplies to send to the Continental Army. I don't have much to offer by way of recompense, but if you boys want to help out, the army would be grateful. My father has given grain and meat. He's culled his herd of beef cattle to help the cause."

"We have a full smokehouse back at Beaver Knob. How long will you be here, sir? We can make our way back here in a few days if necessary." Nate looked down at Isaac from his great height, a smile of satisfaction on his face.

"That would be fine. I'll be sending wagons north at the beginning of the week."

We returned to Beaver Knob and raided our smokehouse. We had a copious amount of venison and wild boar, more than enough to keep us until summer. We loaded Daisy's back with as much as she could bear and took it to the fort, thankful we could do our part, small as it was, to help the army.

We were overjoyed at the news of the defeat of the British by Washington. I feverishly hoped that this was a good sign for the coming year. I was too young to understand how the fortunes of war can change without notice, and had no way of knowing the coming year would be one of the hardest of my life.

It was the waning days of summer, with its soft sweet smells of browned grasses and dry earth, smells that rose from all around. Nate and I had spent the hot months getting ready for the cold, dreary winter ahead by drying and smoking meat and pickling fresh vegetables we bought from Shelby's store. We parched corn and stored it in crocks, ready to be stuffed into pouches before we went to the mountains in the fall. Nate always found it peculiar that I insisted on being prepared before we even journeyed into the hills and mountains of the great Blue Ridge. I always asserted, in return, that we had no way of knowing if our successes in the past would be repeated. We must be prepared for any eventuality.

We got word of the Treaty of Long Island in August of that year. Engineered to the west of us, on the Holston River, the Cherokee conceded our rights to remain on the lands that had been settled west of the Blue Ridge.

We breathed a sigh of relief, and in our immature minds thought perhaps our Indian troubles would be over. At the same time it was understood that the British wouldn't respect the treaty, which was all the more reason to win our independence.

In mid-September we heard a "halloo" from the edge of the clearing around our cabin. It was early morning, and we had just begun to stir. I stuck my head out of the door and spied Hugh McDonald approaching.

"How goes it, Hugh?"

"Well enough I suppose," he replied.

"What brings you out here?"

"Colonel Shelby sent me."

"A colonel now, is he?"

"Yup. Governor Henry appointed him not long ago."

I opened the door wide for him to enter. "What is his message?"

"He got news of Dragging Canoe doing some raiding well south of here. He's coming up from the Cherokee settlements along the Chickamauga River and attacking our people at random. He is leading an expedition to assess the danger and wants you boys to ride with us."

Nate, who had quickly roused himself from his slumber and placed a kettle on the fire for coffee, spoke up. "Sounds fine to me."

"If so, we are to meet at the crossroads leading south to Sycamore Shoals at daybreak tomorrow. Bring plenty of provisions and shot and powder. The Colonel says we may be out several weeks."

"Let him know we will be there," I replied.

We arrived early at the designated location, well packed for the journey. We had Daisy fully loaded with extra supplies, as we figured some of the men might be hard pressed to supply themselves. Just as the sun rose, its early rays of pink and gold peeking from behind a few low hanging clouds, Evan and fifteen other riders approached. I was happy to see McTavish among the fifteen.

"Glad to see you boys," Evan said. "Now that we are all here, this is my plan. We ride west from here, on the road here leading to the new western frontier. We will then veer south and see what we cannot afford to be surprised." He stopped and looked keenly around us, gathered in a circle with him in the center. "Any questions?"

Nate coughed loudly and spoke up. "Do we know for a fact he is about?"

"I have it on good authority that Dragging Canoe was seen with a number of his warriors about twenty or twenty-five miles south of here. This is not a fool's errand." The words came out with a gruff edge to them. Evan did not like being tested.

We rode west, the road before us already well worn with deep ruts, signifying the many settler's wagons that had already made the trek west. After a few miles Evan led us off the main road, along a less-traveled path that wandered south, through a dark forest of pine and hardwoods.

We spent the first night out in as fine a campsite as I had ever seen. There was a bubbling stream, and deep drifts of soft pine needles on which to put our blankets down. We had a roaring fire, sharing our provisions with the others. Some of the men broke out their bottles, including Evan himself. He entertained us with stories of his past encounters with the Indians in the northwest, and I drifted off to sleep content.

We spent the next week in a fruitless search, stopping by homesteads – crude cabins settled amongst small fields of ripened corn, the husks turning brown and withering in the heat. The folks we met were friendly enough and happy to see us. We could see that some were in a hard struggle for survival, and we willingly shared any extra provisions we had. Children capered about us with glee when we approached their homes. Oftentimes, they were thin and looked bedraggled, their clothing worn and threadbare. I wondered at the time why their parents would bring them into the howling wilderness, with marauding Indians and little to live on. I suppose each man had decided that freedom was more important than doing without, and that somehow they would be better off in the end.

We had struck off to the southwest and then circled around and headed northeast as we began our journey back to the fort. It was obvious to all that Evan was not happy that we had failed to engage the enemy. His orders were short and crisp, with an edge to his voice that I had never heard before.

We had about given up that we would find what we hunted, when early one afternoon we heard the sound of gunfire in the distance to our left. We pulled up and gathered around Evan as he spoke.

"Sounds to me that we've finally caught our prey. I believe that fire is coming from the Wilson place, about a mile or so from here. I need a couple of you fellows to ride forward and see what the situation is. Hurry back here as soon as you can."

McTavish and Hugh McDonald spurred their horses forward and headed in the direction of the gunfire. They were back in about thirty minutes with news.

"The Wilson place is under attack, all right. They're holed up in the main house. From what we could see there were a dozen or more Cherokee in the tree line around the pasture closest to the house," McTavish reported.

Evan thought a moment, and then spoke. "Here's what we'll do. We will ride as close as we can without detection, and then two of you fellows will hold the horses while we sneak up behind them. They will have nowhere to go. Those blockaded in the Wilson place will be in front of them, and we will in a position to catch them in a crossfire. Be sure to have your hatchets handy. Once we're up close, we won't have time to reload."

We rode as close as we dared, the shots getting louder,

and then dismounted and handed the bridles of our horses to Tom and James Waters, brothers who had trekked south from the state of New York to begin a new life in a new land. They were none too happy to be assigned horse-holding duty, but they grudgingly complied with Evan's orders.

We each held our rifles in the crooks of our arms and made sure our hatchets were loosened in our belts. We crept forward slowly, with Evan in the lead. I tried desperately to make as little noise as possible, although it was not an easy task as we waded through the forest floor of small bushes that clung to our leggings, and dry leaves that rustled and snapped beneath our moccasins. My heart leapt into my throat when I spied the first Cherokee, crouched down behind the trunk of a big oak, his rifle raised to his shoulder. Soon others came into view, all half-shielded by the forest that surrounded us.

When we were within fifty or sixty yards of the edge of the clearing, Evan raised his rifle and fired. That was the signal for all of us to let loose.

The first Cherokee I had spotted let out a howl and fell to the ground, gasping, as blood spurted out the front of his buckskin shirt. I picked out another and thought I at least winged him, but the enemy were now aware of our presence, and we were set upon by more than a dozen of them, howling bloody murder, their hatchets snatched out of their belts and upraised. The distance between us soon disappeared, and I found myself in the middle of sheer madness.

I let go of my rifle and quickly drew my hatchet. I used it to slash away at the man who first emerged through the smoke. He was large for a Cherokee. His face was contorted in rage, and had clear black markings on it. His topknot swayed behind him as he swung his hatchet at my head. I managed to parry his lunge but felt the full power of his strength as our hatchets clashed together. Desperately, I dodged his next thrust, and then he stopped with a look of surprise and shock on his face. Just as I was ready to strike, he slowly fell forward. I saw Hugh McDonald behind him. As the Cherokee fell, I saw a bloody gash in the back of his neck.

Hugh turned and faced another foe. Everyone was shouting or shrieking. At that moment, I sensed movement directly behind me. Instinctively I moved my body to the right, but not soon enough. I felt a sharp blow to the side of my head. As I fell forward I heard Nate's shrill bellow, and as I hit the ground darkness descended.

⮑⮔

Chapter Twenty

I slowly became conscious of my throbbing head. I lifted my hand to it and felt a bandage tightly wound around it. I blinked open my eyes, only to see the round face of little Timothy Hayward, with his red hair straggling down to his shoulders. As soon as he spotted my opened eyes, he shouted. I winced as the noise of his voice resonated through my aching head.

"He's awake, Ma!"

I realized I was lying on a thin pallet in the corner of a small cabin. Chastity hastened over to me and leaned over. "Quick!" she told Timothy. "Run tell your Pa and Nate." Then, more calmly, she said, "I didn't know if you would make it, Caleb. That red devil gave you a powerful blow. Now lay still. I have some broth ready, just in case you came to."

She bustled over to the fireplace. I closed my eyes and nodded off. Soon enough, she was back. She gently shook my shoulder, then situated herself beside me on the packed dirt floor and began feeding me with a spoon.

Nate burst through the door, as he was wont to do, with Samuel at his heels. He knelt down beside Chastity and gently spoke.

"Are you still in one piece, partner?"

I blinked at him.

"Don't worry about a thing, Caleb. Chastity has been taking real good care of you."

I struggled to speak. "What happened?"

"Well, you got a tomahawk to the side of the head. Don't you remember?"

I thought a moment and then the memory flooded back. I blinked again.

"I took care of that red scoundrel for you, partner. He got my hatchet to the back of his skull."

Samuel spoke up. "We were most grateful the lot of you showed up when you did. We didn't know how long we could hold out."

"Lucky for you we were right here, where someone could take care of you. Evan and the rest of the fellows have gone back to the fort. Only two of the louses escaped. We killed the rest." Nate had a tone of satisfaction in his voice.

"How long ago was that?" I asked.

"It's been three days," he replied.

Chastity interrupted us. "Now you boys get back to your chores. Caleb needs his rest."

We spent another two weeks at the Haywards' cabin. It was smaller than the one inhabited by the Wilsons' and not as well fortified. The two families had huddled together in the Wilsons' to face the onslaught of the Indian raiders.

Chastity was quite solicitous in her nursing duties. She helped me sit up after a day or so, and supervised me as I took my first hesitant steps after four or five days. I was most grateful for her care and consideration.

While I mended, Nate and Samuel were busy making the clearing around the cabins larger. They cleared brush and chopped down trees, hauling them to the back of the crudely built barn that the two families shared.

There was an air of sadness in the Hayward family. There had been no word on the fate of their son Ezra, and they were hesitant to let any of their other children wander more than a few feet from their stoop. In the evenings the talk as we sat before the fireplace was of politics. Samuel's view of the state of the country had changed. He was bitterly angry at the British, because it was now a known fact that they were responsible for stirring up the Cherokee, supplying them with the weaponry used against us.

"I dare a Redcoat to come anywhere near this place.

I'll put a bullet in his head just as quick as I would a Cherokee," he stated emphatically on several occasions.

"Hopefully that situation will never arise out here," Nate would reply. "It's a far distance to any redcoats from these parts."

When I felt strong enough to ride, we saddled Bessie and Sadie and strung Daisy the mule behind us and made our way back to Beaver Knob. The Haywards waved to us from their stoop, and shouted we were welcome there whenever we were in the area. I was happy to have their friendship and grateful for the care I had received in their home.

By then it was well into the month of October. We were unable to make our usual hunting trip into the Blue Ridge, as I was still mending from my wound. I felt the long gash on the side of my head, an ugly scar that would remain with me the rest of my life. Even today, it will throb unmercifully before a storm arrives. My wife says it is a reliable harbinger on laundry days, letting her know when to bring in the clothes from the clothesline. I can only laugh and exclaim at least it is good for something.

In November, Nate traveled to Shelby's Fort for supplies while I continued to mend from my wound. When he returned he had sad news. Evan's wife, Letitia, had passed away from a mysterious illness while we had been off on our raid south. She had gone to visit friends while Evan had been preoccupied with our foray. He had been informed of her passing upon his return.

She had been a good woman. She stood behind Evan and raised his children while he was often gone, fighting Indians and tending to the business of fur trading and raising cattle. It was sad news, indeed. I felt a special pain, remembering the loss of my own mother. Although I did not know Mrs. Shelby well, I knew her loss would be a great one.

The New Year of 1778 dawned, and I was in fervent hope that this would be a happier one than the year that preceded it. In March, I reached the milestone of adulthood – the age of twenty one. I was now a full-grown man. I had added an inch or two in height since I had fled my home in Maryland, and thanks to the ruggedness of my existence had gained in muscle and mass as well. Of course, I could never attain the massive size of my partner and companion Nate, but I was still a good inch or two taller than most men I encountered.

By April I was well enough to mount Sadie and decided I would make my way to the fort on my own. My head felt as if it would burst open as I made my way from our cabin to Shelby's fort. I had Daisy in tow, fully loaded with the pelts and furs Nate had procured for us while I recovered from my wound. The road was well worn by now, as it led its way through field and forest to the safety of the blockhouse. I must admit my strength was not as it should be for the small task I was performing, but I was intent on forging ahead despite my weakness.

Just as I came into a clearing along the road, I noticed a girl. Her back was towards me. She looked to be no more than a child from the angle at which I viewed her. She was slight of build, and was clothed in a blue dress, her head covered with a cap of white. Before her lay a horse, whinnying and thrashing about. Just at that moment, she raised a musket to her shoulder and fired. The sound reverberated, and the poor animal lay still. Her shot had been true.

Her shoulders slumped as she lowered her gun. As I drew closer she must have heard my approach. She turned to look at me. As her facial features came into view, I realized I had been wrong about her age. This was a fully grown woman, with soft brown hair peeking out from under her cap, and large brown eyes with long eyelashes, tears clinging to them.

"Here, here!" I said. "What's happened?"

"His leg was broken. Somehow he managed to find a hole in this field. I had to shoot him."

I leaned down and examined the horse. A fine brown stallion with a pitch black tail and mane. "What a shame. A waste of a good horse. I see that you had no choice. I'm sorry."

She leaned over him and began to try to retrieve her saddle and bridle from the poor dead creature.

"Let me help." I unloosened the cinch and managed to yank the saddle from his back. Not an easy task, as his body covered one of the stirrups. She worked on the bit and bridle, and before long they were free.

"See here, Miss, let me help get you home. I'll load your saddle onto Daisy. Whereabouts do you live?"

She looked at me peculiarly. "I'm Caleb Anders," I stuttered quickly. "My partner and I have a place not far from here. I would be happy to see you home."

"Lydia Burton," she answered quickly. "My Pa and I live but a half mile from here, across the road and over yonder." She nodded southward. "Thank you for your help." She looked down at the dead animal at her feet. "He was such a good horse." Tears began to well up in her eyes again.

"My father loved this animal. He even built a pen alongside our cabin, to keep those dreadful red savages from stealing him at night while we slept. All we have left now is our oxen." She gulped. "It will be a big loss to him."

I didn't know if I should pat her shoulder or offer mine for her to cry on. Instead, I got busy loading her gear onto Daisy's back, on top of the skins and pelts she already carried. Once that was accomplished, I offered my hand to help her into Sadie's saddle.

"I'll get you home, Miss Lydia. Your family might be worried if they heard that shot." She consented to my hand

and climbed into the saddle easily. I lead our little train away, and she quickly explained how to get to her place.

As I walked beside her, I asked. "I've never seen you before. Are you new here?"

"No. I don't suppose you can say we are new. We've been here over a year."

"I haven't seen you at the fort or at church meeting."

"I've been too busy nursing my Ma. She passed away last month. My Pa isn't much of one to socialize. His name is Joseph. Joseph Burton," she continued. "I haven't had much of a chance to ride. I was out today for the first time in a long time." She bit her lip.

"Where do you all hail from?"

"New Jersey. We weren't here very long before Ma got sick. It was just the three of us, you see." She continued, "Pa certainly was proud of Barnaby. We've had a time keeping him out of the hands of the Indians. He will surely be upset that I had to shoot him."

We arrived at her cabin. It was a small but sturdy affair. The yard was neatly raked, and I saw a smokehouse and other outbuildings behind it. As I helped her dismount, I heard a male voice call from inside the cabin.

"Lydia!"

"Yes, Pa, it's me."

A tall, thin man with a craggy face and heavy eyebrows appeared in the doorway. He wore buckskin, stained from much wear, and a full beard, sprinkled with gray. "What's happened? Where is Barnaby?" he asked.

"I'm sorry, sir. I found your daughter in a field not far from here, just as she shot your horse. He had broken a front leg and was in a wretched condition."

Lydia spoke quickly. "Pa, he trapped his foot in a hole. There was nothing I could do." Her voice quivered, and her eyes filled up with tears once again.

"There, there, Lydia." He reached over and patted her clumsily on the shoulder. "I suppose there was nothing else to be done. You're home safe, which is all that counts."

I walked back to Daisy and began unloading Lydia's saddle and bridle from her back.

"Thank you kindly, stranger, for bringing Lydia home." He walked over and stuck out his hand. "I'm Joseph Burton. I hail from New Jersey."

I grasped his hand. "Caleb Anders. And it wasn't much of a bother. She seemed distressed when I happened upon her."

"You're welcome to come in and rest awhile," he responded.

"Mighty nice of you to offer, sir. But I have this load of furs and pelts to deliver to the fort. I best get it done, so I can get home while there is still daylight."

He nodded understandingly.

Without thinking, I uttered, "I wonder if it would be

okay if I called another time." I flushed. "Just to check in and see that you and Lydia are okay."

"That would be fine. You are welcome to stop by any time. Again, my thanks for assisting my daughter."

With that, I climbed into my saddle and was on my way. After a short distance I looked back over my shoulder. Lydia was standing on the small stoop attached to the cabin, watching me ride off.

CHAPTER TWENTY-ONE

It was some months before it dawned on me that my interest in Lydia was more than compassion. I would find myself guiding Sadie towards the Burton home whenever I departed the fort, almost without thinking. Once there, I would discuss the news of the day with her Pa, and help with any little chores that needed attention while I was there. Sometimes, if it was late enough in the day, I would be invited to share their supper.

During one such meal, Joseph Burton explained to me his reasoning for leaving his established farm in New Jersey. "I was worried about my womenfolk. We were in the thick of things there. Soldiers everywhere, always hungry. I have two full grown sons, Joseph and Henry. Left the place with them and headed down here. We moved a might further south than I reckoned we would. I got this hundred acres and barely had time to get our cabin built before my wife Sarah took sick."

I had great respect for Mr. Burton. He was a hardworking fellow and had managed to carve his own place out of the wilderness. Yet silently I questioned his reasoning. Surely he had known the dangers of moving to Indian country. He was not a young man. Had he ignored what he had been told to satisfy a longing to start afresh, without truly thinking of the consequences? I thought perhaps so.

There wasn't much about Lydia that I wasn't drawn to. She had an easy laugh – one that tinkled like the ringing of a bell. She had the largest brown eyes I had ever seen, ones that were soft and inviting when happy, but grew increasingly dark if she got angry. Her small hands were quite lovely, and capable at anything they attempted. She was a good cook and seamstress, and ran a tidy home that I found very welcoming.

We often sat together on the stoop, with her father watching us from inside their cabin. Our conversations would grow lively at times, and I grew to respect her clear head and judicious opinions.

Unlike most women, she wasn't shy in expressing her opinion on matters usually reserved for men. Most particularly, the politics of the day. "I think George Washington is a great man," she would proclaim, her hands folded neatly in her lap, her head nodding determinedly.

"How so?"

"Look how he's managed to keep his troops in order. Before the war, it was inconceivable that men from New York and men from Pennsylvania could agree on much of anything."

"True. But I hear there are still disagreements among the men. Some of the troops don't like being thrust into battle with troops from other colonies. At least, I've heard of such."

"Don't you see?" she would reply earnestly. "That is exactly why Washington is a great man! Somehow he cajoles them all to keep up the fight! I have my doubts that any other leader could accomplish it. As I said, a great man!"

"Perhaps," I conceded. "But it will all be for naught if we don't win this war. He'll be strung up, along with Ben Franklin, Thomas Jefferson and all the rest."

"All the more reason they should remain in our prayers, Caleb."

We were fortunate in those days to have a man such as Evan Shelby close by. Because of his status and his prolific letter writing, we were privy to the latest goings on of the war. We had word of the defeat of Washington at Brandywine in Pennsylvania, followed closely by the victories at Saratoga and Bemis Heights by General Gates. By late spring, we were aware of the efforts to

draw the French to our side, thanks to Shelby's contacts. We rejoiced at the surrender of Burgoyne after his defeat at the hands of Gates, but were somewhat trepidatious of possible entanglements with the French. Evan Shelby well knew what they were capable of, having faced them and their Indian comrades during the French and Indian War, and he didn't have faith they would keep any bargain we made with them. I myself felt the same. Could we trust those who had set out to destroy us but a little more than two decades past?

During this time there was a steady stream of traffic along the road we had come south on. There were large family groups with three or four wagons, loaded with household goods, as well as single riders – men out to carve their fortunes. We heard terrible stories of Tories across the mountains in North and South Carolina persecuting those who subscribed to the Patriot cause. Some families had been driven from their communities, often after a father, son or brother had been murdered.

Many of these people stopped for respite at Shelby's Fort. Along with Patriots were those of Dutch origin, barely speaking any English. Others were illiterate farmers, seeking a better life for the straggly children that romped and played in the clearings inside the fort. Shelby's store did a brisk business in those days, with wagons of supplies arriving almost daily. Evan himself was frequently absent, as he had been appointed a justice of the peace and was called upon to carry out his duties in the state of Virginia.

Shelby's Fort became a sort of crossroads. Some groups headed west, into the new frontier formed by Henderson's purchase of Indian lands. Others headed west and south, down to Sycamore Shoals and the Watauga settlements. Still others headed east, into the foothills of the mighty Blue Ridge.

It was early summer before my partner and I wound our way through the lush, green foothills of the mountains, heading towards the familiar spots on the closest slopes where our past hunts had been successful. Occasionally we would spot the spiraling white smoke of a cabin, nestled quietly among the fields and small hills. We did our best to avoid them. In our minds, it was best not to approach. We had heard tales of other trappers and hunters that had shots fired at them by wary settlers, who nervously kept an eye out for any sign of Indians.

By this time, there were very few Cherokee to be found in the Blue Ridge. The ones that remained had resigned themselves to sharing the land with the white man. They caused no trouble. The treaty of Long Island in the last year had settled their disputes, and they simply wanted to be left alone to pursue their traditions and way of life.

Personally, I had no quarrel with them. It seemed to me that the vast wilderness of the mountains could be shared by all. Although the buffalo had grown scarce, there was still plenty of game to guarantee survival for those who wanted to share in the bounty. Peace was better than war. Once attained, it was worth holding on to.

Occasionally on that trip we would run into other pairs of hunters and trappers. If we knew them from the fort, we would stay awhile, sometimes erecting our tents for a day or two and sharing a campfire in the evenings. If we did not know them we would do our best to avoid them. We had become adept at spotting strangers, and knew that some of the people we ran into were not of good character. There is a myth that holds all hunters and trappers were of good cheer and played fairly. This could not be further from the truth. Like all groups of men, there are always scattered amongst us individuals who are best avoided. We had heard too many tales of other fellows who had been swindled out of their catches by dishonest charlatans who made a living stealing from others. Nate and I decided we would not be the victims of such reprobates.

By this time, we had established a routine, Nate and I. Since I was still the better shot I spent more time in the saddle, scaring up game and taking it down. Nate spent more time working our traps and skinning what we caught in them, as he was much better with a knife than I. I would never stray too far from him while hunting. It was folly to be in the mountains totally isolated. Occasionally we would both take to our horses if I spotted signs of bigger game. During those times, we would work as a team, particularly if I found signs of buffalo or big bear. To do it safely, it often took the rifles of the two of us when it came to larger prey.

We moved our campsite frequently, not choosing to stay too long in any one spot, unlike our very first hunting trip into the Blue Ridge. The results were satisfying. We found a wider range of game that way. Our piles of skins and furs grew faster than at any time in the past.

It was midsummer by the time we headed back to the fort. It was extraordinarily hot that year. The leaves and grasses that lay on either side of the trail home drooped in the heat, listless and limp from the sharp rays of the sun. We endured a tremendous thunderstorm the second night back, with flashes of lightning and the boom of thunder crashing around us. It spooked our animals, and somehow Daisy escaped her tether and skittered off into the night, braying and kicking up her heels. In all the years we had traveled with her, we had never seen her act in such a manner. We made no attempt to retrieve her during the storm, but as daylight broke and the rain abated, we set out to find her. Within an hour or two we spotted her, grazing peacefully beside a bubbling brook as if nothing had occurred. Nate, who had known Daisy longer than he had known me, breathed a sigh of relief at the sight of her.

"Hey, old girl!" He said as he approached her and grasped her ears. "What has got into you?"

She bobbed her head up and down, as if happy to see us.

"Now, let's head back to camp and get you loaded. You cannot run off like that again."

"We would be lost without her, Nate, that's for sure. Not many mules to be found. At least, not good ones. She has done more than her share to contribute to our success."

Chapter Twenty-one

"True. Especially in these parts. And she's not as young as she used to be."

The oppressive heat continued on for the rest of the summer. We had some relief at our cabin on Beaver Knob, but whenever we headed to the fort it felt as if a hot, wet blanket had been dropped upon us from above.

I found as many excuses as I could to stop by frequently at the Burton house, and continued to help Mr. Burton out with his chores. He was full of complaints about the heat and the damage it did to his straggling corn and beans in his fields. He had not replaced Barnaby, the horse Lydia had been forced to shoot after it broke its leg. Horses were scarce in those days, and quite expensive to purchase. The shortage was mainly due to the constant Indian raids from the south.

"To be honest, Caleb, I would just as soon not get another horse. It would just be another thing to lose. I will make do with my pair of oxen. Thank the Lord the Indians have no use for them."

"That may be true, sir, but I would still pen them up close to the house. They may have no interest in stealing them, but they would still be willing to kill them. The harder they can make life for us out here, the better for them."

On every visit, I would do my best to steal a few minutes alone with Lydia. My heart would thump mightily in my chest whenever we had a few moments alone. There was something about the tilt of her sparkling brown eyes and the flush of her cheeks that caused it. She always smelled so sweet, yet spoke her mind freely. I was drawn to her like I had never been drawn to another woman.

I spoke of her to Nate, and he just smiled at me cagily. At times he would stop by with me, when it couldn't be avoided. To be honest, I was a little jealous of his presence on those occasions. I didn't want to share Lydia with anyone. Nate was a big lumbering fellow, but he was more sociable than I. After one such visit, as we headed back to Beaver Knob, he reassured me.

"No doubt she's a fine-looking woman, that Lydia. But she doesn't have enough meat on her bones for me," he stated firmly. "I like women with a few more curves, if you catch my meaning." He winked at me slyly.

"To each his own," I replied with a certain relief.

I had word that fall that Martha and Jacob had added another baby to their family. I was happy for them, but somewhat concerned when Jacob also told me he'd received a wound the previous fall when the British stormed their way through Baltimore City and the surrounding countryside on their way to capture Philadelphia. Jacob wrote:

> *I did not want you to be concerned for my well-being, brother. Thus I had Martha promise not to relay the news to you. Our little militia company put up a stiff resistance, but most of them had no firearms, as most had been sent on to the Continental Army. I received a shot to my*

left leg, but it has healed nicely, thanks to the tender nursing care I received from your sister. Let it not trouble you. Be more concerned for our troops in the field. The loss of Philadelphia has put a strain on all concerned. All Patriots abandoned the city at the approach of the enemy and anything of any value was taken by our troops. A hollow victory for the enemy, but a victory nonetheless.

I could not fault them for not sharing the news of Jacob's wound, as I had done the same, choosing not to share my own close call with the hatchet of a Cherokee. Some things are better left unsaid.

Chapter Twenty-Two

During the fall of 1778 the Cherokee attacks upon the settlements west of us became more brazen. No one was safe from the ravaging hordes. Bands of Indians rode north from their settlements on the Chickamauga River, some two hundred miles southwest of Shelby's Fort. They were led by Dragging Canoe and Big Fool, fierce warriors who had captured countless scalps from helpless settlers all along the frontier. Weapons and ammunition were sent them from the British settlements of Pensacola and Mobile, hundreds of miles further south along the Gulf of Mexico, as well as stores sent from as far away as Canada.

Nate and I chose not to pursue a trapping and hunting trip, as we were wont to do, that fall. We discussed the possibility of being called upon to perform our duties with the militia, and thought it best to stay as close to the fort as we could. When the cold northern winds of early winter began to howl around us, bringing smatterings of snow and ice, word went out that Colonel Shelby had been assigned the task of attacking the wild savages that had plagued us for years.

In preparation, we smoked meat and made pemmican, being sure to mix in all the parched corn we had on hand. We worked diligently to see that all our gear was in good order, repairing our bridles and saddles. We did our best to fatten up our horses and Daisy, not knowing if their services would be required. During the long winter evenings, I finally finished the carvings I had started on my powder horn. On one side was a view of the Blue Ridge. On the other, my name in big bold letters with curlicues and spirals. I was proud of it. Proud enough that I still use it to this day, and have promised it to my oldest son when I leave this earth.

Once the horn was finished, I began reading aloud from the two books I had purchased at Shelby's store. By tallow candle, I read aloud from Thomas Paine's "Common Sense" and Benjamin Franklin's "Poor Richard's Almanack." I was never one to spend my hard-earned money foolishly, but enriching the mind through the written word was important to me.

Sometimes while reading, my mind would drift back to the days I spent in my mother's kitchen, leaning over her little primer while she patiently explained its secrets while stirring a pot over the fire, her face flushed from the heat, her bright blue eyes seeking mine when making a point. Occasionally, I would also recall my father's disdain and disgust with what he considered a foolish waste of time, and his harsh words whenever he caught us having lessons. I did my best to block those thoughts out of my head. I could not change the past, but only learn from it.

Nate enjoyed my reading. He would often interject with questions and comments. Lively discussions on the wisdom of Ben Franklin or the audacity of Thomas Paine would ensue. He was prone to stroke his bushy black beard and furrow his brow while deep in thought, before interrupting me.

"Read that part again where Paine says savages don't make war on their families," he would say.

"Let me see." I would stop. "Even brutes do not devour their young, nor savages make war upon their families."

"Isn't that what those lousy lobsterbacks are doing to us now? Sending the savages against us?" he would respond.

"It would seem so!"

He would then mutter under his breath, "Lousy lobsterbacks."

"Early to bed and early to rise, makes a man healthy, wealthy and wise," he would repeat. "Makes sense to me. How about you, Caleb?"

"Mr. Franklin does have a way with words. I can see no sense in living life any other way."

Not long after the new year of 1779, while at the fort, we came across Isaac Shelby. Now healthy and fit, with a spring in his step so like his father, he approached us while we were purchasing supplies at the store.

"Hey there, boys. I haven't seen you about much these days."

"We've been busy at the cabin, knowing we'll be called out soon to serve with your father against the Cherokee," I responded.

"Yes. We will mount up as soon as the weather warms. Meanwhile, I've been tasked with gathering supplies for our expedition. We've been informed we must provide for ourselves, as the treasury is empty. What little money the Congress can scrape together is being used for General Washington's efforts against the redcoats. We are storing what supplies we can gather in my father's barns." He paused. "I'll be leaving tomorrow and making my way to the foothills east of here to see what I can find to help us. If you boys are willing, I need extra drivers for the wagons."

We looked at each other, then nodded.

"We can help. We'll go home and gather our belongings. What time will you be leaving?"

"I don't think we will be underway until mid-morning. Be prepared to be out for a few weeks. I'll need you to provide your own rations."

Early the next morning we stopped by Lydia's place on the way to the fort. We had our provisions tied down on the backs of our saddles, and brought Daisy with us.

When Mr. Burton appeared in the doorway, we greeted him and asked if he could tend to the mule in our absence.

"I would be happy to."

"Make sure you keep her close to your cabin. I don't want the redskins getting hold of her," Nate said. "She's a very valuable animal, you know."

While the two of them talked, I had a few moments to speak privately with Lydia. I told her I would be absent for a few weeks, and hoped she would be careful while I was gone.

"Stay close to the cabin. The redskins could be about."

She promised she would, and then blinked her soft brown eyes rapidly. "Be careful yourself, Caleb. I will miss you."

I gulped and replied the same to her.

When we reached the fort, we found Isaac waiting for us with three wagons. Simon Eakins was seated with the first one, so Nate and I hitched our horses to the other two. Before we left, Isaac gave us counsel. "We are on the hunt for foodstuffs that will keep for a short while – until the weather warms. We'll take just about anything that can be carried in these wagons or herded along with them. Bags of grain or beans, corn, kegs of flour or salted meat, anything we can get our hands on. Let me do most of the talking. I've gotten pretty good at it, as I've spent time gathering supplies for the Continentals north of here."

"How many men are we looking to supply?" Nate inquired.

"We've got authority for one thousand, but I don't know if my father will be able to gather that many. Many will be loath to leave their families for such an expedition. Many will insist on staying to put their crops in during the spring. We will do what we can, however. I have a little hard money from my father, but I will try to get as much donated as I can."

With that, we were off, plodding along behind teams of oxen. They were slow creatures but kept a steady pace. Stronger and less finicky than horses, their use along the frontier had become more popular. Since they had little speed, they were less than appealing to Indian raiders, who much preferred horses.

We had all brought our own rations and shared a common pot each night, throwing in whatever we had on hand. Sitting before the fire each evening, we swapped stories about earlier times, when life was less uncertain.

Isaac was quite the storyteller. He shared stories of his youth, when he grew up Maryland, before his father lost all he had due to the fur trading business during the Pontiac rebellion and the burning of his home, which destroyed the records of Evan's business dealings and thus lost all account of his finances.

He spoke fondly of his mother, who had maintained the household during his father's frequent absences. "She was a strong woman. With five boys, she had her hands full," he chuckled. "She could look at us with a fierceness that few men can even muster. Not only did she oversee the upkeep of our farm, but she saw to it that we each had an education." He sobered. "She is sorely missed."

One evening, he told us about his grandfather, Evan Senior. "There aren't many like him. He was one determined man. How many men would risk all he owned to sail across an ocean with eight children in tow? He died when I was an infant, but my father always speaks of him with pride."

But he mostly spoke of his holdings in the new lands he had acquired northwest of us, as payment for the surveying work he had done for Richard Henderson. He regaled us with tales of Daniel Boone and the road he carved through the wilderness, accompanied by other settlers from Watauga and Sycamore Shoals.

"It is fine country, gentlemen. Very fine. There are more and more settlers there every day. The Indians are fierce, though. Cherokee, lots of Shawnee, some Miami. They'll do their best to keep us out, but I don't believe they will succeed. There are too many of us. I hope one day to make my home there."

"Sounds mighty fine."

"It is," he replied with satisfaction. "And not a Tory to be found."

"None?"

"None. Since the British have decided to use the Indians

as weapons against us, you won't find hardly a one around these parts, or in the new territories. On the other side of these mountains, boys, it's a different story entirely. You can't throw a rock twenty yards without hitting one of those skunks."

"Why is that?" I asked.

"Pretty simple. They don't have any Indians to bother them, at least not many to speak of. Most of them are new here and haven't witnessed the abuse those bastards in Parliament have heaped upon us. No, they are all safe and snug in their beds at night and dream of ways to stab the backs of our fellow Patriots. There are all sorts of Tory militias rampaging about, stealing livestock, destroying homes and attacking our folks. It's downright discouraging."

Nate spoke sharply. "Our people aren't just taking it, are they?"

Isaac laughed ironically. "Oh no, they're fighting back." He grew quiet for a moment. "I hope the trouble stays on the east side of the Blue Ridge. But there are no guarantees, boys. No guarantees."

During the day, we would keep our eyes out for any telltale signs of chimney smoke. We had headed straight east of the fort, in an area Nate and I were unfamiliar with. We were both surprised at the numbers of settler cabins that were there. Isaac, however, seemed to be familiar with each and every small enclave we came across.

Sometimes there would be a lone cabin, stuck as inconspicuously as possible among the hardwoods and pines. We would make our presence known well in advance, in hopes we wouldn't be shot at. More often than not, Isaac would call them out by name, and then approach on his horse.

Other times we would happen upon three or four or more cabins grouped together for safety. For this, I could not blame them. Although there were few Indians about those days, there were still enough thieves and rogues to be cause for concern.

It was usually the cabins set off by themselves that caused us the most trouble. In such cases, we would let Isaac approach alone while we waited with the wagons, as there was rarely a discernible wagon track that allowed us to advance closer. More often than not, he would return with a sheepish grin on his face and with empty hands.

"Some folks are just short sighted," he would often complain upon rejoining us. "As these folks no longer much to fear from the Indians, they see no sense in helping their neighbors in times of need.

Let's move along."

"Did they try to shoot you?" Nate would ask.

Isaac would laugh at that, a deep full-throated laugh. And sometimes his response would be yes.

"They never lowered their rifle, if that's what you mean. Looking down the barrel of a gun is not pleasant. Not in the least."

We stumbled upon a few groups of homesteads that were inhabited by people who spoke very little English. These were folks who spoke German almost exclusively. They appeared to be quite prosperous despite being in the middle of nowhere. Their cabins and barns were neat and tidy. The beginnings of lush kitchen gardens behind their homes were weed-free and planted in neat rows, with promises of a continuing bountiful harvest. They usually had a shed or other small structure where we could glimpse the rudimentary means of a blacksmith shop, with an anvil and various tools hung in good order along the walls.

Surprisingly, these were the places that were most generous with us, despite Isaac having to resort to hand signals to convey our purpose. Isaac, undeterred by the method of communication he was forced to use, was quite animated and engaging while conversing with them. These conversations, more often than not, yielded us bags of corn and grain, and small kegs of various foodstuffs these settlers had put away for their own use.

We were often invited to camp the night with these Germanic peoples. They would feed us and provide grain for our horses and oxen. Their young women would smile and nod at us.

"I like these German girls. They all have curves, the

kind a man good get used to grabbing hold of," Nate would elaborate, with a nod and a wink.

We even managed to pick up a couple of recruits from them. Two young men, brothers, joined us, toting their muskets and hatchets. Their names were Herman and Bernard Schmidt. They spoke a little better English than most we encountered, and were quite unconcerned about how long they would be gone or how they would return home. They simply hopped into one of our wagons and grinned and nodded at us. Isaac told us that as long as they could shoot his father would be happy to have them.

Nate grumbled a little at their presence. We had been told the stories of the Hessians who were fighting for the British in the northeast, and he was uneasy with them riding along.

"If their women are good enough for you, I don't see why their menfolk aren't," I would reply.

"I don't know, Caleb. I suppose we will just have to wait and see."

Our wagons began to fill. This slowed our progress somewhat because of their weight, and the freezing rain and sleet we encountered were not of much help. It caused the rutted wagon trails we followed to turn to mud, the deep cloying kind that dragged at the wheels of our wagons and stuck stubbornly to the hooves of our beasts of burden. At night, we stretched ourselves as close to the fire as possible, huddled in our soggy blankets and furs.

We were slowly wending our way back to the fort. We had made a circuitous route through the foothills to the east of it. Our wagons were nearly full, and Isaac was happy with what we had been able to gather.

Quite unexpectedly, we were approached by two riders. They hailed us and asked who we were.

Isaac quickly told them, and they asked if they could ride along.

Thomas Wells and Abe Smallwood were seasoned fur traders. They had a hard look about their eyes, and their rifles fit easily across their saddles. We were suspicious of them at first, but our worries were soon laid to rest. They had a good knowledge of the Blue Ridge and had spent years in the back country. They were familiar with the ways of the Cherokee and had no fear of them. When we camped that evening, they joined us readily enough at the fire.

"We were heading to Shelby's fort anyway, so I hope you don't mind our riding along," Abe explained.

"Not at all," Isaac replied.

"We heard about the expedition south. We wanted to join up."

I was somewhat surprised at their knowledge. How did men deep in the back country get wind of it? Isaac had the same question.

"We have our ways," Abe smiled mysteriously.

Thomas laughed. "It is not that strange. One of the cabins you approached belongs to an old friend of ours. He relayed to us the information you gave to him. You remember him, Jackson Campbell."

Isaac replied, "I remember him well. I've met him before. I stared down his rifle barrel for a short while as he explained he wasn't interested in helping us out. Not even hard money could induce him to lend a hand."

Thomas laughed again. "You'll have to forgive old Jackson. He can be a little ornery. But he did inform us about you. That's why we're here."

We arrived back at the fort with three full wagons and four recruits.

Chapter Twenty-Three

It was the beginning of March when we arrived back at Shelby's fort from our expedition to gather supplies. Simon, Nate and I, with the help of our new recruits, unloaded what we had gathered into one of Colonel Shelby's barns, already almost bursting with goods that had been gathered for our expedition. Isaac went directly to his father's house, and before we had finished unloading he was off again, his horse headed north at a fast pace.

Evan found us sweaty and exhausted, as he came out to inspect the new men we had brought. He talked briefly with us, and said our preparations were almost complete.

"Be ready, boys. You new men can make camp here in the enclosure of the fort. Nate, you and Caleb will be notified when we need your services. I'm sure Isaac told you we will have to supply ourselves. Bring extra shot and powder if you have it, and rations if you can." He smiled broadly. "We might be shorthanded, but I believe we will have an easy time of it."

We made our way to the Burtons' and picked up Daisy on the way home to Beaver Knob. While Nate and Mr. Burton conversed, I drew Lydia to the side.

"Are you well?" I asked tenderly, as her brown eyes met mine.

She nodded. "I've missed you."

"And I you," I gulped. Just being close to her set my heart to pounding.

It was in the waning days of March that we received a visit from Ian McTavish. He hailed us from the path that led to our cabin, and jauntily dismounted from his horse as we approached.

"Good news! We will be moving out in a day or two," he stated gaily. I was a little shocked at his cheerfulness. Going against the Cherokee was not a happy occasion for me. But then, I wasn't McTavish.

We invited him into our humble cabin and sat before the fire. He pulled out a bottle and offered it to us. Nate took a long drink before handing it back to him. I shook my head at the offer. "The colonel has a plan in place. We'll be meeting at the mouth of Big Creek, west of here. No need for horses, so it would be best if you find someone to take care of yours in your absence."

"No horses?" Nate interjected. "How are we going to get to the Cherokee with no horses?"

McTavish laughed. "We're going to float down to them. So take care of your livestock. Make your way to our rendezvous place as quickly as you are able. Now I must go. I have others to notify." And with that he was off.

"Doesn't make any sense to me," Nate grumbled as we gathered our supplies. "We don't even know where Big Creek is!"

We saddled our horses and led Daisy back to the Burtons'. I was pleased to see Lydia again, even if it was for a short while. Mr. Burton was happy for us to leave our animals with him, especially since we brought several sacks of grain for their feed.

"We don't know how long we'll be gone. It could be for some time," I told them somberly.

"No matter. We are just happy to do our part to help you fellows. Those red rascals need to be taught a lesson," Mr. Burton replied.

"Do be careful," Lydia said worriedly.

"Keep the livestock close to your cabin. Keep your guns loaded and ready. Most of the fighting men in these parts will be gone. There is always danger of an Indian attack from another direction," Nate said gravely. "If you see any activity that is suspicious, take the horses and head to the fort. There will be a few men there for your protection."

They nodded in reply.

"Now we must be off." I boldly reached over and took Lydia's hand in mine. "Please be careful. Try not to be overly worried about us. Colonel Shelby will ensure our success. Of that you can be certain."

I gave Lydia's hand a final squeeze, and then Nate and I made our way to the rutted path that led to the fort. I was not happy leaving Lydia. Her father was an old man. What if something were to happen to her while I was gone? My heart hurt at the prospect.

We had just started down the road, heading west, when a wagon approached from the direction of the fort. Mr. Eakins, his shriveled bald head shining in the sunlight, was at the reins. In the back were half a dozen men, talking and laughing together. He stopped when he reached us. "Climb aboard, boys! There's still plenty of room for you!"

We traveled the rest of the day rather uncomfortably, pitching to and fro in the back of the wagon with our fellow soldiers. The road headed almost straight west, and we traveled through country I had never seen before. Nate regaled the company with tales of our adventures in the mountains, which he embellished with impunity. Others joined in, and despite the uncomfortable conditions of the ride, the time passed easily enough.

As darkness fell, we all pulled out rations and ate. Mr. Eakins spoke little but kept a steady hand on the reins. We asked him who was minding the store while he was gone, and he told us one of the Shelby servants was tending to it while he was away.

"I'll have the devil to pay when I return," he complained. "The books will be a mess, no doubt."

It was close to midnight when we spotted fires in the distance. As we approached, we could hear the chop, chop, chop of dozens of axes, and the shouts and exclamations of men busy at work. We happily climbed down from the wagon, our limbs sore and stiff from the hours we had spent in it.

The scene that unfolded before our eyes was outlandish and astonishing, almost as if a scene from hell had somehow escaped and landed on the banks of Big Creek. The night sky was overcast, but there was no need for the weak light it would have furnished. There were fires everywhere, both large and small, with dozens of men scrambling around them. We could glimpse on the periphery of this bedlam men with axes in hand, swinging hard at the bases of large hardwood trees, and heard the crash of these huge monsters when they fell. Before the fires were dozens of what seemed to be canoes in the making, with men slashing at the insides of great fallen logs with adzes and hatchets. I turned, thinking of escaping this madhouse, but Mr. Eakins had already turned the wagon around and was heading back the way we came. It would be morning before he was safely ensconced in the enclosure of Shelby's Fort.

As we looked around in amazement, the small, hard

figure of Evan Shelby appeared before us, as if by magic. His normally neat and clean buckskins were awry, with black smudges of soot upon them. His eyes shone brightly through a layer of ash and grime. He was in high spirits.

"Welcome, boys! Glad you have joined us!" he said cheerfully.

"Yes, sir," I replied with some hesitation.

"Now you and Nate follow me. You other boys, find a canoe and give a helping hand." We followed him as he led us deeper into the vast forest of hardwoods that lay beside the creek.

"Look sharp now, boys. I've marked the trees that need to be felled. Did you bring your axes?"

We nodded yes.

"Fine. Pick a tree – a nice big one – and get to work bringing it down." With no further explanation, he turned and disappeared back towards the fires.

Nate and I kindled a fire to see by, and then looked around among the giant trees that surrounded us. We picked a good sturdy oak with markings on it and set to work.

It was hard going, even with the added benefit of Nate's huge muscular frame and long arms. It took us a couple of hours to fell that tree. When it finally teetered over and fell with a crash, we sat ourselves down by the fire, weary from a long day and night. Nate broke the silence. "I don't know what Evan has planned, but he sure seemed excited about it."

"Yes, he did. I hope at some juncture he'll share his plans with the rest of us."

After a few moments of rest, we left our spot and headed into the center of the commotion. Daylight was still some hours away, but the frenzied work continued. I spotted McTavish, busy hollowing out a log, and approached him. Before I could speak, he arose and smiled.

"You boys should get a couple of hours of sleep. Find a spot and rest yourselves. There will still be plenty of work to do when you awake."

"Can you tell us what is going on?" Nate inquired.

"Colonel Shelby will explain it all tomorrow. For now, rest. The details of our endeavors will be clear soon enough."

We took our blankets and found a spot closer to the creek, to the north of the madhouse around us. As I closed my eyes, I fervently hoped a large tree wouldn't come crashing down upon us.

The first rays of the sun, weakly struggling to show through the hazy smoke that poured out of the many still burning fires, awoke us. We freshened ourselves in the creek and filled our water flasks and headed back to the spot where we had felled our first tree. It was no longer where we had left it, dragged and pulled by our comrades, and already set upon to shape it into some sort of water craft.

"Until we're told otherwise, I suppose we should continue chopping," Nate said.

And so we found another large tree, with a clear slash in it to indicate it must come down, and set to work. This one wasn't as thick as the first, so we were able to bring it down much more quickly. We continued onto the next, and then the next. Almost as soon as we felled one, a group of men would appear with small logs they used to roll it back towards the fires.

Around noontime, the call went out that the Colonel wanted to speak to us. Nate and I were grateful for the respite, and headed for the center of activity, where we found Colonel Shelby standing on the stump of a large oak, his face and appearance somewhat improved from the evening before. There were at least a hundred men gathered around him as he began to speak.

"Men, I understand there are many questions about what we are doing here, and it is my desire to answer them for you, so that you can understand the importance of the journey on which we are about to embark."

"As you all well know, the most fierce and warlike of the Cherokee have fled south in defiance of the treaties that were agreed to by all parties. These renegades refuse to abide by them. They have set up their own towns and villages in an area known as the Chickamauga, some two hundred miles south of here. They have continued to send war parties north, harassing our people, destroying property, stealing horses, killing and burning. They have made it nearly impossible for the good folks who have traveled here from all parts of the colonies to rest easy at night." He stopped and his voice grew louder. "Well, it is our intention to put a stop to it! If those rascals want war, then we will give it to them!" There was a rumble of assent from the crowd of men.

"Do not think these savages are doing this on their own," Shelby continued. "They've been supplied and encouraged by the British. They provide arms and ammunition and have instructed them to carry out their own wicked plans. By attacking the frontier, they hope this will weaken our own forces under Washington. It is up to us, men, to put a stop to it."

A loud cheer arose from us.

"Now, don't think I have not planned this out, and that your work here is for naught. My spies and scouts have spent the last few months scouring the landscape between here and there. Men like Ian McTavish, Jonathan Smith and Moses Laythem. It is a dense wilderness between here and there. In order to accomplish our goal, we will need the element of surprise. And to the savages, what would be more surprising than to be attacked from the water?" He laughed.

"You see, Big Creek here feeds into the Holston River, which then merges into the Cherokee River. Most of us have never seen that river, but my scouts have assured me that it is navigable all the way from here to the Chickamauga towns. Now, no one has attempted such a feat. But I know the hearts of you men. I know we can do it!"

He raised his hand to quiet us as we cheered. "We need canoes, men. Lots of them. I have the authority to oversee a thousand volunteers, but I don't believe we will be able to get that many to join us. But however many we have, we must have the boats to carry them south."

Someone from the edge of the gathering shouted out, "How will we get back?"

Evan Shelby smiled. "We will make our way back through the forest. If those bloody savages can do it, so can we." A hearty laugh arose from the crowd.

"I have supplies to feed us while we work. We will bring what is left with us, whatever can fit in our canoes. Once we reach Chickamauga, we will live off the land." He paused. "Any more questions?" There were none. "Alright then," the Colonel concluded, "let's get to work, boys!"

Chapter Twenty-Four

In the following days, more men joined us. They would drift in by the dozens and set right to work. I was pleasantly surprised to see Samuel Hayward and Mr. Wilson join us a few days after we arrived. Their wives and children had been sent to the fort for safety while their menfolk were gone.

It was hard work, fashioning those canoes. Once the trees were felled and stripped of branches, they were either split in half, if they were large enough to make two canoes, or the tops were simply sheered off and they were used for a single vessel. A flat bottom for the soon-to-be canoe was hacked away.

An adze was used to form a trench down the middle of the log, and then small fires were set in those trenches. Once the fire was burned out, we would use our hatchets and axes to chip away at the charred portion of the log. This process was repeated many times for each log, until it was hollowed out enough for one or two men and their provisions. Then the prow would be fashioned and the rear flattened. The final step was stripping the bark and setting it into the water to be sure of its seaworthiness.

Most of the time, Nate and I were assigned the task of cutting down the trees. It wasn't hard to understand why. With his large frame, huge hands and powerful swing, Nate was a natural at it.

We all slept in shifts, so exhausted from our labors that the constant sound of axes biting into wood and the clouds of acrid smoke that filled our camp had little effect on us. We had no worry about what we would eat, either, thanks to the provisions provided by the industrious Isaac.

Occasionally I would spot the German brothers we had brought with us while scavenging for supplies with Isaac, Herman and Bernard. Their blond hair had darkened, thanks to the soot that was always in the air from the fires. They seemed content and happy, and were accepted with no questions asked. In those days, we were happy to have anyone who was willing to work, no matter their background.

The camp grew, as more and more men poured in to join us. Some came from as far away as Sycamore Shoals, others from the outer reaches of the frontier, west and north, from the lands that Isaac spoke so frequently of. These were hardened men, most with long beards and weathered buckskins. They all had Pennsylvania long rifles, carried in the crooks of their arms. They possessed an air of assurance and resolve, and most were men of few words. In short, men I would not want to be on the other side of in any battle.

To say I was not anxious about the task before us would be a lie. Although I had grown up close to the Susquehanna River, I had never spent any time upon it, as my father saw to it that my days were filled with work and allowed me little free time. I could not swim, nor did I have any experience with canoes. I spoke about it one evening to Nate, as we curled ourselves up in our blankets before a small fire.

"Don't trouble yourself about it, Caleb. I would say most of us are in the same position. If Evan says we can do it, then it must be so," he assured me. Before a single minute had passed after his statement, I heard a deep, familiar snore from his direction.

The banks of Big Creek had become crowded with the fruits of our labor. By now there were dugout canoes of every size imaginable. Some were big and spacious, with enough room for three men and provisions. Some were so small a single man would be all it could carry. But no matter the size, they would all find themselves heading south before much longer.

The camp site had grown considerably since we had arrived. There were great piles of dead tree limbs stripped from the monstrous trees we had felled scattered throughout. The forest we had spotted when we arrived was unrecognizable. The stubs of the colossal trees we had cut down stood in stark contrast to the younger, shorter trees that had been deemed too small for our purposes.

Levi Withers, our quartermaster, was generous with our rations, though most of us were too tired from our exertions to take advantage of it. We would oftentimes put a pot of dried beans and meat in a kettle to boil as we snatched a few hours' sleep and then gobble down as much as we could before taking up our axes or hatchets again.

Evan Shelby took up his ax as well, and when he wasn't spotted cajoling and encouraging us to make haste with our efforts, he could be spotted hunched over the beginnings of a canoe with a handful of other men, chipping away at the stubborn interior of a downed oak or tulip tree.

About the sixth or seventh of April we were subjected to a thunderous downpour of spring rain. It pelted us with large, fat drops, dousing our fires and briefly pausing our operations. Those canoes that were still being worked on were quickly covered with large tarps suspended on poles, allowing us to continue our work.

On the evening of the eighth, Evan once again mounted a large stump and called us all together.

"Men, we've done what we could. There are about three hundred and fifty of us now. Enough to let the savages and their British friends know we will no longer tolerate their raiding, murderous ways! We will proceed down Big Creek to the Holston and then down the Cherokee River and attack the towns and villages of those who have terrorized us. I want everything destroyed. The foodstuffs that have been stored, the houses and huts of the inhabitants. I want any cattle or livestock we can not use killed. Any warrior who raises a hand against us will be killed." Some of the men cheered lustily until Evan raised his hand for silence.

"The women and children will be spared. I do not condone the murder of innocents. We will send them off into the woods where they can fend for themselves. If I catch any man taking advantage of any woman, he will answer to me personally. Is that understood?"

He was answered with silence.

"We proceed down the creek day after tomorrow, at daylight. Finish the canoes we have started. Bring what supplies you can carry on your person. My scouts will be ahead of us. But be wary, boys. Keep your eyes out for any signs of trouble. Keep your rifles handy."

As the early morning light broke on the morning of the tenth, we began carefully setting the canoes into Big Creek. Nate piloted his own canoe, a big one, as he was almost large enough for two men. He situated himself in the back and we counterbalanced his weight with a few small sacks of corn, and bags of powder and shot. His boat rode low in the water, but not low enough to swamp it. I had my own, smaller canoe. As I was its lone occupant, I situated myself in the middle, still uncomfortable with the thought I might wind up in the water with no idea how I would make my way to shore if that were to happen.

The current was swift enough that our two hundred or so canoes made it to the Holston River with little impediment. I had a long pole to help guide my unwieldy craft, but found soon enough I had little use for it. I breathed a sigh of relief when we entered the larger stream. I could assign myself a position closer to the banks, and thus could feel confident in my ability to make it to shore if necessary.

Once upon the larger river, our company of erstwhile sailors grew quiet. There was no more catcalling or hallooing among us. Nate, riding ahead of me, kept turning his head from side to side, scouring the countryside we were passing with a watchful eye.

I scanned ahead and saw Evan in the lead canoe, confidently maneuvering his own craft, cocky and self-assured as ever, his gray hair ruffled and blowing in the soft, spring wind that accompanied us.

The countryside we passed through was as pretty as I had ever seen. Deep, silent forests gave way to peaceful meadows, the first green of spring appearing like the willowy strands of a new spiderweb, intricate and tenuous, clinging still to the dead grasses of winter. There were mountains, too, with steep inclines and clefts, reserved in their appearance, their hidden secrets still unknown to any man.

We paddled and poled our way south, ever onward, to a fate I had no way of knowing. I often tell my children that great adventures are always ahead of us. To be assured of success, one must have faith and trust in those who share them with us. As I gazed around at the men who accompanied me on that day long ago, I was satisfied my companions were reliable and true. No man can ask for more than that.

The Holston soon gave way to a larger river, the one we knew as the Cherokee. Our passage had been so swift and sure, it was not much past noon when we broached it. Once again, this waterway was rapidly moving south, engorged by the spring rains. By this time, I had become more comfortable in my ability to maneuver the little canoe beneath me. I glanced behind me and could see very few stragglers.

Late that afternoon, Evan called a halt to our watery caravan. We slipped onto the eastern shore of the river and swiftly set up camp. We were instructed to use only small fires to warm our hands in the cool spring air and heat our victuals.

McTavish stopped by the fire Nate and I had kindled and said the Colonel wanted to see us. Unsure of the purpose of our summons, we made haste to his campfire, where there were about a dozen other men already gathered, including Hugh McDonald and a number of other scouts.

"Men, as you know, the first action the Cherokee will take when we approach their towns is to head for the hills. The fighting men will be among those fleeing, as they will want to preserve their strength to continue their wars against us. I have picked you men in particular for a mission. As soon as they make a run for it, I want you all to give chase. Leave the rest of us and hunt down as many warriors as you can and kill them." He spoke calmly but with urgency. "Any questions? No? Then we will see you before dawn."

As darkness fell, Evan gathered us all together once again.

"The Cherokee are but a few miles south of us. The scouts do not believe they are aware of our presence. Now, those of you who have fought with me before will know what I expect of you. For the others, let me be clear – we will destroy anything of value. The only thing we will take will be those supplies we have need of. Any rifles or muskets, powder or shot we find we will take. All stores of foodstuffs will be destroyed, except those we will need for our own personal use. Anyone who raises a hand against us will be shot. Now get some rest, boys. We'll be on the river again before dawn."

Nate and I were huddled over the small, smokeless fire when we were joined by Samuel Hayward. When he took a seat before our fire I caught the distinct odor of liquor about him. I had never known Samuel to be one for strong drink and was therefore surprised.

"Evening, boys!"

"Good evening, Samuel."

Chapter Twenty-four

"I have a favor to ask of you fellows," he said.

"And what would that be?" I asked warily.

"Please keep an eye out for my boy Ezra. I know those red hellions have stolen him away. They may be holding him down here somewhere." The firelight that flickered across his face enhanced the anguished look of grief that was upon it.

Nate spoke gently. "You know we will, Samuel."

"Thank you kindly, boys. His loss has brought such heartache to Chastity and me. We can't seem to get over it."

There was silence for a moment.

"Is that why you came along? To find Ezra?"

"Well yes. Partly, least ways." His voice rose in anger. "If I can't find him, then I want those rotten heathen to pay for it. They had no right to steal my boy! No right at all!"

Nate and I were silent as he continued.

"And what right do those redcoats have in stirring them up against us? Aren't we supposed to be British subjects? By God and all that is holy, they should pay for their perfidy! They've betrayed us, boys. Betrayed us . . ." His voice trailed off.

"Why don't you bed here by us tonight, Samuel," Nate said calmly.

"No, I guess I won't. Mr. Wilson is waiting for my return." He rose and stumbled off into the night.

For some reason, on that night before we attacked the Cherokee and their towns and villages along Chickamauga Creek, I had a nightmare. The poisonous visage of my father came to me, clear as day. He was shouting at me, waving the straps of Sadie's reins at me, ready to strike, when I was awakened by Nate, shaking my shoulder.

"Up and about, Caleb! Time to teach those rascals a lesson!"

CHAPTER TWENTY-FIVE

We loaded into our canoes just before sunrise. We followed the Cherokee River until we reached a smaller waterway and then followed that southeast. The sun began its rise just as we beached our canoes. We followed a narrow trail a good half mile until we came upon the edge of a sprawling Indian conclave. As soon as they sensed our approach the dogs of the village began a cacophony of high-pitched yapping and howling, shattering the quiet that accompanied the early morning sunrise.

We quickly spread out, rifles firmly planted on our shoulders. The Cherokee poured out of their rough log huts, roofed with wooden shingles, rubbing their eyes in surprise at the sight of us. Chaos ensued, the women grabbing up their young children and babies, fleeing before us in terror. Some of the men of the tribe had exited their homes with rifles in hand. We quickly dispatched them with our own raised weapons. Others fled in fear with their women and children. Within minutes, the village had emptied itself of its residents.

I could hear Evan shouting. "Check each dwelling before you set fire to it. See to it no one has been left behind. Gather any weapons or ammunition you find and bring it to the center of town."

Without a thought, I searched out McTavish and the other men Evan had designated for the pursuit of the warriors who had fled, and we were soon off, running through the deep undergrowth that caught at our buckskins as we gave chase. We could hear them in the distance, thrashing through the same undergrowth as us.

Nate panted beside me. "They got their women and children with them. We'll catch up before long."

Within minutes, we had broken through the forest wall and came upon a field, littered with the green of the new spring and the yearning stalks of early spring flowers. Just as we entered the clearing, shots rang out from the opposite side. I could see ten or so Cherokee warriors, kneeling down as they took their shots at us. We quickly dropped to our knees and returned fire. I placed one warrior in my sights, half-clothed, his dark chest bared in the bright sunlight. I took aim and squeezed the trigger. I saw him fall as I quickly reloaded.

The others with me also fired, and then there was silence. Those who survived had fled. We quickly sped across the field and found the bodies of five warriors, all dead or close to it. I didn't watch as a flurry by some of our men quickly dispatched the wounded. Those Cherokee that survived our onslaught had quickly turned and continued their flight.

McTavish shoved at one of the dead Indians with his foot. "Muskets. The British gave them muskets. No wonder none of us were hit. Gather their weapons, boys, and check for any powder or balls. They will be useful to someone, I'm sure."

We did as we were told. A gruesome task, to be sure. We took their muskets but found little in the way of ammunition. Our quick descent upon their town had hastened their departure, and thus they had not brought much ammunition with them.

"No need for further pursuit. The Colonel will want us back at the town," McTavish stated.

We could smell the acrid odor of the burning village long before we reached it. Tendrils of black smoke curled up into the sky before us, guiding us back to our fellows. As we entered the clearing, a sight reminiscent of hell met our eyes. Numerous huts were fully engaged in fire, their roofs sagging and collapsing all around us.

Upon reentering the Indian town, I became aware of its tremendous size. It extended a good half mile along the creek, with a rather large cylindrical meeting house close to the center of it. As we advanced upon it, I could see Evan shouting directions to the men around him. "Don't forget to check the lodges for firearms and ammunition before you fire them up! Bring what you find here, to this spot!"

Already, there was a small stack of firearms in a pile not far from where he stood. There were a handful of muskets, and some powder horns and small sacks of balls. We dutifully placed the muskets we had captured to the pile.

"Any luck, McTavish?" Evan queried him.

"Some. We got five of them. The rest escaped. I'd say another five or six."

"Good. Every one we kill will mean one less to be sent against us."

"Any sign of Dragging Canoe?"

"None. He either got safely away or is at another location. We captured a couple of squaws and have been questioning them, but haven't gotten a response. Now, you boys get to work. I want this town swept clean. Leave nothing standing."

The Cherokee were still in their winter quarters. The sturdy homes they used were somewhat different from the log cabins built by white people. Although the foundation of logs was the same, their outsides and insides were plastered with a mixture of mud, leaving a smooth surface both inside and out. Each was set deep into the ground, so one had to step down to enter. They were tidy on the inside, with low benches for sleeping. Each dwelling had an array of baskets and earthen jugs containing the necessities of life – food and water.

I had a sense of dismay as I went about my work that day. The eternal questions plagued me – why must the innocent suffer because of the actions of the men living amongst them? What is it about man that we must conquer and destroy, always seeking the upper hand whenever we encounter those different from ourselves?

And yet, I knew the job had to be finished. I steeled myself with the memories of those I had found murdered and scalped, their homes burned and the livelihoods of the living that were left destroyed. As I concentrated on those memories, the faces of Samuel and Chastity flashed before me, heartbroken and desperate at the plight of their son Ezra.

Our first step was to rummage through all the containers we found inside the lodges we entered, thoroughly searching for weapons of war. Then we would make a pile of all the items in the interior and set them afire. Once they ignited and were briskly burning, we threw lighted kindling onto the bark shingles of the roofs and then set out to destroy the next one.

It was grim work. A few of the men found some members of the tribe too old or infirm to take to the woods. They were carried outside of their dwellings and placed on the ground, far enough away to ensure they wouldn't be engulfed by flames. Most made not a sound, but watched stoically as the village they called home burned to ashes around them.

Once a dwelling had been consumed by the fires, we

were instructed to push over any walls that remained standing. All around, I heard the chop of axes and the crashing of walls that had stubbornly remained erect despite the fires that had licked at them from above and below.

On the outskirts of the sprawling village we found a pen that contained at least a dozen horses and several cows, no doubt pilfered from some poor frontier family. Following Evan's directions, these were all slaughtered.

"I don't see no sense in killing these horses. They might come in handy," Nate said.

"We can't use them. We came by canoe, remember?"

"Yes. But we can't go back by canoe. The current runs too strong."

"But what do we do with the horses in the meantime? There aren't enough for all of us," I replied. "And we can't be busy tending to them. Not now, anyway."

By mid-afternoon, we looked back at what we had created. Piles of burned dwellings lay before us, with tendrils of smoke still wafting skyward. The stench of the dead animals we had butchered filled our nostrils, with hordes of flies already busy doing their work on the carcasses.

I could see Evan standing with his scouts, surveying the damage we had caused while carrying on a heated conversation. A few minutes later, he called for us all to assemble. His voice rose as he spoke.

"This is the largest Cherokee settlement along this creek. I am satisfied with the results of your efforts. But we are not finished. Not by a long shot. Get back to your canoes. We will make camp a few hours south of here."

We made camp that evening. Scouts were sent out and guards were posted. We arose before dawn and canoed our way south a few miles. At Evan's direction, we again banked our canoes. The scenes of the day before were repeated but with fewer Indians. Nate and I were once more sent out after a group of warriors that tried to escape our clutches, but were unable to catch them. A few managed to break free by horseback, leaving their loved ones behind without ever glancing back.

We had finished with that village by noon, and once again found ourselves upon the water. The next village we attacked was placed a mile or more inland from the waters' edge. Our rifles loaded, we snaked our way through the landscape to a small clearing, with a dozen or so dwellings surrounding a small council house. This time the village had been abandoned. News of our expedition had spread.

We made camp that evening among the smoldering ruins. We had found a pair of cows wandering aimlessly not far from the town. We butchered and roasted them for dinner, each man receiving his own portion to do with as he wished. Nate and I had brought a small kettle, and we set ours to boil over a fire. As it cooked, Samuel Hayward made an appearance.

"How are you and Mr. Wilson faring?"

As he sat down by us, he replied, "No sign of Ezra. You haven't seen him, have you?" he asked anxiously.

"No, we haven't. We will search you out if we see any sign of him."

"We're faring as well as can be expected. Mr. Wilson says I shouldn't lose hope."

We three stared at the fire, silent.

It seemed as if I had barely closed my eyes before I was being shaken awake. McTavish was leaning over me. "Get up! The Colonel wants to see us!"

Both Nate and I arose and stumbled to a spot on the outskirts of the camp, where there was already a dozen or so men standing, rubbing the sleep from their eyes. In the center of the group was the short-statured Evan Shelby, his arms folded across his chest.

We waited a few moments for the arrival of a few other men.

"Scouts are in. There's a village about a mile or so away from here. The women and children have been whisked away. There are about forty or fifty warriors left. They're waiting for us, fellows." He eyed us before adding, "I have a plan."

He said, "Nate, I want you to take twenty or so men and go back and destroy our canoes. I don't want a single one to be of use to anyone. Take axes to them and destroy them. Understood?"

He continued. "They are of no more use to us anyway. Trying to beat our way back up the river against the current is a waste of time."

"The rest of you – we have a full moon tonight. The Cherokee do not fight at night, so we have an advantage. I want you to get as close to them as you can. There are a few posted in the woods between here and there. Be quiet about it – use your hatchets on them. Then, when you are within two hundred yards of them, I want you, McTavish, to pick four or five of your best shooters and put them in the trees. When they have a good clear shot, I want them to take aim and fire. We will not be far behind. As soon as we hear those shots, the rest of us will advance."

We headed south, forming ourselves into a long, thin line. We crept as silently as we could through the dense undergrowth, crouching to make ourselves as small a target as possible. Occasionally I would hear the inadvertent snap of a twig, and would freeze, as fear of being discovered gripped my heart. Before long, I heard a strangled gurgle coming from the left of me, and knew someone had discovered a Cherokee scout and had taken him out.

McTavish drew next to me. So silent was his approach

I jumped when he touched my arm. "Caleb, we're getting close. Pick out a tree and hide yourself as best as you can."

I found a sturdy oak and climbed until I found a good spot with a fork that I could rest my rifle on. I peered into the darkness, trying to discern any sign of an enemy. The moon, bright and beckoning, lighted the land, illuminating what lay before me. I could see the shapes of the village in the distance, silhouetted as it was by the moonlight. As my eyes adjusted, I could see a few sleeping forms laying before the embers of a fire. I supposed these were men who had been set as a watch before slumber overcame them. I checked my rifle again to be sure the powder and shot were set properly before I took aim and squeezed the trigger. The sound of my shot reverberated through the trees around me, and was quickly followed by three or four more. I glanced to see if my mark had been true before I shimmied down the tree.

At the sound, the rest of the forward advance rushed into the clearing near the center of the village. There were shots fired from inside a few dwellings, but within minutes I could hear the crashing of men recklessly heading towards us from behind. Soon our entire army was in the village. Those warriors that had not been shot already were quickly dispatched.

All told, we killed thirty Cherokee warriors. Their lifeless bodies lay in heaps around us. Evan ordered us to take their muskets and search the buildings for any other weapons before we set fire to them. It was with disgust that I watched a few of our men cackle with glee as they scalped our victims, holding them up as some sort of trophy, blood dripping down onto their leggings and moccasins.

I didn't hold with such displays. If we deemed the Cherokee as savages for such deeds, I could see no advantage for us doing likewise. Who were the savages, here among the looming forest bathed in moonlight: us or the Cherokee?

CHAPTER TWENTY-SIX

Nate and his crew were successful in destroying all the canoes we had spent so much time fashioning out of the forest near Big Creek – so much so that we had to cross the Chickamauga further downstream, our rifles and supplies held high over our heads as we crossed on foot. The rocks in the bottom of the creek were slippery, which resulted in several men losing their footing and plunging into the cold rushing waters, blustering and cursing as they resurfaced from its depths.

Fortunately for us, our scouts were familiar with the pathways the Cherokee used to head north and harry our settlements. We had not been on the trail long before one of those sudden, swift thunderous spring rains was upon us. Drenched with rain, the path became a river of mud. The mud clung to our moccasins and splashed up our leggings. Evan called a halt and ordered us to make camp.

We were all grateful for the respite. The days' exertions had taken a toll on us. We were all hungry and exhausted, as we had not taken the time to eat since the night before. Instead of camping in one of the meadows that opened up along the path, we camped under the trees of the forest to help shield us from the continuing downpour.

Dozens and dozens of small fires were soon started, and kettles were placed among them. Mr. Wilson, Samuel, McTavish and Hugh McDonald joined Nate and I at the fire we had kindled. Each threw into our kettle what they had in their packs in the way of victuals, and soon a nice stew was bubbling away, its aroma tempting our grumbling bellies. We ate hungrily, silently, all weary to the bone.

Soon enough the storm eased and the weak sun appeared for just a few moments to the west as it traveled to its resting place. We lay about the campfire on the soggy ground, grateful for the heat it threw out.

Nate began to quiz McTavish as to our whereabouts and how much longer it would take before we found ourselves back to the safety of our homes. "We still have a long way to travel, boys," he answered tiredly. "With this number of men, it will take longer than it would under other circumstances."

"How much longer, do you think?" Samuel prodded. "I need to get back to my wife and children." There was a catch in his throat. A deep look of sadness spread across his face as it was illuminated by the firelight. There had been no sign of Ezra.

"What do you think, Hugh?"

"If the weather holds, perhaps two weeks."

"Don't forget we have to ford the Cherokee River."

"True enough. But we know a good spot for crossing. It shouldn't slow us down much."

I changed the subject. "How many braves got away from us back there?"

"No more than a dozen," McTavish replied. "Not enough to follow us."

"What if they seek help from their neighbors to pursue us?"

"Not likely. They would be foolish to attempt an attack. And if there is one thing the Cherokee are not, it is foolish."

Despite the damp conditions we all nodded off, our buckskins steaming from the heat of the fire. When we arose early the next morning, we were all dry enough. Those who had saved some parched corn chewed on it as our column moved north.

Evan and his scouts led us at a goodly pace that day and managed to keep our column mostly together. There were a few stragglers, most of whom had sustained minor injuries during our expedition, but they were not of a mind to be left behind. I'm sure they spent a good part of the day looking over their shoulders. The retribution for our raid was sure to come, and those men had no desire to be part of it.

There was not a white man to be found in that part of the country. Virgin forests and flourishing meadows opened up before us, and there was plenty of wildlife around us. Evan sent parties out to hunt, and we could hear their gunshots echoing through the stillness.

Great clouds of duck and geese flew overhead, returning from their winter resting grounds. There were meadows full of wildflowers, and we could hear the scurrying of squirrels in the trees that sheltered us.

After a few days, we crossed the mighty Cherokee River, our scouts having led us to the most likely spot. Here the river was wide, but not deep. Just as we did when we crossed the Chickamauga, we held our supplies over our heads and forded it, taking advantage of the sandbars we came upon. I recalled our canoe trip through this very same spot just a short time ago. I had been uncertain, then, of what lay before us. To some of the men in our party, the raid brought exhilaration and delight.

But I had no such feelings. War, I thought, was a dirty business. Unfortunately it was necessary at times, which proved that man had no keen desire to get along with his neighbors.

I had other thoughts as we penetrated the wilderness along the footpath worn by raiding Cherokees. I thought about Lydia most of all. Her image would rise up in my thoughts as I first beheld her, leaning over her horse with the broken leg. The look on her face when I first saw it, those big brown eyes with tears clinging to her lashes. A picture of her sitting next to me on the stoop of her father's house, laughing gaily at some lame attempt of mine to retell a story shared by Nate.

I wondered if my mother would approve of her, and decided she would. Lydia was all anyone could hope for. She was smart and hardworking. She was tender and caring. And she was beautiful and charming. A man could not ask for more than that.

After we had been on the trail for about a week and our scouts had confirmed we were not being followed, Evan split up our expedition. Those hardy men who had joined us from the wilderness to the west split off onto a trail that would shorten their walk home. Another group headed east on a worn trail that led to the east, towards Sycamore Shoals. The bulk of us headed due north, towards Big Creek where we had started from.

Our scouts had gone before us and alerted the area of our triumph. When the slashed remains of the trees we had used to craft our boats came into view on the banks of Big Creek, our eyes were greeted by numerous wagons and horses waiting for our return. It had taken us two weeks to make our way back from the Chickamauga towns, just as McTavish had predicted.

Nate, lumbering beside me, let out a joyful shout: "Home at last!"

I couldn't help but agree with him.

We gratefully deposited our heavy packs and rifles into the back of a clumsy wagon piloted by a local farmer. There were a dozen or so of us and it was a tight fit, but we didn't mind. Before long, Evan passed us by on a horse that had been brought to him. He looked none the worse for wear, although I noticed his hair, flying in the breeze, was grayer than I had ever seen it. He shouted and waved at us as he passed.

"Take care, boys! I am grateful for your help!"

"Sure thing, Colonel! Next time we need a holiday, we'll be sure to look you up!" Nate replied jauntily. Snickers and guffaws from inside our wagon greeted his retort.

We were a sorry sight to behold when we were dropped off close to the Burton cabin to retrieve our horses. Our buckskins were stained and filthy, holes appearing where no decent man would want them. As we approached, I hastily tried to pull my leggings up further and did my best to drape my leather shirt in such a way as to show as little skin as possible. There was not much left of my moccasins either, and a razor had not touched my face for weeks. Nate noticed me adjusting my clothing and trying to make myself presentable. He laughed.

"Let her see you at your worst, Caleb. That way, there will be no surprises in the future."

"Easy for you to say. You aren't aiming on marrying her."

He stopped and looked at me. "Marry?"

"Yes, marry. I've been doing a lot of thinking. I do believe Lydia is the woman for me."

As we approached, Mr. Burton was in the field putting out hay for our horses and Daisy. Suddenly, Lydia appeared in the doorway of their cabin, and upon spying us, lifted her skirts and flew down the path to greet us. As she came closer, I could feel a lump in my throat, rising up and choking me. She stopped a few feet in front of us, her chest heaving with the exertion.

"You're back," she said.

I walked towards her and gathered her into my arms for a brief moment. I could smell the goodness of her and feel the softness of her body. She returned my embrace, briefly. Suddenly, remembering my manners, I let her go.

"Yes. I hope our animals were no trouble to you and your father."

Her eyes shone up at me. "Of course not. We were happy to do our part to help."

Mr. Burton strode up and shook Nate's hand. "Glad to see you boys are back safe. The news we had was that your trip was successful."

"It was. We hope to have stopped the raiding for a good

while. We most certainly gave them a helping of their own medicine."

"Come in and sit a spell. Lydia has a stew on the fire. I know you boys must be starved."

We ate hungrily, grateful to be under a roof and inside four walls again. Lydia watched us happily, her eyes meeting mine with a frequency that set my heart racing again.

After we ate, we gathered our animals and expressed our gratitude for their keeping. As I mounted my saddle, I looked down at Mr. Burton and asked if I could come calling in a day or two. He nodded his assent and we rode off, back to Beaver Knob.

We arrived back at our cabin just about sunset. Our horses quickened their step as we approached, sensing home was near.

The cabin was much as we had left it. We could see no sign that it had been disturbed by either man or beast. Thankfully we had left a few supplies behind in anticipation of our return. Once we had tended to our animals, we tumbled into our beds and slept the deep, dark sleep of exhaustion.

The next morning, Nate went off to see if he could find us some fresh meat while I spent the morning doing my best to repair my rent clothing. I would have to make do until I could purchase more garments on my next trip to Shelby's store. I got busy with needle and thread, while my mind was all in a fever deciding how I would approach Mr. Burton to ask for his daughter's hand.

Nate returned with a fat turkey and I busied myself with cleaning it before setting it over the fire. While we ate, I asked Nate's advice.

"How do you think I should go about asking for Lydia's hand?"

He ruminated for a moment. "I have no experience, you understand. But to my way of thinking, a direct course of action is necessary. If I were you, and thankfully I am not, I would just come right out and ask it."

"Do you have no desire to have a wife and family?"

"I haven't yet met the woman who meets my expectations."

"And what would those be?"

"Well, for one, I want a woman with plenty to hang on to. And I need one that is willing to allow me my freedom to hunt and roam. Not many of those to be had."

It was with trepidation that I made my way to the Burton homestead the following day. My face was clean shaven and I had done a decent job on the repairs to my clothing. I had tied my hair neatly back in a queue, and had dusted off my tri-cornered hat and placed it on my head and hoped I was presentable enough for the important question I had to ask.

I found Mr. Burton in his garden, a hoe in his hands. He was busily planting seed when I approached him.

"Good morning, sir."

"Good morning, Caleb. Does Lydia know you are here?"

"I don't think so. I wanted to speak with you about an important matter before I made my presence known to her."

"That's fine, son."

My words came out in a rush. "I know this probably isn't the proper way to say it, but I've come to you to ask for your daughter's hand in marriage. I have had strong feelings for her for some time, sir. I know I don't have much to offer her yet, but I hope . . . "

"Slow down there." He laughed.

"I'm sorry for my haste, sir. But I have a need for your permission."

"Have you talked to Lydia about this?"

"Not yet. I was hoping to get your permission first."

"Seems to me you've got this backwards." He leaned against his hoe. "Seems to me you should talk with her first. Lydia is a strong-minded young woman. At my age, I've learned it's best to let women make their own minds up. As for me, I have no objections. But I suggest you talk with her." He smiled.

"Yes, sir," I gulped.

"Now go on to the house and talk with her. I will abide by her decision."

As I approached the front door, it was suddenly slung open, and there stood Lydia. She was wiping her hands on her apron, her sleeves were pushed up and wispy strands of hair escaped from her mop cap as she greeted me.

"Hello, Caleb. I am busy kneading dough. Pa likes a loaf of bread when I can manage to make one."

"Can I come in? I would like to talk to you."

I entered and we went immediately to the kitchen at the back of the house. The table had a large wooden bowl resting on it. She went back to kneading the ball of dough inside it. As her small fists worked the dough, I stood opposite her.

"Lydia, I have an important question to ask you."

She nodded, barely looking up from her work. I reached over and lifted her hands from the bowl.

"It's important, Lydia."

She looked into my eyes as I continued.

"I haven't shared much of my past with you. To be perfectly honest, I am a little ashamed of it."

"Ashamed? How so?"

"No one wants to admit they escaped from their home because their father was a brutal beast."

Chapter Twenty-six

"I don't understand. Why would you be ashamed of that?"

"I didn't want you to think I was like my father. You see, he is a hard-hearted, cold man. He was very cruel to my mother. When she passed away I vowed to run away and start my own life, which is what I have done."

"You've been calling here for some months now. I would never assume you were like your father. I know you are not like that. I've seen how you are with people, Caleb. I see no indication that you are cruel or cold."

"Will you marry me, Lydia?" I blurted out.

She laughed, a high tinkling laugh. "Father and I have been wondering when you would get around to asking me."

I looked at her, dumbfounded.

She withdrew her hands from mine and placed them on her hips.

"You've been making moon eyes at me for months. Your feelings were as plain as the nose on your face, Caleb Anders." She laughed again at the look on my face.

"You knew?"

"Of course I knew. Women have a sense about these things."

I grabbed her hands back into mine. "Will you marry me?"

"Yes, Caleb. I will marry you."

After a short while we were joined in the kitchen by Mr. Burton. He had a pleased look on his face as he spied us.

"I see the matter is settled."

"Yes, father, it is."

"This is great news. Congratulations to you both."

"Thank you, sir," I replied.

"Now let's get down to business. Let's sit on the stoop."

The bread bowl, its contents forgotten, stayed on the kitchen table while we settled on the steps of the stoop. Mr. Burton, his gray head and beard nodding as he talked, began the conversation.

"You young people need a decent start. Times are hard, with the war and all," he began. "It has been hard for a man of my age to manage this place. One hundred acres I have here, and there is much left to be done until it becomes a suitable farm. My boys in New Jersey have no interest in this place. They have their hands full with their own. Lydia, you well know that I have already deeded my place there over to them." Lydia nodded. "That leaves me with this piece of land here."

"What I propose is this – I will get some help from Colonel Shelby to make a will and leave this place to the two of you." He waved me off as I started to protest. "Enough of that, Caleb. I've set my mind to it. You two are young and strong and can make a go of it."

"That is very generous of you, Mr. Burton."

"I have to leave something for my Lydia. It isn't much, this place. But it is something," he continued. Have you decided when you will marry?"

"Not yet."

"We need to have a place to stay first. A place of our own," Lydia said.

"There is a nice spot right over there." Mr. Burton pointed to the east. "Not too close, but a nice level plot, perfect for a cabin."

And so it was decided. Lydia and I would marry as soon as I could get a decent cabin raised.

Chapter Twenty-Seven

As spring turned into the summer of 1779, I began the arduous task of building a home for Lydia and I. Nate helped when he could, and he allowed me the use of Daisy whenever he was able. I scoured Mr. Burton's farm for the necessary rocks to start the process. I laid the foundation of stone and worked tirelessly on the chimney after seeking advice from Lydia's father and the men that gathered around Shelby's store. By the end of July I had a good, sturdy chimney and the foundation laid. Our first home would be sixteen feet by twelve, with a slanted roof kitchen added to the back.

News of the war that summer was both good and bad. General Washington won a tremendous victory over our enemies at Stony Point in New York. However, this was balanced out by the loss of Savannah to the British the previous December. This loss caused consternation among our people. While the battles raged far north of us, we could carry on our lives without much thought. But Savannah was too close to us for comfort. The war had shifted south.

Whenever I traveled to Shelby's Fort that summer I would find groups of men gathered on the stoop of the store discussing the latest war news.

"Those Britishers are getting too close for me to stomach," Nate would growl.

"But what's to be done? We have none but ourselves to protect us. Washington is too far north to provide us any comfort."

"That's what worries me. We can't expect any help from up north. Washington has his hands full."

His face would flush with anger. "Those damned Tories! It's their fault! They would rather stay under the boot of that lousy King George than seek their own independence! It's intolerable, I tell you! Intolerable!"

Others would join in on his grousing. "Lousy Tories! Back stabbers! Turncoats!"

Soon enough the crowd would grow restless, and it was never a help when a bottle would appear and be passed around. I did my best to stay focused on the matter at hand, but I too was concerned about what the future would hold. I would soon have a wife to protect, and the restless anger of my fellow countrymen boded ill.

When fall arrived with its cooler temperatures, and

having helped Mr. Burton gather the crops in the field, I bid Lydia a fond farewell and headed off with Nate into the wilds of the Blue Ridge. She was hesitant as she sent me off.

"Why must you go?" she pleaded with me.

"I must. I have responsibilities now."

"But the cabin is more than halfway completed. Surely you should stay and finish it?'

"The roof is on now. I can do the finishing work when the cold weather comes." I stopped and looked at her. "Never fear, Lydia. I'll return soon. There is nothing that could keep me away."

Nate and I spent four weeks in the wilderness of the mountains. We observed more settlers in the foothills than we ever had before. Some had escaped over the mountains from such places as Hillsborough and even Halifax. Each we spoke with had their own story, but the fear of the British and the unsettling relations among their Loyalist neighbors is what drove them westward.

"A man can't make a living anymore unless he's willing to stand with the King's army," one straggly-haired man told us. His cabin was rough and his children barely clothed, but he told us it was worth it. "I've had all of King George I want. I'm a simple man. Me and my family are better off here in the mountains than we were back there. We can provide for ourselves and we don't have to answer to anyone."

When we arrived back at Shelby's Fort, Daisy's back piled high with the fruits of our labor, I was most anxious to get back to Lydia. I must admit my bargaining with Mr. Eakins didn't go as well as it had in the past, but my mind was preoccupied with other matters.

As we settled in for winter, Nate had more time to help me with the cabin I was building to start my new life with Lydia. We fashioned three windows and covered them with oil paper to let in light. We added a fireplace to the room I had set aside for the kitchen. We planed the wood for the floors and set about carving a mantel for the two fireplaces. The most arduous task of all was chinking the logs. We used a mixture of straw and mud, a devilishly difficult mixture to make during cold winter months. By early spring, the cabin was ready.

As friends gathered round, Lydia and I were married by a traveling preacher on March 30, 1780. We were given a party by our friends at the fort. Colonel Evan Shelby made an appearance and gave us a set of silver spoons that are still my wife's pride and joy. As I settled down into married life, I knew I could not ask for more than the good Lord had already given me.

Those first few weeks of wedded bliss were soon followed by the news of that bastard Tarleton and the fall of Charlestown in South Carolina. A few days before our wedding, Lord Cornwallis, with thousands of troops and a full fleet of warships descended upon the city from New York and laid siege to it. Our troops under General Lincoln did their best but were soon overcome by superior numbers and firepower. In mid-May, the Continental Army had no army at all in the South.

To make matters worse, Colonel Tarleton was let loose upon the civilian population of South Carolina. He burned and destroyed his way through the state. At the Battle of Waxhaws it was reported he gave no quarter to surrendering troops, just killing them indiscriminately.

The news spread like wildfire through our settlements. Neighbors visited neighbors to spread the news, and Shelby's Fort was flooded with folks trying to get the latest information. The war, it seemed, was drawing close.

That summer, Isaac Shelby appeared. He had been west, doing survey work and securing land for himself and others. After he heard of the fall of Charleston, he hurried home, determined to do his part for the cause of freedom. I happened upon him one day while I was at the fort. He strode up to me and held out his hand.

"I hear congratulations are in order."

"Thank you, sir."

His reddish hair had grown to his shoulders, and there was stubble on his face. Despite that, his neat dress and direct manner exuded confidence.

"I'm here for only a short while. I'm recruiting men to

cross over the mountains. The Patriots in South Carolina are in a desperate situation."

"So I've heard."

"I would call on you, Caleb, but I know you are newly married. Where is Nate?"

"He's up in the mountains hunting."

"Hmm," he peered at me quizzically. "Unusual time of year to be hunting."

"He says he has to make up for my absence, since I now have duties at home and cannot break away."

He nodded thoughtfully. "Perhaps next time, then?'

"Yes sir."

To be honest, I was relieved. When Lydia and I spoke about it later that day, she expressed her happiness at my decision.

"The war is closing in on us, Caleb. But I'm not yet ready to let you go. The time will come when I will not have any choice, I know. But for now, I'm just happy to have you here."

Isaac had encouraged almost two hundred men to join him, and within a few days they headed east, across that vast mountain range that had called to me so clearly since I first laid eyes upon it.

Within weeks of his departure, the disastrous news of the defeat of our troops at Camden reached us. Evan

Shelby's network of correspondents relayed the news. The defeated troops were those of General Gates, who had come south to attempt to defeat the British and put a stop to their northward expansion.

A cold fear ran through us. Where was Isaac and what had become of him and the brave souls who had so willingly followed him across the mountains? Had they been caught up with the Continental Army? Would our men be returning home, or were their lifeless bodies left scattered across the barren wasteland of the battle?

It was with much relief that I spied Nate spurring Bessie into the yard of our little home one day in late August. I had worried he would have somehow been found and encouraged to join Isaac on his jaunt across the mountains.

"How goes it, partner? How is married life?" he called out jocularly.

"Just fine. I was hoping to see you. I was afraid you had been called into service."

"No, not me. I heard the news in town. Bad news, all the way around."

"Has there been any word of Isaac and his men?"

"Not yet. But I did learn he was appointed a Colonel in the militia last year. Did you know that?"

"No. I spoke with him shortly before he left and he made no mention of it. He's mighty young to be a colonel."

"Figures. But I wouldn't worry overly much. Isaac has

a way of making it through. Besides, he and his men are militia. Not likely to be fighting with Continental troops."

As he eased his way out of the saddle, Lydia appeared in the doorway. "Nate! So good to see you safe and sound! I have a stew on the fire. Come in and eat!"

Never one to turn down a good meal, he joined us at the table I had so carefully crafted for our new home. He ate heartily and shared his opinions on life, the war and any other subject that crossed his mind.

"I hope your trip was successful."

"It was. I surely missed your rifle, though. I stumbled upon a small herd of buffalo but was only able to get three of them."

"I'll be more than happy to go with you in the fall, after harvest."

He clapped me on the shoulder, nearly knocking me off my chair. "That is good news indeed!"

Of course, at that time I had no idea I would be far busier with things more important than a mere hunting trip. Life is like that, I have often found. Sometimes it is best not to lay plans too far into the future. Events have a way of hindering them.

CHAPTER TWENTY-EIGHT

It was not long after Nate returned home that Shelby's Fort and the small hamlet of Sapling Grove began to host groups of militia, on the run from over the Blue Ridge, from the British forces that had decimated the Patriots at Camden. Some brought their families and encamped them within the fort's walls, and it brought back memories of our arrival at the fort back in 1774. Then, we had gathered there to protect ourselves from raiding Indians. Now, members of the South Carolina militia had gathered in hopes of protection from the British.

Stories circulated of the great defeat. How Gates foolishly placed his least experienced troops against the veterans of the British Army. How the Virginia militia ran away when presented with the bayonets of the professional soldiers of Great Britain. How the bravery of the Continentals was displayed, standing firm, while Gates and his underlings fled like dogs before the onslaught. I daresay there is not a curse in existence that wasn't used to describe the General who ran and left his fighting men on the field.

We heard of the bravery of militia units still at war within the state, led by such men and Sumter and Marion, busy harassing the British at every opportunity, holding out hope for the brave souls – the Patriots of South Carolina. Yet little word had reached us about Isaac and the men he had led across the Blue Ridge.

It was the first week of September when Isaac finally made his appearance, along with the men who had soldiered with him. He had been skirmishing with the British in western South Carolina, and came home with the majority of his force intact.

I hurried to the fort when I heard of his return, kissing my wife as I left, my rifle in hand. "Don't do anything foolish, Caleb," she entreated me as I left.

After I entered the tumult of the fort, I soon spotted Isaac with a group of men surrounding him. He was deep in discussion, his red hair in disarray, his face animated and fervently red.

"I tell you, boys, we had some close calls. Those Brits are devils in disguise. There is no degradation they will not employ. We witnessed the most vile acts. Homes burned, men strung up, livestock slaughtered. They mean to do away with anyone who opposes them."

There were moans and groans from the dozen or so who clustered around him.

"Have I told you about Ferguson yet?"

"Not yet."

"Major Ferguson. British. He's got an army of Tories he's using against us. Tories. People who have lived among us our whole lives are now engaging in the most awful of crimes against their own people. Down country they've taken over whole towns, killing or pillaging anyone who stands in their way."

Cries of "shame!" and "disgraceful" arose from the group, as well as a few curses I won't detail here.

"Matter of fact, Ferguson's also threatened us, here across the Blue Ridge. He says he will be heading our way, and promises to string up any Patriot he finds on the western side of the mountains!"

As the group gasped, Isaac's voice rose. "I will not have it, boys! I will not!"

His statement was greeted by shouts of encouragement.

"Do any of you men know John Sevier?"

"We all know of him, Isaac. He lives over in Jonesborough, doesn't he?"

"Then you know of his prowess in the field. He's been fighting the Cherokee as long as we have. A good man, with a steady hand."

There were noises and nods of agreement.

"I've just come from his place. He agrees with me. We must act, men. We cannot have our lives upended any longer by those blasted British. To hell with them, I say! To hell with their Parliament and with their demented King! We must take a stand for our freedom! We must!"

There were cheers all around.

"Sevier and I have agreed to this. We are to meet at Sycamore Shoals on September 25th. We must be well armed and ready to ride. I am beseeching each and every one of you. Spread the word. We need as many as we can gather. We will join forces and march over the mountains and show Major Ferguson that we mean business! Are you with me?"

There were nods and cheers all around. It was at that point I realized I had no choice. I would be going to war against the British.

I made a stop at Evan Shelby's house in hopes of speaking with him. I was led into his study by a servant who nodded graciously at me as I entered, despite the rifle I still carried in my hand. He was seated at his desk, bent over, quill in hand.

"Good morning, sir."

"Hello, Caleb. How is married life treating you?"

"Just fine. I wished to speak with you a moment about Isaac and his proposal to travel east across the mountains."

"Ah, yes. Quite an undertaking."

"Will you be leading us?"

He sighed. "No, my boy. My fighting days are over. It's well past time for me to give that job over to those younger and more able."

"But sir…"

He interrupted me. "No buts about it." He sighed again. "My age has caught up with me. I can no longer tolerate the physical stress that would fall upon me if I were to go."

"You will be missed."

"Well, thank you." He smiled. "But don't fret. Isaac is perfectly capable of being the leader you will need. Assuming, of course, you plan on accompanying him."

"Yes. I haven't told my wife yet."

"Some advice. Be firm yet gentle when you relay the news. And don't worry. There are still a few of us older men to keep the women and children in these parts safe. Do your duty, son."

I left him and made my way home.

Lydia was dry-eyed and calm when I explained the

circumstances we now found ourselves in. I simply told her the truth, which I find to be most helpful when dealing with women, especially when it comes to matters of such magnitude as war.

"So you see, my dearest, I must go. The British have threatened us all with death if they breach the mountains. I see I have little choice in the matter," I explained to her as I held her close.

"Yes, Caleb. You must go. You will be needed. All the men hereabouts will be needed."

As we drew apart, she looked up at me. "I have news for you too. I am with child."

"What?"

"Yes. I waited to tell you so I could be sure. But it seems to me unfair if you didn't know before you left."

I hugged her close. She clung to me. "So you see, you will be fighting not just for our freedom, but for the freedom of our child."

"Will you be all right with me gone?"

"Perfectly. Don't worry. I have some months to go before the baby arrives."

"Perhaps you and your father can stay at the fort while we're gone."

"Nonsense," she replied forcefully. "Pa can stay with me here in the cabin. We are close enough to the fort to reach it quickly if trouble arrives."

I rode over to Beaver Knob and consulted with Nate. We agreed to ride first to the fort and then leave with the other men gathering there for the campaign.

"It's finally come. We'll get to fire at those lobsterbacks!" he gleefully stated. "They've stirred up a hornet's nest and don't even know it yet!"

Nate arrived at my door on September 20th, Daisy in tow. He was well stocked with all he would need for the expedition. I loaded bags of corn and meal on Daisy's back, as well as some extra smoked meat I had on hand.

I shook Mr. Burton's hand and then held Lydia as close as I could. I whispered in her ear, telling her of my love and my determination to return. "I will be back as swiftly as I can. Don't worry overly much. I will make it home. I promise."

And with that, Nate and I rode to the fort. By then, it was full of families determined to stay within its protective walls as they saw their men off to war once again.

I spotted Samuel and Chastity, their wagon fully loaded with their children and most of their prized possessions. Right next to it was the Wilsons' wagon, also loaded to the brim. On spying them, I had an idea. I approached them and explained that my wife and her father were well situated not far from the fort.

"It would be most helpful if they had company. You could set up camp there easily. Mr. Burton's cabin will be available for your use, as he will be staying with Lydia while I am gone. Both he and Lydia are good shots and are well armed in case of trouble."

Samuel and Mr. Wilson quickly agreed.

"Better there than here in these cramped corners of the fort," Samuel said.

Convinced, the women accepted the proposal, and I breathed a sigh of relief as they maneuvered their wagons out of the fort. It eased my mind to know Lydia and her father would not be alone if trouble arose.

A group of about fifty of us headed south the following morning, just as dawn broke over the mountains we would soon be crossing. Many familiar faces rode with us. Both Ian McTavish and Hugh McDonald were there. I spotted the Schmitt brothers – Herman and Bernard – who had joined Isaac and I as we searched for supplies for our expedition to attack the Chickamauga Indians. John Williams and Henry Fallwood, who had ridden south with us when we first arrived at the fort were also in attendance. And of course, Samuel Hayward and Mr. Wilson.

We arrived at Sycamore Shoals, the designated meeting place late that afternoon. I was surprised, almost shocked at its appearance. It was teeming with men, many with their families in tow. The center of town was crowded with all manner of carts and wagons. People milled around outside the walls of the stockade. There were tents set up by scheming merchants, selling their wares at exorbitant prices in the hope of making quick money from those who had rushed off without fully supplying themselves. Dairy cattle were staked out in the fields, pigs squealed and chickens crowed. Dogs ran in and out among the people, barking and yapping endlessly. All in all, Sycamore Shoals had become a madhouse. I was glad I had said my goodbyes to Lydia at home instead of bringing her here to this bedlam.

Already encamped there were the sorry troops of two Colonels – Hampton and McDowell – who had fled from the onslaught of Major Ferguson and his Loyalist troops. Dejected, they told tales of the brutality of the men we would face. This news did not deter us. It only served to further inflame our desire to meet the enemy in the field. There were hundreds of us, and we would soon be joined by hundreds more.

Some of the men carried their old muskets, new when their families first reached the shores of the New World, hatchets firmly attached to their belts. Many were on foot, without the benefit of a horse, hoping to find one while there, to take their shot at the British who had dared to threaten them with death if they were caught and found to be a Patriot.

Amid the chaos, stood Isaac Shelby and John Sevier.

Sevier I remembered from our foray to help Sycamore Shoals after it had been attacked by the Cherokee. He was a clear-eyed, determined man, with an air about him of competence and strength. He and Isaac had known each other for some time, and it showed. They worked easily together and were busy forging order out of the chaos.

If I had to leave home and family to defend what I knew to be the truth – that we had the right to determine our future for ourselves and not leave it in the hands of a distant king and a Parliament who did not have our best interests at heart – I could not have found men more worthy to lead me in such an endeavor.

CHAPTER TWENTY-NINE

Lydia says that every man that fought at King's Mountain was a hero. I personally don't hold with that view. We were not heroes. We were determined men, with our hearts set on protecting our homes and families. We did not take the crossing of the Blue Ridge Mountains lightly. It would be a dogged task to get us safely across, with pitfalls and dangers along the way. Hundreds of men crossing that wilderness was no easy task. But we were driven. Driven like the summer rain from a stiff southwestern breeze.

As the day of September 25th dawned, Isaac and Sevier drew their forces together. Both had about 240 men. Some of those who rendezvoused with us were sent home, as their age or infirmities precluded them to be fit enough to travel.

"We will need you to stay home and protect the women and children from any actions taken by the Cherokee in our absence. Your service is just as vital to the cause as ours. Take heart! Be wary! Protect us from the rear!" Isaac told them. Mollified, they quickly left and returned to home and hearth.

Our two companies were joined by two companies of 400 under the command of Colonel William Campbell. Joined by the troops that had fled that devil Ferguson, we had a sum total of a thousand men, all eager to pursue those who had threatened us with our very lives.

We set out on the morning of the 26th of September after a religious service. We were in high spirits that day, as we set off to climb Yellow Mountain. Each of us carried our own supplies, as the paths and trails we would follow would be of no use to wagons. A herd of cattle was driven behind us to supply us with fresh meat.

Not all the men had the benefit of a horse. A goodly number followed on foot, their rifles and muskets slung across their shoulders. I was thankful to have Sadie, who had been a faithful beast all these years, and still had more years of loyal service in her.

That first night we camped at Shelving Rock. Some of the cattle we had brought were slaughtered and provided us with supper to cook over our campfires. A meeting among the leaders was held a short distance away, and soon enough Isaac joined us around our fires.

"Boys, I have news," he began. "We are not satisfied

with the pace of the march. We've decided the herds we brought are slowing us down. We need more speed if we are going to surprise and trap the British. So we propose to slaughter and save what meat we can and send the rest of the cattle back to Sycamore Shoals."

Samuel Hayward spoke up. "That sounds reasonable to me!" I looked at him as he spoke. Ever since the loss of his son to the Cherokee, Samuel had hardened. There was a glint in his eye that spoke not just of pain, but also of determination. His hatred of the British was now well known among us, and I could sense a deep need of revenge in the way he spoke.

After we bedded down I shared the news of my soon becoming a father with Nate. He seemed happy for me, and said, "Don't worry, partner. I will do my best to see you get back home safe and sound."

We spent the following morning slaughtering, skinning and cooking enough of the cattle to see us through for a few days. The remains of the herd were sent back to Sycamore Shoals with some of the men who followed us on foot. They would try to join back up with us later.

Freed from the burden of shepherding cattle on the narrow winding trail, our pace quickened. We reached the top of Roan Mountain by early afternoon and were soon set to drilling. We were divided into companies and the rolls were called.

There was already snow on the ground at the top of the mountain. Disagreeable enough because of the cold wet flakes that clung to our ankles, some of the men grumbled about drilling at all. "Why are we stopping here? We don't need this. The lobsterbacks are waiting! Let us get to them!"

"Now, now. We got to know who all is here. When we whip those lousy Tories you'll be glad to have your name listed!" Nate would cheerfully reply.

I was happy to see most of my friends in the same company as I. We were divided into about fifty men to a company, and we were proud to be under the command of Isaac. He was well known to us, and we felt comfortable under his leadership. All in all, he had four companies at his disposal.

After the roll call we moved quickly down the mountain to our next campsite, which was at Bright's branch where it joined Roaring Creek. There were six of us gathered around a single campfire. As there was a distinctly cold chill in the air that evening, we had built our fire up to a roar to warm ourselves. There was McTavish, and Hugh McDonald, Samuel Hayward, Mr. Wilson, Nate and myself. Out of the darkness, Isaac Shelby appeared and plopped himself down among us. We had just finished warming some of the beef we had saved in our saddle bags and we offered him a share. He ate hungrily.

"Sure do wish your father was here with us."

"As do I. He would most certainly be enjoying himself," he replied.

Nate guffawed at this rejoinder. "That he would!"

"If his health had been better, or if he was ten years younger, nothing could have kept him from being here."

A silence then descended upon us. All of us, at one time or another, had put our lives in the hands of Evan Shelby, and he had seen us through. In my minds' eye I could see his dynamic, muscular frame astride a horse, shouting commands and leading the way.

Isaac interrupted my musings. "Boys, I spent several hours in consultation with my father before we started on this venture. I can assure you he gave me some good advice." He poked at the fire, and the flames that arose illuminated his face. "He is a wise man, and knows more about war than all the rest of us combined. You don't fight Indians for 30 years and not know about war. You can have confidence he is here in spirit, if not in body."

"How close do you reckon the British are?"

"According to our scouts, closer than we thought. We will see action soon enough," he replied soberly. And with that, he arose and wandered off, headed to the next fire with men gathered round.

The next morning we followed a narrow trail called Bright's Trace. It wandered through the rough woods, narrow and winding. It was difficult going, as this trail had never seen the likes of hundreds of men passing along it.

We found an excellent spot to encamp after a difficult 20-mile march the day of September 28th. We scraped together some parched corn and the last of the beef we had carried with us and set both bubbling in a pot over our fire. We slept the sleep of exhausted men that night.

The following morning we were saddled up and ready as soon as the sun made an appearance. It had been decided we would split up into two groups. Those of us under the command of Isaac and Sevier would continue on as we had come, while the others under Colonel Campbell would advance on a different route, in hopes of gathering intelligence about the movements of the British we would soon face on the battlefield.

It was on that day, September 29th, 1780, that I and my fellow soldiers reached the peak of the Blue Ridge Mountains. The vistas that lay before and behind us were a most magnificent sight. Rolling hills, lush with greens and blues, were tinged here and there with the colors of fall – bright yellows and oranges splashed among the solid phalanx of greenery stretched as far as the eye could see. Scattered among the undulating hills were taller mountain peaks, feathered with snow at their tops. I drew a deep breath as I took in the scenery around me. No other place on earth could have touched my heart like the sight of the Blue Ridge in all its fullness stretched out before me.

We descended and made camp for the night. As we lay before the fire – it was a cold evening, and we bedded down as close to its warmth as we could – I began to ponder what lay before us. My mind reviewed the life I had led to that point. My difficult childhood, the loss of my mother, the happenstance of meeting Nate while I fled from home, the luck in stumbling upon Shelby's Fort and the welcome I had received from my fellow frontiersmen. The skills I had learned while making a living in the fur trade, and the other ones I acquired while stalking and fighting the Cherokee. The men I had met who had seen my worth and taught me how to hone my skills and to be a man. All these things, I determined, had led me here, to the eastern foot of the Blue Ridge. No matter what we faced in the coming days, I knew that Providence had provided what I needed to survive, and even conquer what lay before me. As I looked about, I knew the very same Providence had prepared each and every one of us.

We resumed our march on September 30th. Before the morning was over, we had rejoined with the forces under Colonel Campbell and surged forward, heading south by southeast. That evening we made camp at the home of McDowell, the commander of the local militia who had scattered across the Blue Ridge and made their way to Sycamore Shoals and joined with us. We had a good meal that evening, and the Colonel even insisted we use his fences to build our fires.

McDowell was a likable soul, although we questioned his military ability. Surely he could have done his part against the British before he tucked his tail and ran. To be clear, he had fought in several small engagements the preceding summer, but had not stayed the course.

That evening, our forces were strengthened. A couple of militia companies from close by joined forces with us. We were now about 1400 strong.

But there were fractious contentions among our ranks. Not being used to the discipline necessary in such a military effort, many among us grumbled and griped about following orders, and argued repeatedly with those in command. This caused us more delay than necessary and was a cause for concern.

"We will be of little use against the British if we cannot stop the squabbling." McTavish stated.

"What we need is a single leader. What we have now is four men in charge. That's three too many in my opinion."

"Truer words were never spoken, my friend," Nate replied. "We may be forced to take matters into our own hands and knock some heads together." We laughed as he demonstrated to us how he would personally go about accomplishing that. But in truth, it was no laughing matter.

CHAPTER THIRTY

The next morning we struck out. We made quick progress until noon, as the road was a good one. It was wide enough to accommodate more than two or three of us at a time, and so our journey south was swift and sure.

Ever since we had crossed the mountains and descended down into the foothills on the other side, we regularly spotted cabins and homes, tucked into secret glades and glens, smoke rising steadily from their chimneys. At times we would be greeted by the waves and shouts of the farmers and families who made their livelihoods there. They exchanged pleasantries with us and encouraged us in our endeavors. But sometimes we would come across a homestead that remained silent and withdrawn as we approached. These places, we knew, were most likely peopled by Tories who sided with the British. As we passed, some of the men could be heard sending curses and condemnations in their direction. These were always met with silence. The inhabitants knew what folly it would be to stick their heads out and return the insults.

Early that afternoon we were inundated with a tremendous storm, with crashing thunder and a hard, pelting rain. We slogged on as best we could, but our columns were halted early because of the weather. We made camp that night in the pouring rain.

The next day the weather had not improved. A steady rain fell, dampening the spirits and causing many of us much grief. Some of the men pulled out bottles and drank liberally to pass the time, as it had been decided we would go no further that day. As they drank, they became rowdy, and fights broke out. This should not have been surprising, considering the circumstances. Men with time on their hands, cold and wet and with no means to keep warm in the midst of a chilly, numbing rain, are bound to find something to occupy themselves. If the bottle is applied at the same time, it is like a flame to a pile of dry kindling.

Nate and I managed to nurse a small fire under the branches of a large elm tree. Its intertwining branches provided us some shelter, despite being denuded of its foliage.

Lydia was much on my mind that day, as I huddled as closely as I could to the flickering flames. As some of the men caroused around me, my thoughts were of her. I missed her warm touch and the feel of her in my arms. What would she think of me if she had sight of me at that moment, sodden and unshaven, hunched over a small fire in the middle of the wilderness, with wild men cavorting and carrying on around me? I decided it would be best if she thought of me in the saddle, rifle in hand, soberly chasing our enemies, and I decided that if I willed it, she would think it.

By late afternoon, those of us still sober had resolved to put an end to the squabbling. I saw Nate demonstrating his ability to knock heads together on numerous drunken soldiers, and had to smile as I remembered, how just the night before he had shown us his technique. I must say it worked out quite satisfactorily.

That evening, a conference was held among the four colonels of our enterprise. Colonel McDowell had the most experience, and he led the meeting. Colonels Sevier and Campbell, as well as Issac, spoke earnestly to one another as they tried to decide what our next steps would be.

Despite his great bulk, Nate managed to position himself close enough to catch most of the discussion as these four men decided our fate. He positioned himself behind a great log that had conveniently fallen beside the canvas tent they were under.

He hurried back as quickly as he could to our little campfire. McTavish and Hugh McDonald and Samuel Hayward were there with me, in great anticipation of what Nate would have to say.

"It's been decided. Colonel Campbell will be our leader." The pitch of his voice rose as he spoke.

"Why him?"

"McDowell wanted us to wait until we sent off for an officer from the Continentals. He figured they'd have someone who could take charge. But Isaac was having none of it." He chuckled. "He let them other fellows know we didn't have time to wait. The enemy is close at hand and we are ready for the fight."

"McDowell is the senior man. I'm surprised they didn't pick him," McTavish said.

"That don't make any sense, McTavish. McDowell is the one who ran all the way across the Blue Ridge rather than face Major Ferguson. It wouldn't be right to pick him."

"Why not Isaac?" I asked.

"That wouldn't be right either. He's the youngest one amongst them."

"I don't see what age has got to do with it."

"Well, you aren't a military man. How do you think the others would feel if they let a young whippersnapper lead them? It wouldn't work out."

"So Colonel Campbell it is."

"Yup. Colonel Campbell. It was a little hard on McDowell that they passed him by, but he's offered to head north himself to seek out a man with more experience to lead us."

"We don't need anyone with more experience," Samuel complained. "We have what we need right here."

"Perhaps," McTavish piped up. "But there's no harm in trying."

We were gathered together, all fourteen hundred of us, on the morning of October 3rd. Striding into the center of us were our leaders – an array of colonels that any army would be proud to fight under. Without hesitation, Colonel Cleveland who had joined us with a number of men, spoke first. He was a heavy-set, jovial man, and as he spoke McTavish leaned over to me.

"Don't let his looks fool you. He knows how to fight." I nodded as I strained to hear his words.

Next up was Isaac. His youth, as compared to the other colonels, was apparent. He was clean shaven, his red hair set ablaze by the morning sun. He did not hold back.

"Men, we believe the enemy under Colonel Ferguson is camped at Gilbert Town, but a few short miles from here. His force is smaller than ours and composed entirely of Tories. Tories that have robbed their neighbors blind. That have destroyed the livelihoods of our fellow Patriots – their own neighbors. Who have taken the lives of men, women and children without cause." His voice rang out louder as he continued.

"Just two weeks ago, a force of our men arrived at Augusta, Georgia, determined to confiscate the weapons and provisions stored there by the British to supply the Cherokee and Creeks. Those supplies and those Indians were to be used against our own people. Our forces were overrun and compelled to flee, bringing along their women and children. We lost several good soldiers that day. They were hung by those damn Tories. Do you understand? Prisoners of war, twelve of them, were hung!"

A loud growl could be heard as the rumors we had heard were confirmed. It began slowly but increased quickly as Isaac spoke. He held up his hand for silence.

"Now is our chance to strike back. I do not believe they can withstand us. We must strike with all we have." A cheer rang out. Isaac raised his hand again.

"As I look around this circle, I want to speak plainly to you men. If any of you have a reason why you cannot commit fully to this cause, I simply ask that you take three steps back. No one here will fault you for it."

There was an eerie silence. I glanced around the circle. Not a single man among us took those three steps. After a moment, a cheer arose among us. We were bound to the task, wholeheartedly.

Isaac resumed his speech.

"I am proud to see each and every one of you committed

to fighting our foes. Now, here is what we will do. When we come upon them, don't wait for any command from us. You know how to fight. You've proven it over and over to us. Every tree, every stump you will take advantage of. Use the skills you have learned from fighting the Cherokee, the Creek, the Shawnee, the Delaware. Advance from tree to tree. Your officers will be right there with you. But, once the enemy gives way, you will then take your orders from us. Does everyone understand?"

Another hearty cheer arose. I lustily joined in. Then, McTavish leaned over once again in my direction.

"Anyone who doesn't understand that Evan Shelby isn't here in spirit is a fool."

Filled with patriotic fever after Isaac's speech, our force moved out in great anticipation of what we expected to be a battle at Gilbert Town. We reached its outskirts the following day, October 4. Much to our chagrin, however, when we arrived we found the British had escaped. Loud groans and rumblings erupted throughout our little army.

"Those dirty, filthy turncoats!"

"Turned and ran, they did! They know we're coming."

"They can't hide from us forever, boys. We'll hunt them down," Isaac shouted to us gaily.

It was determined that Ferguson had most likely traveled

south, and so we preceded in that direction. Along the way, we were happy to see more small groups of militia, astride horses and with a look of resoluteness about them, join us. As our numbers grew, the likelihood of victory only increased.

Late that afternoon, we forded a small creek and then the Broad River. Our scouts reported disappointing news. The trail of the British had been lost.

By then, our arduous journey had taken a toll on both man and beast. The soldiers on foot that had followed us all the way from Sycamore Shoals were exhausted from the strenuous marches. Many of the horses were in a bad way. Hard, difficult miles over treacherous terrain had put a strain on them. For Nate and I, we were most fortunate. Bessie and Sadie had withstood the difficulties well, as we had always seen to it that they were properly fed and watered. Many of our men would learn a hard lesson in the coming days – those who fail to take proper care of their beasts might well pay for it in the end.

On October 5th we were greeted with a steady downpour of rain. Halted, we did our best to safeguard our firearms, many of us wrapping the coats off our backs to protect them. Meanwhile our scouts scoured the landscape looking for any sign of the enemy.

A council among our leaders took place late that afternoon and continued well after darkness descended. Those of us nearby could see them gesticulating wildly under the cover of a rain-sodden tent, each man taking a turn in expressing his opinion.

About ten o'clock, the council ended abruptly and each leader left to consult with his men. As Isaac approached us he had a spring in his step. We gathered round as he spoke.

"As you know, some of the men have had difficulty keeping up. It will not get any easier as we move forward. After a long consultation, we've decided to let the best shots with the best horses move forward ahead of the rest. I expect each and every one of you to appear before me for inspection. We cannot jeopardize our chance of victory. We must catch Ferguson. We've come too far to allow him to slip through our fingers."

And so, the process began. Each of us, with our horses, appeared before Isaac. The same was done with the other companies. Every soldier was inspected. Those who passed were gathered in the center of the camp. Those who didn't were charged with following as quickly as they were able.

Before the rays of the sun appeared, we each rested as best we could. I had difficulty and did not sleep a wink in those few hours. Both Nate and I had been selected.

CHAPTER THIRTY-ONE

There were about seven hundred of us that rode out of camp early the next morning. Before we left, I made a point of stopping by and saying goodbye to Samuel Hayward and Mr. Wilson. Neither had made the cut due to the condition of their horses. They wished me well. "Aim true for the rest of us just in case we don't catch up!"

We moved quickly, our speed having been increased substantially without the need to wait for those with poor horses. We were headed in a southeastern direction when we were joined by Colonel Lacey and his four hundred men from South Carolina. Two hundred of the best of them were hand-picked to join with us. We were close to a thousand strong when we stopped for the evening in a cattle-grazing area known as the Cowpens.

We had found ourselves in the vast fields of a Tory by

the name of Sanders. We made free with his livestock and fed ourselves well that evening. Our horses, too, were well taken care of, thanks to an abundant cornfield. We stripped it quickly, to ensure our animals were properly fed.

We remounted and continued on. The weather clouded, and soon we were inundated with a heavy downpour of rain, which made our march challenging. The faint trace of a trail we followed was difficult to see in the dark, and the hooves of our horses turned it into a river of mud. To make matters worse, the temperature dropped, so as we slogged through the cold and wet, a murmur arose from our ranks.

Some of the scouts that had been thrown out in front of us took a wrong turn, resulting in several companies veering off in the wrong direction. The sun finally peeked over the eastern horizon, and with its rise the missing men were found and rejoined us. We forged ahead and crossed the Broad River at a place called Cherokee Ford.

Isaac was in a foul mood that morning. The scouts had done their work, and we knew the enemy was not far from us. He cursed the rain that continued to fall, and shook his fist at the heavens.

The other three commanders of our expedition – Campbell, Sevier and Cleveland – approached him while in the midst of his cursing.

"Surely you can see, Isaac, the men are worn out. We've ridden almost twenty miles during the night. They are cold and hungry. A stop would be in order," Sevier tried to placate him.

"I will not hear of it!" he shouted. "I'll follow Ferguson all the way to the British lines if necessary. These men can take it, I assure you!"

Without answering, the three of them returned to their places in the line.

As luck would have it, two Tories were captured after we had left the Broad River about seven miles behind us. They were enticed into spilling what information they had. Ferguson and his soldiers had encamped at a place called King's Mountain. Now, at last, we knew where our enemy was.

At noon, the ceaseless rain that had caused us so much discomfort stopped. The sun appeared in an almost cloudless sky, its rays warming us, steam rising up from the rain-soaked ground. Now that we knew our final destination, our enthusiasm for the mission returned.

Our leaders drew themselves aside, along with the scouts we had that were familiar with King's Mountain. They had detailed descriptions of the lay of the land, vital information needed in order to draw up a battle plan. I could see Isaac seated at an impromptu table, quill in hand, as those around him gesticulated as he busily made notes. The meeting broke up not long after it began. Each commander returned to his men to explain our next steps.

I have never pretended to be a military man. I've not spent much time arguing or discussing the ways of war, as I find the entire concept repugnant, if necessary at certain times. But I can most assuredly say that it is a rare occurrence for leaders to give all the details, including the overarching strategy, to the common soldier. Most only obey the immediate orders given by their superiors, without a thought to the meaning of it.

But this was no ordinary army. We had been informed that once we met the enemy on the field, we were to act as our own officers. Each man was expected to do whatever he felt was necessary to ensure our victory. That is what made the difference at King's Mountain that day.

Isaac returned, and all two hundred of us gathered round him as he explained what would soon take place. He scratched away a large patch of dead leaves with a stick, and drew a diagram while he spoke.

"Colonel Ferguson and the turncoat Tories that make up his army have taken a fine position, at least in his mind. They have encamped on the top of a mountain with a large meadow and water close at hand. The sides of the mountain are steep and rugged, with fallen timbers and plenty of trees for cover. Being British and unfamiliar with our ways, he believes he can hold his position against our rifles. I'm here to tell you gentlemen, he has taken us for granted."

A snicker rose up, with much shaking of heads and a few full-throated guffaws.

"Here is our plan. Each of us will place our commands around the perimeter of their position like a noose around the neck of a condemned man." He drew a large oval in the dirt." We will place ourselves here, at the northwest corner." He drew an X. "Sevier and his men will be to our right." Another X. "Williams to our left. Then Cleveland, Lacey and Hawthorne." He marked their places. "On the end, Chronicle. Then Winston and McDowell. Straight across the field from us will be Campbell." He paused. "The trick is, boys, we must hold our fire until all of us are in position. No matter the provocation, you must hold your fire until I give the signal."

He raised himself up. "When we reach about a half mile out your orders are to tie up your horses and leave behind your blankets and coats. Most importantly, have your rifles primed and ready to fire." He grinned. "I don't believe Ferguson understands the advantage we hold in our hands, gentlemen. They will have to fire downhill with their muskets. We with our rifles will be far more accurate shooting uphill."

We eagerly went to our horses and mounted up. Within moments we were riding hard. Unbeknownst to us, we were heading towards one of the most uneven battles ever fought upon our soil.

We rode as quietly as we could as we approached the mountain. We could see it rising before us, its steep incline and tangled undergrowth sprouting trees that reached skyward and littered with the debris often found amidst the living things of a forest.

As we closed the distance to our destination, a soft shout was heard ahead of us. Isaac's scouts had surprised the pickets that had been placed to warn of our coming. Without firing a shot, they were captured.

We dismounted less than a half mile from the mountain and tied up our horses. I gave Sadie a pat on the neck, for luck. I half feared I would need it that day. A picture of Lydia flashed in my mind as I joined Nate, striding forward with eager anticipation.

To the right and to the left of me, I saw my comrades tackling that mountain, their rifles strapped to their backs or tucked in the crook of their arms as they struggled through the undergrowth. Slowly and carefully we made our way ever upward, climbing over boulders and fallen timber, clutching with our free hands branches to help propel ourselves forward.

We were about a quarter mile from the top when we heard the ominous sound of the British drums, rattling out a message that surely meant we had been spotted.

"Here's to our success, partner!" Nate said, a wide grin showing through the black darkness of his bearded face. "Let's give 'em hell!"

Our company was fired upon first. The loud crack of gunfire sounded out, and we took cover as musket balls whizzed past us, over our heads. We could hear Isaac shouting. "Hold your fire, men! Hold your fire!"

We dutifully waited for the signal, although I did hear complaints grumbled out along our line. We had come a long way for this moment, and all the pent-up anger at the British and the atrocities they and their Indian allies had heaped upon us bubbled and simmered within us, ready and waiting to boil over.

In a few moments, we heard gunfire emitting from Campbell's company, positioned almost directly across the mountain from us. Blood curdling yells, mimicking the cries of Indian warriors, erupted all along our lines.

Isaac yelled, "Go get 'em, boys!"

We moved forward. We saw the British troops clearly through the haze of gunsmoke, at the top of the mountain. Moving from tree to tree, boulder to boulder, we let off our rifles at the enemy as they slowly descended the mountain. I saw bodies, some clothed in scarlet, fall in crumpled heaps as our rifles rang out true. Ever closer we crept forward, and I saw the flash of bayonets as we closed the gap.

As the enemy drew closer, I heard a loud yelp from my right, where Nate stood. As I reloaded, I glanced over and saw that he was down. "Are you hit?"

"Yes," he replied, as he clutched at his right leg. "Right straight through my leg."

I could see blood pouring out of a hole in the right leg of his buckskins, splashing down to his moccasins. I crouched and crawled over to him, just as his giant body gave way and hit the dirt.

There was a large boulder not far from him, and I pulled and tugged his huge frame behind it as he gasped in pain. "Give me your belt."

I took it from him and wound it tightly around his thigh, just above the gushing hole.

"Wouldn't you know it, I get hit first thing," he gasped.

At that moment I could hear our comrades rushing past us, headed back down the mountain in retreat. I finished loading my rifle and peeked around the boulder and saw redcoats not twenty yards from me, their fixed bayonets gleaming in the sun. They were chasing our men, who were falling back down the slope. As they passed, I carefully took aim and fired, seeing the man in my sights fall silently, face down.

Nate tugged at my leg and handed me his rifle. He sat with his back on the boulder that shielded us. I fired it at the onrushing British, and another fell. I handed Nate's rifle back to him and he fumbled with his powder horn and shot bag, reloading slowly, his rifle stretched out before him at an angle, as I quickly did the same. I peeked again around the safety of our boulder and dropped another one just as they were heading back up the mountain. The rifle fire coming from our comrades below us was too much for them, and it was their turn to retreat.

I could hear Isaac not far below us, bellowing to reload and advance. Again, our men crept forward, although it was hard to spot them amidst the billowing gray clouds of smoke that hung over us. Soon, Isaac was there beside me.

"Caleb, stay here. We will provide cover for you and Nate if we are forced to retreat again. Aim at the officers if you can. The snake can't do much without its head."

Within a few minutes our men were again tumbling past us, trying to evade the bayonets of the enemy, poking and jabbing at them as the two sides came close. Nate grimaced as he reloaded his rifle and handed it to me, perspiration flowing down his face and soaked into his beard, so that I was able to get two shots off within seconds. I could hear scattered fire below me as the enemy advanced, our comrades willingly providing cover for us as we huddled behind the safety of that rock.

For nearly an hour, the battle continued the same way – advance and retreat, advance and retreat. Every time the Tories charged our men would fall back, not allowing them to close. Then the enemy would have to fall back or be picked off in the woods. Our ears rung with the sounds of the guns, both ours and those of our enemies. Whenever I steadied my rifle on the edge of the rock in front of me, I could see more lifeless bodies clothed in scarlet or homespun, scattered every which way on the side of the mountain. Wisps of smoke clung to them, and around the trees and fallen timber and the giant rocks and boulders.

I have heard of other soldiers who claim in the midst of a battle they thought of home, of their families, of their past mistakes and future plans. Perhaps so. But for me, I had no time to think. My mind was simply fixed upon reloading, aiming and firing, reloading, aiming and firing. Thinking could wait. Survival was uppermost in my mind.

Chapter Thirty-Two

Slowly, steadily, the noose we had placed around the neck of Colonel Ferguson tightened, until suddenly we found ourselves on top of King's Mountain. News passed from mouth to mouth that Ferguson had been killed. As I sat beside Nate, tucked safely behind our boulder, McTavish appeared out of the smoky mist and told us the news. With his help we managed to get Nate to the top of the mountain, me supporting him on his right and McTavish on his left. As we climbed to the top, about a hundred yards from the place Nate had been hit, he spoke.

"Blast it all! Blast it! I was hoping to take that skunk out myself!"

McTavish laughed. "As we all were! But never you mind, Nate. The job is done. That's all that matters."

Huddled together in the center of the flat plateau at the

top of the mountain were hundreds of Tories, the so-called Loyalists. Men who fought for King George rather than their own country. The smoke still lay heavy, and we could hear a few scattered shots as we approached. Dead bodies lay every which way, and we could hear the wail of the wounded. Littered about were the remains of a defeated enemy. Broken muskets, pieces of clothing, discarded canteens, blood-soaked rags blanketed the ground on which we stood. As we eased Nate to the ground, Isaac, seated on his horse, whizzed past us. His head was singed on one side, and his buckskins were all askew, stained and dirty from the battle. He headed directly towards the cluster of British soldiers in the middle of the field. McTavish and I advanced, and as we did we could hear calls of "Quarter! Quarter!" from the defeated men.

Isaac shouted from his horse. "No quarter until you give up your arms!"

Within the crowd was a circle of what remained of the officers. They had given up their swords and they were being collected by Colonel Campbell and his men. As Isaac drew closer, all the others began to lay down their arms. They were thrown into jumbled piles, as useless then as they had been during the battle.

The sniping fire of a few of us at the enemy stopped. Shouts from our officers rang out clearly. Slowly more bands of our little army gained the summit, their appearance rough and coarse compared to the captured British, although their neat uniforms were neat no longer. We had no uniforms. We were dressed in buckskin or homespun and each carried the weapons of his own choosing.

There was much jubilation over our quick victory. The officers had a difficult time controlling the crowd of frontiersmen that gathered around our captured enemy. There were shouts raised of "Tarleton's Quarter." Angered by the murder of so many of our fellow Patriot soldiers when they were captured, it was only natural for many of our number to demand retribution. Tarleton, who many thought would be hot on our trail after our victory, was well known for shooting and hanging any Patriot soldiers that fell into his hands.

I left McTavish there and went to tend to Nate, who we had left at the edge of the meadow. He lay still, but was breathing heavily as I approached. He opened his eyes as I knelt down.

"It's done, then?"

"Yes."

"Is it true Ferguson is dead?"

"It appears so. Now, let me look at your wound."

The right side of his leggings was soaked in blood from the middle of his thigh on down. I drew my knife and cut away what remained of it, and carefully peeled it away. There was a purple hole on the left side of his thigh, bright and angry looking. It had quit bleeding by now, and was only oozing but a drop or two of blood. As he winced and groaned, I carefully lifted his leg and looked at the back of it.

"It seems to me you are one lucky man, Nate. That bullet went clean through you."

"Are you sure?"

"Yes. Let me find a bottle of whiskey somewhere to clean it." I arose and glanced around. There were dead bodies in all directions, so I had hopes of finding some sort of alcohol amongst them. I rifled through pockets and packs searching for what I needed. It was not a pleasant task to rummage through the remains of the dead. If they hadn't made war against their own people they wouldn't be dead, I reasoned.

Soon enough, I found a bottle on the body of a sad young man, his chest torn open from a bullet. His knapsack yielded what I needed and I returned to Nate. I poured whiskey on the wound from the front, and he yelped in pain.

McTavish appeared, and between the two of us we were able to turn Nate over. I then poured what was left of the bottle on the backside of his wound. Nate emitted more groans of pain.

With that done, McTavish and I headed back to the edge of the clearing and back down a few feet and gathered moss that grew on the trunks of the trees that had managed to survive amidst the rock-strewn side of the mountain.

We returned and used Nate's belt to fasten them to his wound, front and back.

"I'd offer you fellows something to eat, but these fools have none."

"No supplies?"

"None. They must have sent off foraging parties but there are no signs of them."

"Any plans decided upon yet?" I asked.

"Isaac said we are to remain here on the battlefield for the night. Colonel Campbell has assigned a strong guard for the captured soldiers. We will head back at first light."

The captured wagons were used as firewood for the evening fires. There was no food to cook. The silence of the night was continuously interrupted by the cries of the wounded, which was pitiful to hear. Only one British doctor had survived the battle, and I saw him moving from fire to fire, administering to his downed comrades. As for our injured, we tended to them ourselves.

There were crews of Patriots busy burying our dead all through the night. We had not many, and for that we were thankful. Some thought we should also bury the dead redcoats, but it was finally decided they would be buried by a contingent left behind for that purpose. The fear of retribution from Tarleton and his Light Horse Legion was strong among us, and the bulk of us had no desire to tarry longer than necessary.

Before morning light, McTavish, Hugh McDonald and

I managed to maneuver Nate down the mountain to our horses. We cut two poles from the forest and slung a piece of canvas between them. We lashed Bessie and Sadie together, and tied the poles to them, one on each side. We eased Nate into the sling we had created. When the army started to move, we were ready.

We rode along the same path by which we had come. The main army, herding along some seven hundred prisoners, was ahead of us. There were many wounded among us – about sixty, I recall. We trailed our army as best we could. We left the British wounded on the top of King's Mountain with their doctor and a few hundred of us to bury the dead redcoats.

I rode on Sadie and helped guide the makeshift litter we had fashioned for Nate. The going was difficult, but at least the trail we followed had been well trampled on our way to the battlefield.

The sun blazed brightly, lifting our spirits. We had done the impossible and were happy for it. We made many miles that day, considering the size of our entourage. We arrived back at Green River, where we had left those with weak horses that afternoon.

Samuel Hayward found us at the rear of the army.

"Well, boys, you made it!" he greeted us gleefully.

Nate replied for us. "But not in one piece. It could be worse, I suppose."

"No matter. I'm happy to see you fellows. I've got a nice pot of stew on the fire. I'll fetch you some."

I eased out of my saddle and unhitched Nate from the horses. When Samuel rejoined us, and as we wolfed down the stew he brought on bark plates, he shared some news with us.

"Do you fellows remember George Simmons?"

"You mean that shifty eyed fellow that we rode south with?"

"Yes. You remember him?"

"I recall he had a keen eye for our horses and rifles. And your wife, too," Nate replied.

"I saw him amongst the prisoners. McTavish and Hugh were having a word with him."

"I remember they caught him stealing from their traps," I replied. "What kind of word were they having?"

"All I can say is there were fists involved," Samuel replied with a note of satisfaction in his voice.

"Well, it's no more than he deserves. Lousy turncoat," Nate remarked. "I hope it's the last we ever see of him."

And it was.

We moved Nate beside the fire of Samuel and Mr.

Wilson, and then I tended to the horses. As I was relieving them of their saddles, Isaac Shelby slipped up to my side.

"Mighty fine shooting up on that mountain, Caleb," he said, startling me.

"Why thank you, sir. Just doing my part."

"Yes, you were." His eyes narrowed as he studied me.

"Some around here are saying they expect Tarleton to make an appearance before long."

"That's what they say."

"Do you believe them?"

He scratched the side of his head and shook it. "No, I don't. General Cornwallis has his hands full as it is. The news of our victory will spread far and wide, and will only strengthen the resolve of our fellow Patriots here in the Carolinas. No, I think Tarleton will have other orders besides chasing a band of mountaineers through the foothills of the Blue Ridge."

"So what will be our next steps?"

He sighed heavily. "We've got seven hundred prisoners on our hands. We'll have to take them north somehow, and deposit them with the Continentals. Meanwhile, I and our other officers will have to do what we can to quell the discord over the fears of that bastard Tarleton. How's Nate?"

"He will make it, if we can keep the fever out of his wound."

"Keep it clean and a poultice of moss applied to it. Works wonders." He paused. "I have a proposition for you."

"What's that?"

"Who's to say that if you and Nate fell to the back of the army when we return to the march, and wander off, say, to the west, towards home, if anyone in particular would miss you?"

"Samuel and Mr. Wilson would." (To this day, I have no idea why everyone called him Mr. Wilson instead of using his given name of Jedadiah.)

"Here's the situation, plain and simple. We have about sixty wounded with us and seven hundred prisoners. The wounded need tending to, but it's nearly impossible to do so while we're busy with the prisoners. Although I would be happy to have you and your rifle ride with us, Caleb, in the interest of what's best for this army, it would be fine with me if the two of you head for home. You know the woods as well as any man, and I don't doubt the ability of the two of you to make it across the mountains safely. One less wounded man would be one less for us to care for. Explain it quietly to your friends. They will understand."

I broached the subject as we gathered around our evening fire. Mr. Wilson was the first to speak up. "Sounds like a fine idea to me. Samuel and I missed out on the fighting. It's almost like we're taking your place. Go ahead, I say," he said with some satisfaction.

Samuel nodded in agreement.

The next morning as the army started to move, I steered Sadie and Bessie back onto the trail by which we had come, while the rest of the army moved north.

The trail was well trodden, but difficult to navigate because of the countless hoof prints left by our eager army in their chase of the enemy. I moved slightly off the trail in an attempt to keep from jostling Nate any more than necessary, but it was slow going. I heard little or nothing from Nate, and I stopped at noon to check on him. He was dozing peacefully as I approached him with a canteen of water. He awoke and looked at me. "Where are we?"

"We're about four miles west of where we were this morning."

I checked his wounds. "There's a scab forming, which is a good thing. You'll be able to ride in a few days." He nodded weakly but made no reply.

I watered the horses at a nearby creek, and we continued on. The weather that first day was a fine one, despite the cool, stiff breeze that came out of the north. Mid-afternoon, I found a grove of trees that still had some green grasses, so I stopped to let the horses eat. It was cool and pleasant beneath the overhanging branches.

We had no food with us. We were both hungry and tired.

"Partner, we are close to some settler cabins. Perhaps I should go and see if I can find us something to eat."

"Most likely you'll need to steal anything you find, Caleb. Remember, we came through these parts but a few days ago and picked it clean."

What he said was true. I waited until darkness fell and left on foot. After an hour, I found a cabin, clothed in darkness. I heard the squawk of some chickens coming from a pen hidden away in a small glen a good distance from the house. I helped myself to a couple of fat hens and headed back. I didn't feel good about it, but there it was.

When I arrived back to our makeshift camp, Nate had propped himself against the trunk of a tree. I quickly prepared the hens for our supper and started a small fire and put them on to roast.

We continued our journey the next day and made better time. Late that evening we were greeted by a tremendous thunderstorm, raging like mad against the humble tent we had fashioned. Undaunted, we continued our journey the next day despite the mud.

We camped alongside the Broad River, hiding ourselves in a grove of mixed elm and oak. We threw some fishing lines into the stream and managed to catch a few trout for our supper. Nate was feeling better, and his wound was healing nicely. He ate ravenously.

We decided to delay our trip for a day, to aid in healing Nate's wound and to take advantage of the trout we were able to catch. There beside the river there was food for our horses as well.

After a day's rest and feeling stronger, Nate eased himself into Bessie's saddle.

"Are you sure this is a good idea?" I asked.

"I'm feeling well enough. And I'm done with bumping along in that sling. The quicker I ride, the quicker we will get home."

We took it slow for the next few days. We generally followed the path by which we had come, although we sought to avoid other humans, being uncertain who was friend or foe. We managed to find some game along the way but used our weapons as little as possible to avoid detection.

Once we reached the steep inclines that led to the top of the Blue Ridge, we both breathed sighs of relief. We knew home was not far away. We moved quickly now and made our way over the top and proceeded downwards, finding familiar trails and cabins of friends we could be sure of.

The news of King's Mountain had spread quickly, even to the backwoods country. Those we encountered were hungry for accounts of the battle and we had to repeat our stories to those we encountered. I grew impatient to share my story with the one I most cared about.

We passed by Shelby's Fort. Nate thought we should stop and pay our respects to Evan and share our news of the battle, but I would have none of it. He reluctantly agreed, noting my eagerness to get home.

As we rounded a corner in the road, I could see the snug cabin I had spent so much time constructing rising into view. I spurred Sadie to a gallop. I saw Mr. Burton by the barn and the wagons belonging to the Haywards and Wilsons parked next to it. But I only had eyes for the small figure who suddenly appeared in the doorway – Lydia. My Lydia.

POSTSCRIPT

In September of 1800 I came down with a terrible fever. I had just come from the fields and was overcome with it, and Lydia quickly put me to bed. After a few days, with me in a delirium, Lydia called Dr. Hargrove from town to assess my situation. He told her there was little to be done but hope for it to pass. As to the cause of it, he was uncertain. He offered to bleed me, but Lydia refused it, certain that it would have done no good.

I awoke from the confusion the first week of October. I saw my dear wife, her head bent over her sewing, in the old rocking chair that had once been her mother's. Weak as a kitten, I asked for water. She looked up immediately, with tears forming in her eyes and rushed to my side. She called for water, and our eldest daughter Sylvia soon appeared in our doorway, relief upon her face, with a pitcher and cup.

My thirst was soon quenched and I drifted off to sleep once again.

The next day, when I awoke, Lydia was there. She lifted my head and offered water. Again, I drank thirstily, but did not drift away. She leaned over and kissed my forehead and expressed her relief.

"Dearest Caleb, you have been gone from us for two weeks. I feared you would not make a recovery." She reached down and grabbed my hand.

"I am sorry for having been such a bother."

"No bother, husband. We were so afraid you were gone." Her voice caught in her throat.

I nodded weakly and asked for something to eat. Some bread and honey was soon brought and I ate it gratefully.

"You missed the celebration in town," she informed me.

"What celebration?" I asked weakly.

"Do you not know? The celebration of the anniversary of King's Mountain."

"Oh."

"Not that it wasn't on your mind. You have talked about it almost constantly while you slept."

I nodded.

I began regaining my strength in the following weeks, although I must admit I was a fractious patient. I paced back and forth throughout the house, grumbling and grousing about my weakness and inability to get on with the chores that so desperately needed to be taken care of. Lydia patiently put up with my complaining.

On a trip to town, she returned home with a sheaf of paper, a bottle of ink, and a half dozen new quills.

"Here, here! What is all this for?"

"I was thinking, Caleb, that since you are unable to go about your business normally, you could occupy yourself by putting down on paper your experience with the battle. There is renewed interest in how it transpired, and I'm sure your children would appreciate a lasting record of your exploits."

"I don't know that my story would be that interesting to my children."

"Of course it would! They have heard some of the details, but reading it from your own hand would help them understand what brought it about!" she persisted. "It's important, Caleb, for our children to understand the sacrifices that were made. Our children's children deserve to know what brought about their freedom and prosperity."

I grudgingly agreed, although I suspect Lydia was only doing her best to keep me occupied during my recovery. Better to have me toiling away at my writing than interfering with the running of the household. And so, I began.

All that I have written here is an honest report, based on my own recollection. I thought it important to not only give the details of the Battle of King's Mountain, but also the reasons we wound up at the top of it, rifles at the ready, to hand a solid defeat to what was called the finest fighting force in the world.

After I returned home, Lydia and I settled down to wait for the birth of our first child, Nathaniel. He greeted us squalling at the top of his lungs a few days before my own birthday, on March 5, 1781. Through the years we have been blessed with two more children – Sylvia and Patience. However, there are two small headstones in the family graveyard, resting beside Lydia's parents. Sickness took our sons, James and John, before their first birthdays.

In the summer of 1782 a post rider galloped his way onto our property with a missive from Jacob and Martha. My father was on his deathbed, and they insisted I make my way back to Maryland before he passed. With haste, we borrowed a small wagon and headed north, accompanied by Nate, as there was still some danger on the road and he insisted on coming along with us for added protection.

We arrived too late. My father passed away three days before our arrival. We were there when he was laid to rest beside my dear mother. For the first time in many years, my sisters and I were together once again. My many nieces and nephews scampered about Jacob and Martha's place while we sat down to decide what was to become of my father's property.

"Your father left no will," Jacob stated. "So by rights, all his property now belongs to you, Caleb, as his son."

"I have no interest in his property. I and Lydia are well situated at Sapling Grove. The only fond memories I have of it are those times I spent with mother."

"Then what is to be done?"

"Father has not kept his place up. The house is in need of repair and many of the fields have been left fallow. I have no interest in any of it. I have mother's New England Primer, and that is all I have an interest in." I paused. "I believe we should sell the place and get the best price we can. Any of his possessions that my sisters have an interest in, they are welcome to."

And so it was done. The money derived from the sale I divided among the four of us. I thought it only fair, since my sisters had been subject to the same abuse as I.

After we returned home, I managed to purchase additional acreage adjacent to my own. When Lydia's father passed away in 1784, we were in possession of two hundred and fifty acres of good land, with a fresh creek that runs through the middle of it.

As the threat of Cherokee raids lessened and then disappeared, I began breeding horses, always aware of the shortage of horseflesh that stymied our early days in Sapling Grove. Later on, in 1795, I managed to acquire two fine jack donkeys and began breeding mules as well. They have been a big success. They are more suited to farm work than oxen, which are too slow to be of much use. I was able to add to our original cabin, the one I built myself before our marriage, and just three years ago I added clapboards, laid over the original logs. It is a fine looking home, I must admit, and an abode I will be happy with until the end of my days.

As for Nate, he now lives between here and Sycamore Shoals. He left Beaver Knob after his marriage to Henrietta Schmidt in 1785. She is a large woman – almost as big as Nate – and has been a great helpmate to him. They have not been blessed with children, but Nate does not seem to mind. He still spends time hunting and trapping in the Blue Ridge, and also has a blacksmithing forge on his property.

Because of my illness this past fall, I was unable to participate in our annual tradition. We go together for two weeks every fall for a hunt far into the mysterious folds of those mountains that have been calling to me ever since I first laid eyes on them. We spend time around the campfire in the evening, reminiscing about the old days and our shared experiences. He is the best friend a man could possibly have, and much loved by my children as their Uncle Nate.

Samuel and Chastity Hayward never found their son Ezra. As to his final fate, no one knows. Despite their terrible sorrow, they went on to have two more children. They still live on the same property, although they now own it outright. Mr. Wilson and his family picked up and moved to Kentucky, in hopes of finding even greener pastures.

Ian McTavish and Hugh McDonald also left for Kentucky not long after they returned from King's Mountain. As it was explained to me, their need to wander and explore was just too strong for them. I can understand that, although I never felt that urge personally. They are good men and good friends. Where they are at the present is not known to me, but I have the utmost confidence they will never have a problem making their way in the world.

Evan Shelby passed away in 1794 at the age of seventy-four. He had remarried, and his new bride Isabella blessed him with three more children. His strength and wisdom have been sorely missed in the intervening years. I am thankful for his time of service to his community and country. Without him, Sapling Grove would never have grown into the bustling and prosperous little town it is today.

Isaac Shelby continued on in the service of his country after King's Mountain. He joined General Daniel Morgan right after the battle and fought against the scourge of the British for months afterwards. After the war he moved north, settled in Boonesborough, and married. He was elected the first governor of the new state of Kentucky in 1791. It has been some years since I have seen him, but I will always be grateful for his leadership during our time of need. I am proud to have had the honor to serve under him.

Shelby's Fort no longer exists as it once was. The walls are mostly gone, giving way to the ravages of time. Sapling Grove has grown and now boasts two churches, a school, and various and sundry other establishments. It became part of the new state of Tennessee, which was formed in 1796.

We are a fledgling country, this United States of America. We fought and won our independence from Great Britain at a great cost. Our wings have sprouted feathers, like the wings of the baby barn swallows that occupy a nest underneath the overhang on our stoop. How we use those wings, once fully grown, is yet to be determined. My fondest wish is that my children, and their children that come after them, will continue to nurture what they have been blessed with. That they will not take for granted what others have fought and died for. And most of all, that they understand how the sacrifices made were not just for our generation, but for all the generations that will follow. May God bless the great state of Tennessee and these United States.

Caleb Anders

May 15, 1801

Sapling Grove, Tennessee

Sources and Further Reading

Special thanks to the Library of Congress, Washington, DC and the Tennessee State Library and Archives, Nashville, Tennessee for their help in obtaining materials.

Alderman, Pat. One Heroic Hour at King's Mountain. Tennessee: The Overmountain Press, 1990.

Boulware, Tyler. Deconstructing the Cherokee Nation. University Press of Florida, 2011.

Burnett, Swan Moses. The Over-Mountain Men. Forgotten Books, 2012.

Compton, Brian Patrick. Revised History of Fort Watauga. Electronic Theses and Dissertations: Paper 1103. dc.etsu.edu/etd/1103, 2005.

Dunkerly, Robert M. The Battle of King's Mountain. Charleston, SC: The History Press, 2007.

Gilbert, Catherine R. and Oscar E. True for the Cause of Liberty: The Second Spartan Regiment in the American Revolution. Havertown, PA: Casemate, 2015.

Henderson, Archibald. Isaac Shelby. The North Carolina Booklet, North Carolina Society of the Daughters of the American Revolution, Volume XVI, January 1917.

Jones, Randall. Before They Were Heroes at King's Mountain. Winston-Salem, NC: Daniel Boone Footsteps, 2011.

Knapp, David Jr. The Chickamaugas. The Georgia Historical Quarterly, Vol. 51, No. 2, page 194, 1967.

Land, Robert H. The Shelby Family Papers. Library of Congress, Vol. 11, No. 3. Quarterly Journal of Current Acquisitions, 1954.

Powell, Allan. Forgotten Heroes of the Maryland Frontier. Baltimore, MD: Gateway Press, 2001.

Ramsey, J. G. M. The Annals of Tennessee, Philadelphia, PA: Lippincott, 1860.

Thomas, Ryan. *The Pennsylvania Long Rifle.* Pennsylvania Center for the Book, 2009.

(pabook.libraries.psu.edu/literary-cultural-heritage-map-pa/feature-articles/pennsylvania-long-rifle)

Tunnell, Josie J. *Cherokee Architectural Traditions: A Southeastern Environmental Design Precedent.*

Chancellor's Honors Program Projects, 2022. (trace. tennesseee.edu/utk_chanhonoproj/2470)

Williams, Samuel C. *Shelby's Fort,* East Tennessee Historical Society's Publications, Knoxville, TN: Volume 7, page 28, 1935.

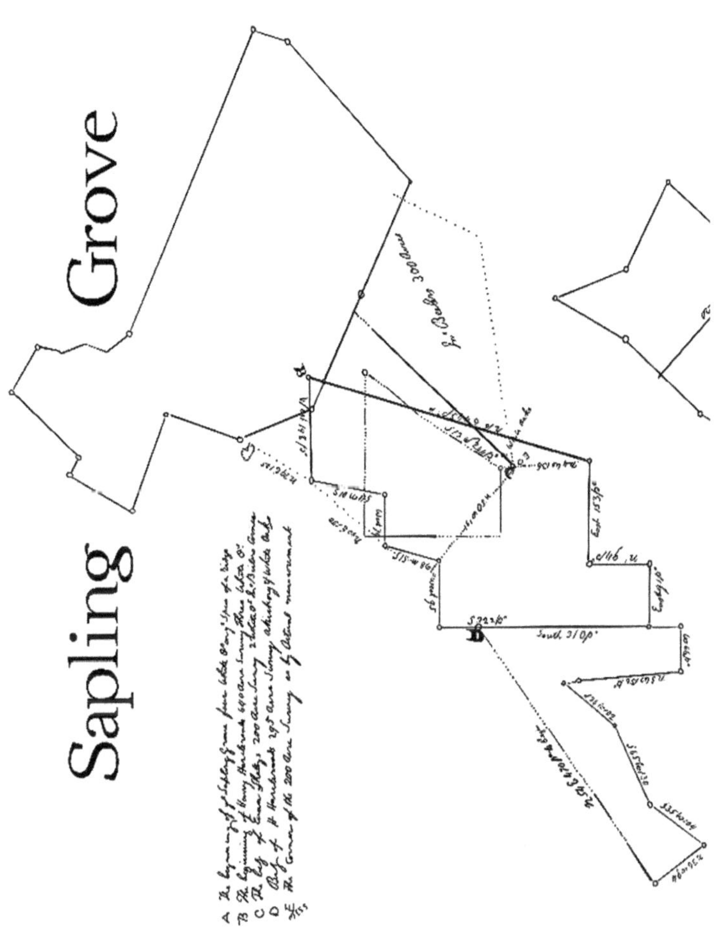

Grove
Sapling
300 Acres